A SAFE HAVEN ON BEAMER STREET

SHEILA RILEY

Boldwood

First published in Great Britain in 2024 by Boldwood Books Ltd.

Copyright © Sheila Riley, 2024

Cover Design by Colin Thomas

Cover Photography: Colin Thomas

A CIP catalogue record for this book is available from the British Library.

Paperback ISBN 978-1-80483-287-5

Large Print ISBN 978-1-80483-288-2

Hardback ISBN 978-1-80483-289-9

Ebook ISBN 978-1-80483-286-8

Kindle ISBN 978-1-80483-285-1

Audio CD ISBN 978-1-80483-294-3

MP3 CD ISBN 978-1-80483-293-6

Digital audio download ISBN 978-1-80483-291-2

Boldwood Books Ltd
23 Bowerdean Street
London SW6 3TN
www.boldwoodbooks.com

I dedicate this book to my family who are patience personified, feed me, and bring me endless cups of tea and coffee when I am writing.

Lavender blue, diddle diddle
Lavender green
When I am king, diddle diddle
You will be queen.
Lavender green, diddle diddle
Lavender blue
You must love me, diddle diddle
As I love you.

— NURSERY SONG

1672–1685

PROLOGUE
LAVENDER GREEN, LANCASHIRE

I was about to leave the cottage to collect herbs from the meadow when Lady Felicia came to seek Ma's advice. I knew I must make herself scarce. Ma and Felicia had been friends for years, albeit in secret, for Lord Silas did not like his wife mixing with peasants – anybody from the village – witches, wise women, or healers, we were all the same to him. Even though he was not above sending his servant to collect herbal medication from Ma every week to ease his gout.

I could hear Lady Felicia and Ma chattering away even though I was in the next room, the scullery door was only closed over as I was collecting my wicker basket and hadn't intended to eavesdrop. And then their voices became hushed, but still carried through to the scullery. My hand was on the latch of the back door, and I knew I should have continued about my chores, but by then my curiosity had kicked in. What could be wrong with Lady Felicia?

'My stomach has been out of sorts for weeks,' she told Ma, 'and I feel quite bilious in the morning.' I could hear Ma's reassuring tone, and I knew I ought to get away. Ma held her consultations in the strictest confidence. And even though Lady Caraway had everything money could buy – a large house in its own grounds, a rich and powerful husband – there was one thing Ma knew she could not give him. They had not conceived the son whom Lord Silas so desperately wanted, even after ten years of marriage. Lady Felicia had mentioned to Ma on more than one occasion, she suspected many of the maladies she suffered were the result of her inability to conceive.

'Let me make you a betony tea to settle your stomach,' Ma said, mixing her finest herb. 'A cure for no less than forty-seven different maladies,' I heard her tell Lady Felicia, and I smiled, knowing Ma liked to add a bit of a backstory with her herbal infusions. 'This herb, widely believed by the ancient healers to be so precious, they should sell their coat to buy it, will make you feel right as rain in no time.'

The two women chatted for a while longer, and, unable to interrupt by going through the front room without letting Ma know I had not yet left to collect the herbs she needed, I was forced to wait in the scullery. Ma's only rule was that I must never interrupt a consultation. A born healer, Ma was widely known as the soul of discretion. She would never repeat the secrets passed on to her by those who came to be healed or seek guidance. When I made to go out the back way, what I heard struck me rigid when Lady Felicia spoke.

'Thank you for the tea.' The sound of her cup being placed on the saucer seemed to reverberate through the cottage. 'Although, I doubt it will cure this malady – I suspect I am with child.'

Panic screamed to the roots of my hair, and I knew Ma would feel the same. Betony must never be administered to a pregnant woman. It stimulated the uterus, I knew.

There was the crash of a jar hitting the stone floor and I could hear Lady Felicia rise to her feet, and she said, 'My dear, are you all right? You have gone quite pale.'

'You should have told me sooner,' Ma gasped, and I could hear her obvious distress as her voice rose higher and faster with every word. 'I would never have given you betony tea if I'd known you were expecting!' Lady Felicia had visited Ma on many occasions over the years for what she called, 'stomach troubles'.

I stepped back and spied through the narrow opening in the door and saw Ma sitting Lady Felicia in her straight-backed chair while she sat opposite. She took hold of Lady Felicia's hands and I could see by her pained expression how desperately sorry Ma was feeling, the pallor of her skin the colour of raw pastry.

'Felicia, this is a most terrible catastrophe, I would never have... Oh my Lord, we should pray...'

'Please, Deborah.' Lady Felicia sounded quite calm at Ma's revelation. 'Do not upset yourself, Deborah, this is not your fault. I should have told you sooner.'

'But there is a possibility you may lose the child!'

'What will be will be, my dear, there is no going back now.' Lady Felicia's words stunned me. She sounded so composed, not like a woman who had just been told she was going to lose the child for whom she had waited ten long years.

'As you know, my marriage has not produced the son Silas so desperately wanted. He was growing more impatient. More forceful.' She was quiet for a moment, as if trying to find the right words. 'The only thing that would negate his powerful urges was for me to conceive... I had no choice.'

'No choice?' Ma sounded confused, as was I.

'Silas threatened to divorce me if I did not produce the son and heir he so desperately wanted, to continue the Caraway name. My husband regards authority with paternity. He would not like it known he carries a fragile seed.' The last part of the revelation was said with bitter mien.

'But how do you know this?' Ma asked.

'He said he was cursed by a woman he sent to the gallows years ago. She said he would never father a child of his own.' I watched Lady Felicia rise from the straight-backed chair through the crack in the door, and she stood with her back to Ma as if ashamed to face her. 'He developed syphilis from a lady of the night and was told by the Harley Street specialist who was treating him that he was barren. It was years before I discovered the truth.'

This conversation was no concern of mine, and I had no right to listen. But I could not help myself. If this news got out the scandal would be remembered for years to come.

'I had a friend, a very good friend... Edwin,' Lady Felicia said. 'He'd been flying one of those new-fangled aeroplanes across enemy lines.' Her voice became wistful. 'So brave and debonair. I loved him so much. He was everything Silas was not, and he adored me, he told me so.' Felicia's voice then turned to ice when she finally said, 'His plane was blown up over Belgium.'

The gasp I heard next came from Ma.

'The child I am carrying is Edwin's.' Lady Felicia was silent for a moment, as if to let the news sink in. 'He was so truly kind, and more loving than Silas has ever been, how could I resist? I never thought for one moment I could conceive. I believed Silas when he told me that not having children was all my fault. So, you can imagine my shock when it happened.'

'Do you want the child?' I heard Ma ask.

'Not particularly, and especially not after Edwin's death,' Lady Felicia answered. 'I doubt I would make a good mother and Silas would make the worst possible father. We are not all gifted with a loving husband as you once were.'

'Oh, Felicia!' Ma gasped. I knew she was so careful when giving advice, her knowledge of herbs was as natural as breathing. 'I would never have...'

'Please,' Lady Felicia said, 'this is neither your fault nor mine.

The decision has been made for us. I can only assume by God's law this situation was meant to be.' There was another silence for a moment. 'This is my penance, Deborah,' Lady Felicia gripped my mother's hand, 'for allowing myself to be loved by another man.'

'Don't say such things, Felicia. I will do my best to bring you and your child safely through the confinement.'

'I don't want you to help me. I want to be with Edwin.'

Over the next few months, Lady Felicia was attended by nurses hired by her husband, yet her strength ebbed, and she became more subdued, but they could do little to help a woman who did not have the will to live.

After the fragile body of her lifeless son was brought into the world, it seemed to all concerned, his mother would soon follow. By the time Ma was called, she could see Lady Felicia had contracted childbed-fever, the infection had taken hold of Lady Felicia, and it was impossible to save her.

Lord Silas was beside himself – not with grief, but rage. He blamed everybody for the death of his child from Ma to the doctor, to the nurses, even to Lady Felicia, herself.

Only later, when we were back at the cottage, and Ma was at the table mixing the cures we needed, did she confirm what I had heard months earlier...

'Lady Felicia was not a stupid woman, by any means. She knew what she was doing when she drank the betony tea, but she did not lose the child, not then...' I knew that having been a friend of Ma's for years, she would have some idea of the powerful effect of herbs. I could hardly believe any woman could be so calculating. 'But who can say if any damage was done that day?'

'I don't understand,' I said, 'surely you don't blame yourself for what happened to Lady Felicia and her baby?'

'Who knows?' Ma answered. 'Lord Silas will stop at nothing to get the truth and the son and heir he wants.' Ma sounded like she was talking to herself, and I worried for the first time that she was filled with doubt. But Ma was one of the finest healers in the county, everybody said so.

'What happened to Lady Felicia was tragic,' I assured Ma, 'and I feel heart sorry for her, but her demise was not caused by anything we did.'

I may have sounded flippant and should have taken more notice. But my head was filled with other things, like love, and Aiden Newman – and the only link to Lord Silas was Aiden being his gardener.

Although, I did not know then how much the day Lady Felicia died would change my life. Ma and I were busy making cures for the injured soldiers returning from the trenches. Many more were wounded than had been expected.

'The War Office decided the country was well prepared to treat incoming casualties,' Ma told me as she worked at the table, 'however that calculation has been misjudged.' And so, after Lady Felicia's death, Lord Caraway spent much of his time in his London chambers, and Oakland Hall was requisitioned. The number of casualties that flooded into Oakland Hall meant Ma and I spent much of our time there, caring for the returning wounded. But apart from collecting the herbs and helping Ma make her cures, the war did not affect me much. Not then...

1

21ST JUNE 1916. AFTERNOON

'Well, that silenced me good and proper, Aiden Newman.' Joy laced my words and no doubt my eyes were full of sparkle. It was my sixteenth birthday, the day of the summer solstice. The sun was high and hot, the ground bursting with life. Brilliant, sharp-coloured flora and fauna erupting all over the meadow, as if in celebration of my special day. And those colours were even more vibrant after Aiden took me in his arms for another kiss, so heavenly I sank into his body, the hard planes of his muscles enfolding me, caressing me.

I felt like I'd jumped head first into an ocean, swimming against the tide. His kiss took my breath away, as I fell deeper and deeper into his very soul, and I had to hold on to him tightly to stop myself pouring onto the floor in a puddle of molten desire.

'Elodie Kirrin, you are the only girl I have ever, or will ever, love.' Aiden's lips brushed my ear, raising goosebumps across my skin, and his words burned into my heart.

'So why did you wait until my sixteenth birthday to kiss me?' I answered breathlessly, and when I looked into his intense blue

gaze, I instantly recognised the mirror image of passionate longing. We both wanted more than just a kiss.

A low, pleasant hum warmed my body, and I suddenly understood. Sixteen, the age of consent, and I so longed to consent. I
wanted so much to give myself to Aiden. He had turned eighteen
only the week before and could be called up at any moment. I
wanted to give him something precious. Something to remember
me by. We were two hearts beating as one, and it would have been
so easy to give in to the temptation and seal our love, both longing
to slake our mutual desire, but dare we yield?

'We mustn't,' he whispered. 'I can't leave you with...?'

Aiden's words of warning were unspoken, but we both knew
what he meant. He could be sent to France, fighting from the
trenches, like other employees from Oakland Hall who had gone
before him, and would never come back. Aiden wanted me, and I
wanted him. That much was clear. Although he didn't want to
leave me with a lasting legacy of our love if our first union turned
out to be our last.

'I can't bear the thought of leaving you,' his voice was stilted,
low and intimate, 'but knowing how much of our love I have yet to
discover will keep me alive.' His words meant only for me would
repeat over and over in my head on the best and the worst day of
my life...

We had been friends in the tranquil Lancashire village of
Lavender Green for as long as I could remember, and I had loved
him for all of that time. I was beyond thrilled when he'd told me
he felt the same way about me. Aiden lived in the centre of the
village with his parents and a gaggle of siblings, whilst I lived with
my widowed mother in Lavender Cottage on the edge of the forest.
Our home, a stone cottage known locally as the apothecary, had
been in my family for three centuries. Three hundred years of
herbal healers – *wise women*.

The most precious gift Aiden could have given me was that first kiss, and he'd waited until my sixteenth birthday because, he said, he didn't want to come up against the feared Lord Caraway, high court judge and his employer, if I should strongly resist him and threaten him with the law. As if I ever would, I'd told him, and we'd laughed at the absurdity.

Always kind, Aiden protected me when the villagers voiced their false opinions that Lord Caraway's wife died in childbirth up at Oakland Hall, because me and my ma got there too late to save her. But the villagers were wrong.

It was the old doctor's nurse who spread the rumours about Ma and me, while trying to cover up her own mistakes after Lady Felicia's usual nurse had been called away. The local nurse had been going from patients who carried infections, and had not even washed her hands, something Ma was very strict about. Not even after laying out the newly dead, before attending Lady Felicia, who had taken to the delivery bed. Neither the doctor nor the nurse gave a thought to cleaning their medical instruments properly, just a quick swill in lukewarm water was the only attempt to clean them, and not the scalding in boiling water they needed.

If nursing soldiers who came back from the battlefields of France had taught me and Ma anything, it was that infection was the biggest killer of all. Ma and I kept our hands and our instruments scrupulously clean at all times. But by the time we got to Lady Felicia, it was much too late to save her or the child.

Everybody knew Lord Caraway had a vicious temper. He had sent more miserable souls to the gallows than any other high court judge in the land. So, the village medics didn't want him pointing his finger at them. The knowledge got me thinking back to that day Lady Felicia called to see Ma...

* * *

After Aiden's kiss, my life stretching ahead of me seemed suddenly more glorious.

'Ma wanted me out of the cottage early,' I said, knowing I must talk of mundane things to quell the burning thoughts inside my head. 'I think she is baking one of her lemon balm cakes for my birthday.'

'Lemon balm cake is my favourite.' Aiden's voice was deep and husky, like he'd just woken from a cavernous sleep and my banal remark had brought him back to earth with a bump. Life could not get any better than this, I thought, reaching out and gently stroking his sun-weathered face.

'I'll walk back with you.' Aiden took my sweet-scented, herb-filled trug and kissed the top of my head. 'There is plenty of time for loving,' he said, wrapping his large work-toughened hand around mine and pulling me close. I knew then he would never push himself on me. He wanted my love, not my compliance. And I knew, I had never loved him more. 'For now, my love, your kisses will sustain me,' he said as we sauntered down the lane, 'and this exquisite longing to make you mine will be all the sweeter when we finally become one.'

'I love you more than life itself,' I answered.

'I'll come over after work for a slice of that cake.' Aiden stopped in the lane before we reached the cottage and turned me to face him, kissing the tip of my freckled nose.

'You don't need an invitation,' I laughed, feeling like I was walking on one of those white frothy clouds. Aiden, the most handsome man I had ever seen, his loving heart mine.

'I made you this.' Aiden was smiling as he took a garland of braided grass from his pocket, and solemnly placed it on my long, corn-coloured hair, like he was placing a crown. 'There, you are now officially queen of the meadows.' His eyes twinkled as his gaze rested on mine. 'It enhances the glow of your beauty.' Then, looking deep into my eyes, his smile slipped.

'I will treasure it forever.' We were both aware there was a war on, and this perfect joy could be a delicate thing.

'You grow more beautiful every day.' *By this time tomorrow I will not be here. I shall be on my way to France. But I cannot tell you such a thing, today of all days?*

'Why, thank you, kind sir,' I laughed. I did that a lot when Aiden was around. I suspected the glow he spoke of was not just down to the braided wreath, and I touched it with my fingertips. 'I'll go and show Ma.'

'Elodie,' Aiden said in a low voice, and I turned to him. He leaned in and kissed me once more, inviting a small giggle to reverberate at the back of my throat. 'I love you,' he whispered, 'and I always will.'

'I love you too, and I always have,' I answered.

His eyes were quiet. Intimate. Their unspoken gaze saying a thousand things.

When I reached the door, my heart was hammering so strongly I could barely breathe. 'Don't forget to come by for a slice of cake.'

'I won't forget,' Aiden said before turning, hands in the pockets of his dusty corduroy trousers.

I was still watching as he rounded the bend and sauntered into the distance, whistling a cheerful tune as he made his way back to Oakland Hall, giving me the impression he didn't have a care in the world. I could not be more wrong.

2

21ST JUNE 1916. NOON

Deborah Kirrin gazed out of the window, and although she knew she should not allow her burning pride, which flew in the face of all that was holy, she could not deny the honour she felt to have reared such a beautiful daughter as Elodie, a compassionate, caring girl who, even now, had the knowledge and expertise of all her wise ancestors put together.

Today was Elodie's sixteenth birthday, and Deborah could see her daughter had not a single care in the world, as she sauntered down the narrow front lane towards the meadow, to collect the herbs they so desperately needed for the brave servicemen, who were being sent back from Flanders' killing fields with indescribable wounds.

However, there was one blight on this otherwise perfect day, and Deborah prayed Lord Caraway would not call for his usual medication – a strong draught of laudanum to ease the pain of his gout-ridden foot.

She had been given strict orders not to supply strong painkilling medication without proper authority. However, Deborah knew His Lordship was a law unto himself and would have much to say about not getting his usual dose of medicine, to which he was most certainly addicted.

The brave young soldiers, coming home in droves, were so severely injured the pharmaceuticals could not keep up with the supply of medication needed. And as a herbal healer, her services were once more required, and she had the letter of authority from the Home Office, to prove she could not administer unauthorised medication, no matter who wanted it.

So, with Elodie's invaluable help, they were both, once more, doing what their ancestors had done for generations, by taking advantage of God's Own Market, freely given, to heal those who needed it most.

Deborah sighed as she turned back to her daily work, weighing, measuring, and dispensing healing herbs, teas and tinctures into glass bottles and jars ready for the collection from Oakland Hall.

Lord forgive me, she prayed, knowing she would rather dwell on the suffering of the young men who were returning home, half dead, than to imagine what may lie ahead for Elodie if Aiden had to go to war. *No, I won't let my mind go there, it is too terrible to think about...*

Nobody expected the masses of young men to be brought back from the battlefields so quickly, and the situation had become critical when medicine began to run out. Herbalists like Deborah and her daughter, Elodie were urgently called for, engaged to supply their own healing cures.

They were busier than ever, with casualties flooding back home every day. Everything and anything that could be used to save their brave lives was desperately needed. The military hospitals were barely able to cope with so many young men who needed treatment, and many large houses had been requisitioned as makeshift hospitals. The infirmaries, workhouses, and asylums, which the government had also commandeered to care for the sick and wounded, were full to bursting.

Initially, the local hospital could only keep hold of soldiers who were assured of being saved, and they were then sent to Oakland Hall for recuperation. However, as the war drew on, the hall was requisitioned by the War Office, as a hospital for the wounded, and required to do its bit. Even the high-born ladies, who did their best to help the sick and wounded, found the burden heavy-going.

Deborah and Elodie were working day and night, making cures in such quantities as never before. As Oakland Hall began to take in and care for even more injured soldiers, the doctors and nurses were in dire need, and their expertise of herbal healing had been called upon almost immediately. All balms, tinctures, calming restoratives, and cures were swiftly collected from the cottage every day, while Deborah and Elodie hardly had time to draw breath. But it was worth it, thought Deborah, to know the earth's natural treatments saved many a young man's life.

Turning from the large, well-scrubbed, wooden table in the centre of the stone-floored kitchen, Deborah busied herself collecting her heavy pestle and mortar from the dresser.

Her thoughts wandered to the weeks after Felicia's death, when Lord Silas would come to collect his tincture – the name he gave to the laudanum-based concoction to which he was addicted.

And for as much as she tried, Deborah could not ignore Lord Silas Caraway's insinuation that Elodie could be the answer to his craving for a son. She had good child-bearing hips, he had said last time he came, and even asked what young maiden would not want to benefit from a life as mistress of Oakland Hall?

When she had protested at such a sickening arrangement, he warned her Elodie could be her saviour – especially if it was decided she had given his wife some kind of tonic that had hastened her death. Deborah took a deep, steadying breath to calm herself. The betony tea she had given Felicia would never have taken so long to kill her. But she could never say for sure if it had endangered the life of the unborn child.

Deborah froze as she placed the herbs onto the table. Skill and centuries of judgement told her nothing she did could have saved Lady Felicia. It had been far too late by the time she and Elodie had been summoned. Much too late for Lady Felicia or her unborn child. However, she knew that if Lord Silas ever got wind of the fact she had administered the betony tea, albeit many weeks before his wife's death, he would show no mercy. The hangman's noose loomed large in her mind.

Lord Caraway would blame her, because she was not conventionally trained in medicine, even though her past record in healing was impeccable, which was why Felicia chose to go to her in the first place.

Lord Silas had been beside himself with rage and recriminations and the villagers agreed with the scurrilous accusations to pacify him, yet when any of them were in need of a soothing tonic or a healing tincture, they would secretly scamper along the back lane, to make use of her services, albeit unwilling to be seen.

Grinding herbs, Deborah was so deep in thought, she barely heard the bellpull, which rang in the scullery.

Laying down her pestle, she wiped her clean hands on the rough hessian sacking she wore over a dark skirt that reached the top of stout black leather boots. It was still early, and her heart flipped in dread, but she must hold her nerve, show no alarm, for his intention was always to instil fear, and Deborah did not wish to let him see she was apprehensive.

Lord Silas would come for two reasons, Deborah knew. The first would be for his weekly dispensary of the potent laudanum tonic. The other, more terrifying. Today was Elodie's sixteenth birthday and so he would want the answer to his proposal, which she would most vehemently refuse.

Her shoulders back, Deborah strode through the brightly lit room, past the polished jars of glistening oils, positioned on clean well-dusted shelves next to bright powders in their bowls, while drying herbs hung from the ceiling rack, stroking her hair as she passed. Once through the forest of twisted spikes and scented roots, she entered the scullery and the air suddenly cooled, the room darkening.

Her head was held high as she went to open the back lane gate, knowing the opium, needed for the soldiers, was becoming scarce. Deborah must tell Lord Caraway she could no longer supply his needs, but her refusal was overshadowed by her worry about her daughter's future. As dread bubbled up inside her, she tried her best not to show it, knowing she must also break the news that she could only dispense morphine-based medicines and cures to the hospital.

Lord Caraway did not have any crucial disorder that would warrant him in need of such medication. Gout, although painful when he had a flare-up, did not allow for the amounts he requested. And she was not going to tarnish her reputation by supplying him with the precious medication needed by deserving soldiers.

Although the news could not have come at a worse time, Deborah thought, fearing his reaction. Lord Silas Caraway had taken full advantage of the opium-based laudanum for many years and had become hopelessly addicted to the reddish-brown liquid.

Nevertheless, the soldiers' needs were much greater than his addiction, and he, of all people, must understand that she could not go against the law to supply his habit. Deborah must tell His Lordship, a high court judge and member of parliament, whose duty it was to do the right thing, when she unlocked the back gate. However, he seemed in a hurry, eager to be inside the cottage, and crossed the threshold unbidden. Being the landlord, he had every right to enter without invitation and there were times when he used his powers to the full. Standing aside, her mouth was pinched, her eyes narrowed, and her stance was stiff and uncompromising.

'You know what I've come for,' he said, ducking as he entered the low-beamed cottage, his tone dark and commanding. Towering over Deborah's slight frame, he was an intimidating sight.

'I am sorry, sir, but I am no longer allowed to dispense your usual tincture, as it is needed for the injured troops.' Deborah stood her ground. Unwavering, and to the untrained eye, unafraid.

'Do not goad me, wench, or you will suffer the consequences.'

'I am not goading you, sir,' Deborah answered, desperately trying to keep the tremble from her words, knowing this man was a bully of the lowest kind. If he saw her crumble, he would take swift advantage in any way he could. She had heard the rumours, and they were not pleasant.

'I am Lord Silas Caraway,' he said as if she needed to be reminded. 'You will do as I say. You will bring me the elixir.'

Again, Deborah shook her head. 'I am not allowed to do that, sir, I have a letter from the authorities...'

'I am the authority around here, and you would be wise not to forget it.' He leaned towards her, his words carrying an unspoken threat. 'I know full well what the authorities are ordering on behalf of the war effort.'

'But you do not accept the rule applies to you?'

He watched her twitching movements, and she was sure he could see she was nervous, and he knew why.

'You recall the day my son died, and Felicia? I vowed that one day I would come for the young wench. And I will have her.'

'You know the date?' Deborah felt the colour drain from her face when he said, 'You will recall the pledge you made on that terrible day, when my wife died at your hands?' Deborah was silent, unable to speak.

'I'm waiting. Do you acknowledge my words and the unspoken pledge that saved you from the hangman's noose?'

'A pledge, sir?'

'Do not play the fool with me, you know what I am here for. I have come to collect.' She could see he was growing impatient. 'I was not going to insist you bring your daughter to me, but you are forcing my hand.'

Deborah stood quite still, refusing to show him the reverence his standing dictated, and she saw a mean smile spread across his face.

'I made no such pledge. You are mistaken, sir.' She would never sacrifice her daughter to make her own life easier. Deborah could not recall him talking of marrying her daughter when she turned sixteen. The only time it was mentioned was on his last visit and she had told him then that Elodie would make her own decisions.

'We had an understanding,' he said, his barrel chest rising and falling, his breath coming in great bursts. 'I am not the most feared of this country's judges for nothing.' His eyes, lost in folds of skin, drilled into hers. His voice was low and threatening. 'You narrowly avoided the gallows on the promise you would give me your daughter on her sixteenth birthday. Now I've come for my payment.'

A thirty-year-old widow, Deborah drew back when his finger and thumb reached for the top button of her blouse, and the revulsion in her determined features was plain to see.

'You are fat, forty and, by the amount of laudanum you consume, I would say flaccid.' Deborah watched his fury darken the expression on his face. She would never allow her daughter to be chained to a monster like Silas Caraway, no matter how rich and powerful. Felicia had warned her what a cruel man he was. 'What could my daughter possibly want from a man like you?'

'You dare to speak to me in such a manner? I could have you horsewhipped.'

His skin mottled with an enraged flush of pink and her eyes narrowed as saliva built up in the corners of her lips, and she saw the loathsome look of lust in his eyes.

'My, my, you are a feisty one,' Lord Caraway said as she shrank from his touch, her silent rebuke apparently heightening his hungry gaze, travelling every curve. 'You fill me with a powerful urge I have not known for years.

'You made a promise after you killed my wife,' he said. His words were deceptively sweeter than honey. 'I suspect you are still of a childbearing age.'

Two things shocked Deborah to her core. The first was that he believed she might offer to have his child, and the second was that he believed she was responsible for his wife's death.

'I did not kill your wife. And I most certainly will not promise to have your child!' Deborah spat the words.

'Do not flatter yourself, Mother Kirrin, it is not you I choose to carry my son.' When his meaning dawned on Deborah, her stomach turned.

'My daughter is her own mistress, Your Lordship. She will have the man of her own choosing. I made no such promise to you.'

'You dare call me a liar?' His words were now a low threatening growl. 'Well, let me tell you, madam, you may regret your high-handed determination, when you realise who has the final say in this matter.' There was no denying the threat in his words and

Deborah knew he had the power to put her and Elodie out onto the street.

'My daughter is an innocent, sir,' Deborah's pleading words were all but a whisper, 'she has no knowledge of the world outside the village, she is just a humble healer, as am I.'

'You allowed my wife to die!' His lips twisted to one side like he was having some kind of seizure and Deborah knew she had to say something to try to make him understand.

'It was the childbed fever, sir,' she explained, 'the infection is passed on by attendants, the worst offenders for not washing their hands when they go from one patient to the next – even doctors!'

'How dare you!' Silas Caraway's nostrils flared, his eyes all but bulging from their sockets. 'You have the temerity to censure men trained by the finest medical minds of the twentieth century. Physicians who stand far above your kind, who would have been executed as a witch, yet you dare to judge them?'

'Your wife already had the fever when I was summoned,' Deborah argued. 'I never once said I would offer my daughter's life to save my own.' Such a thought was sickening, and Deborah knew she would die penniless in the gutter before she would allow this man to make Elodie his wife – or worse.

'You would rather face the gallows than allow your daughter to live in comfort and grandeur she has never known before?'

'The gallows were never once mentioned—' Deborah's words were brittle '—and if they had been, do you think I would still be here, in this village where I have been scorned since your wife died? Although, the villagers are not above using my services. I am a healer to any who need me.'

The air was still, and the room was silent. Deborah sensed he was watching her every move and she felt caught like a fly in a spider's web.

'The day has arrived, and I have come for my dues. Where is she?'

'She is collecting herbs.' Deborah's backbone stretched to its full length as she permeated courage and determination she did not feel. Nevertheless, she must not let him see she was fearful, for that was his usual manner, according to her poor friend, Felicia.

'When will she be back?' Taking empty laudanum bottles from his pocket, he did not wait for her to answer, instead he pushed the bottles into her hands. 'Fill these,' he demanded, and Deborah refused.

'You will supply my medicine without question, and you will do it now!' He was aware that the thump of his enormous fist on the table did not make her flinch as he had intended, instead she stood unmoving, until he went to the shelf and took down the large bottle of laudanum, which was due to go to Oakland Hall. Removing the cork, he downed a long swig of the powerful mixture.

'I can no longer supply your medication without proper authority,' Deborah said, watching his face darken.

'I am the authority!' He spat the words. 'And you will do as you are told.'

'You will not have my Elodie...' Deborah answered. 'I will die before I allow you to take my daughter.' Deborah Kirrin sounded so sure of herself when she spoke, until she saw his expression change from anger to hatred.

Her defiant declaration summoned an overpowering mist to descend in his hazy, laudanum-soaked brain.

'You may well have to stand by those words, Ma Kirrin.' His sagging jaw slackened, his words slurred. 'Now, tell me, where is she?'

'I've told you,' she answered defiantly, 'she is out collecting herbs.'

This woman made no consequence for his lofty status, as he would have expected from anybody else, and he knew that if the law were a woman, her name would be Deborah.

The hot blood rose in his veins as she stood before him, hand on hip, brazen, uncompromising, her hair clinging damply to her forehead. He edged towards her. And when she pushed him away, his rage had no boundary.

The gold, high-sided signet ring he wore on his little finger caught her face side on as his large hand swiped out. She fell. Caught off-balance. Her head making the most sickening crack when it hit the stone hearth. And for a moment she did not seem to move. He watched her lying there, sprawled across the floor.

Then he heard the most unearthly groan, and in one slow undulating movement, she drew herself up and rose from the floor. He watched in a horrified stupor as she gradually stood to face him.

'What witchery is this?' he asked. By the sound her skull made as it hit the stone flags, this woman should be rendered incapable of consciousness, let alone able to stand. But there was no blood, not a scratch. 'You are the enchantress.'

His rage dissipated, replaced by a fear he had not known since he was a child hiding from his alcoholic mother, who was hell-bent on giving him a good thrashing for no reason other than he had disturbed her afternoon rest.

Silas felt the blood drain to his boots. Wiping clammy hands on his coat-tails, he opened his mouth to speak, but his voice deserted him, replaced only by a strong, throbbing pulse in his throat, his chest rigid, his leg muscles turned to stone. He had every intention of fleeing the cottage, but his legs would not move. How could she revive so quickly?

'Get out.' Deborah's words, barely a whisper, filled the room. 'You mark my words – you will never father a child.'

Her words gave him the impetus he needed to move towards her. 'You dare to curse me, witch?' His huge hand shot out and curled around her throat. Pushing her backwards, she came to a halt when her body slammed against the limewashed stone. And as life seeped from her body, he registered what he had done. Pulling back his hand as if she were a hot poker straight out of the fire, he watched in horror as her limp body fell to the floor.

Stepping over her lifeless body, he caught sight of a coil of twisted hemp and flax, which he picked up, the strong fibres woven into a rope, long enough for his needs.

When he left the cottage a while later, he was completely unaware of the figure at the window.

As Aiden's tuneful whistle lessened, the harmony of the surrounding countryside was broken only by the low drone of buzzing bees and the peaceful twitter of the goldfinch as it feasted on teasel and verbena seed heads. When she could no longer see him in the distance, Elodie pushed down the latch with her thumb, eager to show Ma her new headdress.

The cottage was as silent as a church, and the expected aroma of freshly baked lemon cake was disappointingly absent. Placing the trug on the small table near the door, her hand went to the pale golden wreath that haloed her head.

'I'm back, Ma!' Elodie called while leaning on the post that went up the wooden stairs. But there was no answer, which Elodie thought strange, knowing her mother would usually be working in the outhouse at the back of the scullery waiting for Will, the orderly, who came daily from Oakland Hall, to collect the precious treatments that were in such high demand for the wounded soldiers.

Picking up the trug, the sound of her low-heeled boots echoed on the flagstone floor as she headed towards the back door of the cottage. Pushing down the latch, it gave that pleasing clack under her thumb, and she opened it to its full width into the scullery.

At first, nothing registered as any different. Then, as her eyes grew accustomed to the scene before her, Elodie noticed her mother's large mixing bowl had been upended, flour, eggs, and lemon balm scattered on the floor. Jars of herbs and oils were strewn on the flagstones.

Her brow wrinkled. Ma was very particular about the cleanliness of the cottage, especially in the room where she mixed her medicines and cooked the delicious meals they enjoyed. She would never leave it like this. Then, slowly, her unfocused gaze went around the room and Elodie's mind registered more chaos. Her stomach clenched, the only sound in the room was a small involuntary gasp escaping her lips.

An acrid smell gave her cause to cover her nose and mouth. Then she noticed the cast-iron pan had boiled dry on the polished black kitchen range, and the air was filled with the charred smell of the scorched pot.

She spun around and her horrified gaze moved to the end of the upturned table stretching to the outhouse beyond, which Ma used for the apothecary, and a cool breeze cocooned her from the open window, making her shiver. Stepping over the mess on the floor, she was more scared than she had ever been.

Her gaze trailed past the wooden six-lath rack from which her mother's herbs usually hung to dry, infusing her laundry with their scent, but it was now empty, the herbs strewn across the flagstones. And taking a few faltering steps towards the apothecary, the thrust of her gaze skewered the beam of the ancient apex roof, and her body began to tremble.

Her mind desperately tried to reject the scene before her, and looking over her shoulder into the scullery, she expected the action to drive away the ungodly sight before her. But when she turned back, the vision was still there. Hanging by the neck, her mother's lifeless body swung overhead.

She needed to run, to scream, but her body had become petrified stone, and she could not move. How had Ma got up so high when there was no stool. No ladder. No chair! Ma had been singing happily when she left the cottage earlier.

Elodie didn't recall leaving the outhouse apothecary, but then she was in the scullery, then the sitting room, trying desperately not to look back. The cottage was silent, save for a distant rhythmic creaking of her poor mother's body swinging back and forth. That sound would stay with her for the rest of her days.

Elodie did not know how long it was before she realised, the ear-piercing sound filling the room was her own unrestrained screams.

3

The cottage was soon filled with curious, intrusive people. Elodie
didn't know how long they had been there, or where they had all
come from. Most were villagers, but some she didn't recognise at
all. Men in bowler hats were asking questions she could not
answer. They looked official in their dark suits, and when she
opened her mouth to speak, no sound would come.

She wanted to shout and tell them all to get out, but she didn't
feel strong enough to challenge these people. She could not voice
the scrambled thoughts in her head, and all she wanted to do was
crawl into a corner and put her arms over her head until this
nightmare had gone away.

'Elodie!' She heard Aiden's anguished call before she saw him
enter the cottage, and then he was shouldering his way through
the villagers towards her. 'I've only just heard. I saw people
running down the lane.' He put his arms around her, and it was
only then she realised her body was shaking from head to foot. 'By
God, this is terrible.' Aiden held her close, the love and happiness
they felt earlier was now just a memory. Elodie felt completely

numb. 'You can't stay here by yourself. Ma said you must come to our cottage.'

Before she could answer, she watched the undertakers removing her ma's body.

Elodie was being told things she could make no sense of. Someone asked her a question and she stared blankly, trying to untangle the chaos in her head.

'Thank you all for your concern, but I think Elodie needs some privacy right now.' Aiden cleared the cottage and she slumped helplessly onto the fireside chair, only vaguely aware of the spattered blood on the hearth.

I want Ma, she longed to say, but remained silent. Stunned.

Aiden brought her a cup of tea sweetened with honey, and they sat for a long time saying nothing.

'She was the strongest woman I know,' Elodie said, eventually finally managing to voice her thoughts, 'she would never do something so cruel as to take her own life, not today, of all days.'

'What are you saying?' Aiden asked. 'You believe she didn't commit...' His voice refused to say the word 'suicide'.

'Why would she?' Ellie let her tears roll down her face. 'We were secure for the first time in years, we had steady work, steady money.'

'Who knows what goes on in people's heads?' Aiden put his arm around her and held her close, unsure he was saying the right thing. 'I'm as much at a loss as you,' he said. 'Neither of us have ever been in a situation like this.'

'Ma had no reason to kill herself,' Elodie was thinking out loud. 'She was going to bake me a birthday cake. The future looked rosy for once. We have regular money coming in from the War Office, I could hear her singing as I walked down the lane...' Elodie's shoulders shook under the weight of her sobs.

'Maybe there was something she didn't want to discuss, something personal.'

'Something personal? Like what?' Wide-eyed, Elodie looked to Aiden as if he had the answer, but of course, he didn't. 'And if there was something wrong, or she was ill, I would be the first person she would tell, surely. Why would she do such a thing, today of all days,' Elodie said again, 'my sixteenth birthday.'

The immediate shock of her discovery was beginning to ebb, and her mind was beginning to tick over again, asking questions she could not answer.

'Who came to help you?' Aiden said, knowing he could not have been far away.

'One of the orderlies who came to fetch the medicines. I don't know his name, but he raised the alarm and alerted the whole village.'

'Don't concern yourself about that now,' Aiden said, his head full of unasked questions.

'Nobody thought to ask how Ma got up there in the first place,' said Elodie, 'I wonder if anybody knows?'

'After the villagers had trampled all over the cottage, the place looked like it had been ransacked. I remember thinking how your Ma would have gone mad if she could see it knowing she kept the place spotless.'

'It looked like that before the villagers even got here.' Elodie's voice was dull and flat, the mere effort to answer too much. The focus she needed, to grasp the situation, was seriously lacking.

'I should have stayed with you,' Aiden said, rocking her in his arms.

Then, suddenly, she broke free from his embrace as guilt rose up inside of her. Elodie's breathing came out in great gulps. She felt she was drowning. 'If I hadn't wasted time...' she said. 'I should have been here,' she cried. Her thoughts moved back and forth between the moment she walked through the front door, not a care in the world, then, moments later when her whole world shattered into a million pieces. 'Nothing makes sense. I should have read the signs.' She couldn't get her thoughts to line up, the words stilted. 'But there were no signs.'

'I wish I knew how to ease your pain,' Aiden answered. This was not the time to tell her he had been called up to go overseas to serve in the army corps. He discovered last week that he had been enlisted, but there was never a good time to tell Elodie.

Elodie remained silent. Her natural curiosity dissipated. She wasn't ready for talking, not even with poor Aiden, who had been so reassuring when it was the last thing she wanted. She longed to be alone with her thoughts. Try to make sense of the situation. Unable to understand any of it.

'Who reported the—' Aiden began, but she cut off his words.

'Suicide? You can say it, you know, everybody else will.' Her words were barbed, cruel, she wanted him to feel as bad as she did and hated herself for it.

'What else could it be?' Aiden asked and at that moment she wanted him gone.

'I don't believe my mother hung herself. Why would she?' Elodie wanted answers but didn't even know what questions to ask.

'I'll stay with you,' Aiden said, and she held up her hand determinedly.

'No, Aiden. Thank you. But no.' Her voice was stronger than she intended. 'I have a lot to think about and I don't...' She could not tell him his presence was a distraction she couldn't cope with right now. 'I will speak to you tomorrow.'

She walked with him to the door, hoping he wouldn't linger. But even his gentle kiss on her cheek felt like an intrusion into her private grief. She needed to be alone.

'I love you so much,' Aiden whispered, knowing he would not be here to help her through this awful time, and there was nothing he could do about it. 'You can't go through this alone.'

'I will see you tomorrow, Lord Caraway will be wondering where you have got to.' Elodie vaguely recalled seeing His Lordship earlier, he was standing in the lane outside the cottage.

'Let him wonder,' Aiden said curtly, 'you are far more important to me.'

'Tomorrow,' she said, trying to force her lips into a reassuring smile, but it was impossible.

* * *

The next morning, Elodie put her hands over her ears, to ignore the persistent knocking. She could not face anybody. Not even Aiden. Not yet. She had sat in her mother's chair beside the dying embers all night and stared into space, trying to fathom what she should do next.

The floor was still littered with debris. Her mother was so finicky about keeping the place clean and tidy. A place for everything and everything in its place, she would say. Looking through heavy eyes, Elodie knew Ma would be distressed to see the disorder of the room. The place looked like it had been raided. The idea was immediately dismissed. There hadn't been a crime committed in Lavender Green for twenty years.

What about the lack of a chair or stool for Ma to climb up on? Elodie asked herself. Ma could hardly levitate to the rafters! The thought was so outrageous, it caused a gurgle of hysteria to bubble up in the back of her throat and she had to bite the inside of her cheek to stop herself laughing out loud.

Then she noticed the crown, which Aiden had made for her. It was discarded amongst the rest of the debris, and she walked over, sitting down among the chaos. Picking it up, her fingers stroked the silken grasses he had plaited with his own hands. She felt her throat tighten and stinging tears welled up at the back of her eyes. Elodie desperately wanted to show her mother the sweet-smelling halo, before she realised that never again would she share even the smallest of things with her mother, knowing she had lost the one person who would be there for her and who had always made things better.

'Why did you do it on my birthday, Ma?' Elodie said out loud to the silent cottage, longing to know the answer, as scalding tears coursed down her cheeks. Her whole body jerked under the intensity of her sobs.

When she heard the closing of the wooden gate, she stood up, pulling the starched net curtain to one side, her vision blurred by tears, and saw Aiden. He was in army uniform, and he was waving from the crowded charabanc. Realising what was happening, she dropped to her knees, distraught. Aiden was going off to war, to fight on the slaughtering fields of France.

Her heart was so full of regret for many things. She should have been here for Ma. She should have wished Aiden good luck. Said a proper goodbye. Now she knew what he meant when he said he had something to tell her.

Oh God! Please let me see him again!

* * *

In the depths of her grief, Elodie questioned the reasons of her mother's death repeatedly over the next few days. The villagers were saying she had committed hari-kari because she blamed herself for the death of Lady Felicia.

There was no inquest, no post-mortem. Lord Caraway told the ancient coroner the case was cut and dried. He let it be known her mother had committed suicide whilst the balance of her mind was disturbed, due in part to her guilt, with regard to the death of Lady Felicia and their much-longed-for son. The old coroner would never dare argue with Lord Caraway, and Deborah was buried in unholy ground that had not been blessed, which broke Elodie's heart when she went every morning to put flowers on her mother's grave.

Elodie closed her eyes and prayed at her mother's graveside, just a small mound of earth at the end of the woods. No head-stone. Nothing to say that her mother had been the backbone of the village for years. Ma was a good woman, and Elodie knew she did everything she could to save Lady Felicia, so why would she be so guilt-stricken as to take her own life a year later, and on her daughter's birthday, too? It didn't make sense...

4

Silas Caraway gave a sharp rap on the front door and Elodie jumped from the chair. She checked her hair was tidy and her clothes were not rumpled. The aroma of freshly made bread and fruit scones wafted through the cottage. When she opened the front door that opened straight onto the garden, he grunted something she could not untangle as words.

Ducking, he entered the sitting room, and his heavy, over-weight frame filled the room as much as the scent of freesias, her mother's favourite flower, which were placed on the small side table near the front door.

He had not stepped foot inside the place for a year, which had filled her with a false sense of security, thinking she would be allowed to continue the tenancy of the cottage in her mother's absence. But, by the stern look on his face, her dreams were about to be shattered to smithereens.

As his eyes roamed the clean and tidy kitchen, Silas Caraway looked at her in a way she found a little disturbing. He looked from her to the scrubbed table upon which she, like her mother before her, prepared her balms and tinctures.

'Did you see that?' he asked her, and she turned to where he was looking.

'See what, sir?' she asked, and he shook his head, as if trying to throw off an improbable thought.

'It was nothing,' he said, watching her pour tea into dainty cups on the small table near her chair. A level-headed man, he was not in the habit of seeing ghosts. But this particular ghost may have a grievance against him. The thought made him shudder.

'Are you feeling cold, sir?' Elodie asked, eager to fathom if he had come to evict her or to allow her to remain in the cottage. 'Please, sit here by the fire where it is warmer.' The sun was high and warm, the summer's day sunny and bright and there wasn't a cloud in the sky, yet she had lit a small fire to make the cottage more homely, feeling no need for a fire herself, as she spent most of her time in the apothecary. She looked up when he hesitated and noticed him looking at her as if he were examining a rare, delicate object.

'I am not cold,' he said, his eyes appreciatively taking in every curve and dip of her body. She was a sturdy girl, he mused, her childbearing hips were of good proportions, and she was of the same solid stock of women who found no difficulty in pushing out babies every year. He would have his male heir in no time at all. Then she could do as she pleased. There was no sentimentality in his decision. 'I have a proposition, that will dissolve you of the necessary requirement, essential to living in this cottage.'

His verbosity had Elodie mentally running to keep up with his meaning. And she wasn't sure she favoured her own under-standing.

'I don't understand, sir,' Elodie said as she handed him the cup and saucer.

'There is nothing to understand,' he said a little impatiently, 'I am asking you to marry me.'

Elodie was so shocked she had to grip the cup and saucer for fear of losing both. Marry him! She could think of nothing worse. Except losing her home, her job, and her belongings, which he could make happen.

'I guarantee you a roof over your head.' Silas Caraway was talking as if he were closing some kind of deal instead of changing her life forever. 'You will be given an allowance, of course.'

'But I have never given marriage a single thought, sir.' Not to him, anyway. The only person she had ever dreamt of marrying was Aiden. If she accepted Lord Caraway's proposal would that not make her the same kind of woman who sold her body? She could not bring herself to contemplate such a thing. She would not marry this man.

'I promised your mother I would look after you if anything ever happened.' His words carried the gravity of a man who was never contradicted.

'Why would you do that, sir? You have no responsibility towards me.'

'I will take care of you,' he said ignoring her question. 'I will give you anything you want, all you have to do is marry me and live in comfort for the rest of your life.'

Elodie felt she did not have much choice in the matter. Her mother had taken her own life; her best friend, the only man she had ever loved, was fighting in a far-off land, and she may never see him again. Elodie wondered if she would lose everything if she did not comply. He did not elaborate on details, and she feared to ask. The thought of becoming this man's wife was sickening. But did she have any choice? She doubted it. She had been given to understand from Aiden that Silas Caraway did not deal in compromise.

'I need some time to think about your kind offer, sir,' she said, stalling for time. His proposal had come like a bolt from the sky. She had never expected such a thing.

'All I ask is that you give me a son and you can have anything your heart desires.' By offering her a gold band in return for a much-craved son and heir, she was sure of a place to live and plenty of food to eat. Elodie's mind worked at breakneck speed. She could earn enough money from the sale of her herbal treatments to leave the village. There was nothing for her here any more.

'I did not expect or even imagine I would marry such a powerful man as yourself.' The notion appeared to please him, she thought.

'Is it such a terrible proposition?' Silas Caraway asked when the silence lengthened. 'At least you'll have a home for the winter and will not have to sleep under the hedgerows you are so clearly fond of. What choice do you have?' His voice held the supreme confidence of a man who rarely heard the word 'no'.

'I do well financially, selling my cures.' The words were out of Elodie's mouth before she had time to stop them, and she knew in her heart she had said the wrong thing.

'Is that so?' Silas leaned back in his chair, glaring at her, showing a determined belief in his own superiority. 'I can make sure you do not find any more work at the hospital. The people don't trust you the same way they trusted your mother,' he said, obviously trying to shatter what little confidence she possessed.

Elodie knew she had as much experience as her mother. But one thing she had no power over was the dominating influence of Silas Caraway.

He rose from the chair, which creaked under his obese frame, and stood so close, Elodie feared he was about to kiss her. She could think of nothing worse than being in the arms of a gout-riddled widower who drank too much, at forty was twenty-three years her senior and grunted like a stuck pig.

Forcing down the sour bile rising in her throat, Elodie tried to think fast, but her thoughts were jumbled. She must give a refusal without causing offence. Because to upset Silas Caraway would bring dire consequences.

'You are a distinguished high court judge, sir,' she reminded him, 'while I am but a low-born lass.'

'You are young, and strong. It has been proven; a woman of pedigree is not strong enough to carry my seed to fruition.' His words were matter-of-fact. He could have been talking about the mating of the farmyard animals he so resembled. 'I am looking for someone who is strong – and submissive.'

'Then you are looking at the wrong person,' Elodie answered. Strong she may be. But submissive? Never. 'I take orders from no man – and what about my cures?'

'So be it,' Silas said as if the matter were already agreed. 'You can do your work for our injured soldiers.' Although, he did not tell her that he would stop her from doing so as soon as the war was over. 'You will live at Oakland Hall in the manner I expect of a wife. You will have jewels and furs. You will come and go as you please.'

'As I please?' Elodie asked, and he nodded.

'You will treat the hall as your home, you will be entitled to roam as far as you wish.' *But only within the grounds*, he thought. *The forest and the meadows will be out of bounds.*

'But I did not agree to be your wife, sir.' Elodie could not think of anything more repulsive. This man might be one of the most powerful in the land, but he had no power over her. She had the means to support herself. Unless he evicted her. Then, life as she had always known it would be over.

'You mean to tell me you prefer to roam the lanes and

hedgerows without a roof over your head,' Silas was impatient at her hesitation, 'as an alternative to living in luxury for the rest of your life?'

Elodie insisted he give her twenty-four hours to think about his proposal, remembering Aiden had said she could move in with his mother and family.

When she reached the Newman cottage in the centre of the village, there were a group of villagers outside the gate and her trepidation grew with each faltering step.

'Mrs Newman?' Elodie saw Aiden's mother raise her tear-stained face from her apron.

'Oh Elodie, I've just received this.' Mrs Newman held up a piece of paper. 'My boy is missing, the powers-that-be think he's dead!'

'No!' Elodie gasped as the bottom fell out of her world. The shock was so great, she didn't even remember the walk back home. Unable to eat, her head was pounding, and even when she shut herself away in her bedroom, she could not sleep, or even cry, unable to release the volcanic grief steadily building inside her.

Elodie closed her eyes, longing to recapture the feeling of his last kiss, knowing her love for Aiden was what usually held her together. But the memory of their last meeting faded from her mind so quickly as other thoughts crowded in. Questions she could not answer. She opened the drawer in the bedside table and took out the letters he had written to her, and her eyes drank in every loving word. She could not envisage a life without him. He could not be dead.

The news had left her feeling emotionally arid, a dried, disbelieving husk. He can't be dead. Her voice said over and over in her head. He can't be. I would know.

'I would know!' Elodie sat up in her bed and screamed the

words that reverberated around the empty room and bounced off the walls.

Then, the long-awaited tears came. 'He can't be dead!' she sobbed until she could cry no more and eventually she drifted into a fitful sleep, in which Aiden was walking towards her, his arms outstretched, his handsome face bathed in golden sunshine, beckoning her to join him, and they looked deep into each other's eyes, luxuriating in the warmth.

Aiden was so close she could almost reach out and touch him, breathe him in, feel the essence of his love, she felt the tears stinging her eyes as he leaned in to kiss her. His unique touch seeping into her body, her soul. His arms held her close, drawing her to him. Gently rocking her, reassuring her.

'We will be together again,' he whispered, then lifting her chin, his kiss was as gentle as the flutter of a butterfly's wings. Her eyes slowly opened, and Elodie's fingers were flat against her lips. She had been so sure Aiden had kissed her. But he wasn't here!

She could not contemplate a life without him. Stretching out her arm across the bed, her hand caressed the place she dreamt he had been. But he was not there... Shrinking into a foetal curve, she cried until she could cry no more.

Mrs Newman received Aiden's scant belongings weeks later, even his identification tag, still covered in the dried mud of Passchendaele, which she gave to Elodie who wore it around her neck.

When Silas Caraway had asked her to marry him, stating that she could no longer live at the cottage, Elodie, emotionally drained, lowered her eyes to the floor. She knew she had nowhere else to go...

5

OCTOBER 1918

Elodie had married Lord Silas Caraway in a small ceremony, but theirs was not the marriage she had dreamed of, and apart from the fact that there was still no sign of the son he longed for, Lord Silas proved to be a bully and a tyrant when his wishes were not exacted. And, although Elodie had nothing to compare it with, lovemaking should not have been so rough and painful she was sure – otherwise, why would anybody do it more than once?

In anger and frustration, Lord Silas spent more time in his London chambers, while Elodie, like a bird in a gilded cage, spent her days alone, mixing herbal remedies. Then, to take her mind off her impetuous decision to marry Silas, while still mourning the loss of her beloved Aiden, she spent long hours tending the recovering wounded who had been brought to Oakland Hall to recuperate.

* * *

The day had been so busy, settling in the new intake of soldiers, and Elodie felt she could sleep on a clothes line, she was so tired.

There were a couple of empty beds, however, Elodie knew that although they would soon be filled, she felt a stab of shame when she hoped they would not be occupied today. If she didn't get some sleep tonight, she would be in no fit state to do her job properly tomorrow.

'We have one more soldier, Your Ladyship,' Matron said, and Elodie still found it unusual to be addressed in such a manner. 'You look tired, we can admit this one.'

'No,' Elodie said, immediately feeling pangs of remorse knowing all the other nurses were working just as hard as she was. 'I will stay and do my duty, the same as everybody else.'

'You will work yourself into the ground,' said Matron, a kindly woman who had given her whole life to serving the sick and wounded. And, although Elodie felt dead on her feet when the soldier was brought onto the long bed-lined ward that had once been the ballroom of Oakland Hall, she remembered her mother telling her that their life was to help those less fortunate, and these brave men needed all the help they could get.

'I am stronger than I look, Matron.' Elodie managed a smile as the door opened and the patient was brought onto the ward.

'I know that voice,' the soldier said, and Elodie's heart leapt to her throat when she heard the local dialect and, turning, she saw a young soldier in a wheelchair, the bandage covering his eyes telling her he was blind.

'Will? Will Birch, is that you!' Suddenly forgetting her tired, aching body, thrilled to see the hospital orderly. 'You made it! Oh, that is good news, I am so happy to see you.' The last time she saw Will he was making funny faces from the window of the charabanc that day he and Aiden went off to war...

'We put up a good fight, Elodie,' Will told her when he was settled, and she came back with a cup of tea and a packet of cigarettes. Putting one to his lips, she lit it for him.

'Did you and Aiden stay in the same unit?' she asked, her heart hammering against her ribs at the mere mention of Aiden's name.

'Aye,' said Will, 'we went over the top together, and on into no-man's-land, then we got split up. I caught the business end of a toffee apple from their trenches.'

Elodie had no need to ask what a 'toffee apple' was, she had heard many a tale of the trench mortar bombs that caused so much damage to a body.

'I never saw him again.' He gave a low rueful half-laugh. 'Well, I never saw anything or anyone again. But at least I got to come home, that's the main thing.'

'Yes, Will,' Elodie said, trying to keep his spirits up, 'that is most certainly the main thing, and let's give thanks for small blessings.'

'He would be thrilled to see you all decked out in a nurse's uniform doing what you do best,' Will said, as an afterthought.

'Well, now we will never know.' Elodie could feel the tears sting the back of her eyes, but she refused to cry on the ward, grateful Will could not see her distress. Turning, she made an excuse and hurried from his bedside only to see another wheel-chair being brought in. The day was continuing the way it had begun, with a full complement of filled beds.

'You might want to admit this one too,' said Matron and Elodie gave a gentle sigh. These men had been through so much. So, she must not be uncharitable. Their need was much greater than hers. What was a pair of aching feet to a soldier who had none. What was a stiff back to a man who would never walk again because his was broken?

She efficiently took the clipboard that had the names and ranks of the new patients from Matron and looked for his details.

'Sergeant Aiden Henry Newman. Twenty years of age. Shrapnel wounds: head, body...' The words floated before her eyes and Elodie realised she must be more tired than she had first thought. She was beginning to hallucinate.

'Are you all right, Nurse?' the soldier asked and Elodie looked up to see Aiden sitting in the wheelchair. She felt as if she were going down a dark tunnel. The light was beginning to dim. Moments later, she sank into oblivion.

6

NEW YEAR'S EVE, 1924

Molly Haywood's Beamer Street house was so clean you could eat your dinner off any floor. Molly looked around her cosy kitchen and gave a satisfied sigh. A widowed mother of four lively offspring, including her seventeen-year-old daughter, Daisy, her mainstay, then fifteen-year-old Davey who worked in the paper bag factory along the dock road, and fourteen-year-old Freddy who'd just left school and was about to start work as an apprentice at Beamers Electricals. Finally, there was her youngest, eleven-year-old Bridie, who, like the budgie in the cage on the kitchen shelf, was never out of the mirror.

'Where did the years go, Bert?' Molly asked her dearly departed, much-missed husband, who was taken from her on the battlefields of Ypres in 1916, when her children were still young. Then, as now, she strived to do her best by her family, and worked all the hours sent to make sure they were loved, well fed and cared for.

Molly, like most of the folk around Beamer Street, didn't have much, but what she lacked in riches she made up for with two parents' worth of love inside her for her children, who never went without. A full stomach, a clean bed and a listening ear, that's all her family needed.

Tomorrow was the start of a brand-new year and Molly, being a superstitious woman, believed that whatever situation she was in at midnight would last throughout the coming year. So, making sure a fire blazed in her hearth at midnight, there was coal in the scuttle, bread and salt in the cupboard, a fine spread of food on the table, and coppers in her purse, Molly believed the coming year could be a good one.

Once she had all of those things organised, she could battle the greatest obstacles with her usual can-do spirit. And if she couldn't do it, she was sure Daisy would.

The whole place was gleaming in readiness for the new year. From the open fireplace, the coal glowed a deeper red in contrast to the shining black-leaded hob, with the oven to its right sending its glow onto the top of the shiny brass-railed fender. The flames flickered onto the mahogany legs of the table and shed its radiance over the polished chiffonier against the parlour wall, casting a glow in its oval mirror and over the little ornaments her children had bought her, sitting on the polished shelf.

Raising her chin, Molly drew back her shoulders and stood admiring the view of the bustling street from her gleaming, newly polished bay windows, framed by dolly-blue tinted lace curtains, which she had starched to perfection, their folds arranged into identical white billows.

With her arms folded across a motherly bosom, Molly was astonished when she saw Daisy coming out of Mary Jane's Kitchen – the bakery, owned by Mary Jane Everdine who lived next door.

'Mam! Come quick,' Daisy beckoned when she came flying out of the corner shop door across the road like the devil, himself, was after her. A fierce gust of wind blowing up from the River Mersey gave Daisy cause to hold on to the white mob cap she wore as a recently qualified baker, her pristine apron flapping in the winter breeze as she dodged icy puddles in between the cobbles, to cross the road. 'Mam, you're wanted on the telephone!' Daisy's large brown eyes were wide as Molly went to the front door, knowing the telephone was one of only two in Beamer Street. Mary Jane's husband, Cal, had had one installed in the bakery, when Mary Jane had found out she was expecting again, when they moved next door from the flat above the bakery. Cal had also had a telephone installed in their house, in case of emergencies, like phoning the doctor or the midwife. Everybody knew how he loved Mary Jane, and Cal was taking no chances with her health, or that of his offspring.

Molly had never used a telephone in her life and did her absolute best to stay as far away from them as possible. 'I don't know anybody with a telephone,' her eyebrows pleated into a puzzled frown, 'and I can't understand why anybody would want one.' However, Molly's natural curiosity got the better of her when she said, 'Who is it that wants to talk to me on the telephone?'

'Come on, Mam!' Daisy called as her mother lifted her coat off the peg in the hallway. Daisy almost danced on the spot in an attempt to keep warm in the icy breeze that promised snow before nightfall.

Molly was still sprightly in her forties and hurried down the stone steps of one of the larger houses on their side of Beamer Street, pushing her arm through the sleeve of her coat as she headed towards the terraced red-brick bakery.

Unbeknown to the inhabitants of Beamer Street, except the Haywood family, every house was owned by Cal Everdine, who had inherited them from his rich father. However, Cal had put the properties in the hands of agents in Liverpool and never had much to do with them since he came back from the war after living in Canada.

'Somebody wants me on the telephone,' Molly called to Ina King, who was about to go into her own house on the same side as the bakery. Talking on a telephone was a novelty to the residents of Beamer Street, and Molly could not resist the urge to boast, especially to Ina who liked to be the first to know everybody's business.

Then, as Molly suspected, Ina tapped her forehead with the palm of her hand in an exaggerated show of suddenly *remembering* something she 'needed' from the bakery. A telephone call was a huge occasion because apart from officials, nobody else had such an instrument of communication with the outside world.

'Did Daisy say who it is that's calling you?' Ina was eager to know, falling into step beside Molly.

'Did they give you a name, our Daisy?' asked Molly, and Ina quickened her pace to keep up with the two women. She didn't want to miss a thing.

'It's Aunty Rosie's lad, our Aiden.' Daisy knew Ina would not go about her own business until she had squeezed every last ounce of information from her mam, who would practically burst out of her girdle in the race to crow, especially to Ina. Daisy smiled, knowing the two women went out of their way to try to outdo each other at every turn. 'You'll have to hurry, Mam,' Daisy called, nearing the bakery door, 'he said it's urgent.'

'So, Aiden's your sister's lad?' Ina questioned, and Molly nodded, still fastening the buttons on her coat as protection against the freezing, notoriously cold west wind blowing up from the Mersey. Molly might be wearing her best coat, but she was still wearing her carpet slippers, and didn't want to be loitering in the street discussing her business. 'Does she live around here, your sister?' Ina asked.

As reluctant as she was to share her life story at that moment,

Molly could not resist the urge to boast. 'She lives in Lavender Green, a small Lancashire village about fifty miles away.'

'I do hope it's not bad news, Molly,' Ina said. 'For sure, bad news is not welcome at any time of year,' the broad Irish dialect that was so common in these parts was in evidence when Ina added, 'but on New Year's Eve, it's a terrible thing.'

'Why would it be bad news?' Molly asked indignantly. 'The call might be to wish me a happy new year.' In truth, Molly had no idea why her nephew was telephoning her, she had not seen him since he miraculously arrived home from the war after being missing presumed dead for months. Her sister had told Molly that the nurse actually fainted when her son was brought into the huge manor house that had been requisitioned for the use of injured and recovering servicemen. And so, he should have been, he was a hero who had saved his men when he was on the front line being bombarded by Lord knows what! And, as he worked for Lord Caraway before the war, it was only fitting he received the finest of care.

'Aye, I suppose,' said Ina, who was also of the opinion that whatever situation you were in when the old year gave way to the new, that was your lot for the rest of the year.

'It had better not be bad news,' Molly muttered.

'Well, like I say,' Ina, usually began her conversation like she was halfway through it, 'who'd go to the expense of a telephone call just to wish you a happy new year?'

'I'll have you know, Ina, my sister and her family keep in very good contact with me over the telephone, and no expense is spared.' It wasn't true of course, but Molly had no intentions of letting Ina put a damper on such a rare event as receiving a telephone call as she increased her pace, leaving Ina behind to wonder.

'She walks through this shop like the Duchess of Connaught,'

Ina whispered to another customer waiting in the queue, while pushing her shopping basket up her arm before drawing her heavy black shawl around her shoulders, proffering an answer before being asked the question. 'She's receiving a private telephone call from someone in her family.' Ina was dying to know how a member of Molly's family was in a position to make a telephone call all the way from Lancashire. She had never even heard a mention of an Aiden before from Molly.

Beamer Street mothers set great store by propriety, Daisy knew, as she led her mother to the curtained cubicle at the back of the shop. It showed in their clean doorsteps and gleaming doorknobs, knockers and letter boxes, and also in the way they conducted themselves, like they had a pole up the back of their cardigan, never minding that their best curtains might be in Uncle Bill's pawnshop, along with their husband's Sunday best suit. Outside show was everything to these women, her mother especially.

With her back straight and her head high, Molly took the earpiece of the candlestick telephone in one hand, looking to Daisy for reassurance that she was doing the right thing.

Daisy nodded, silently motioning for her mother to hold the black Bakelite mouthpiece to her lips.

'Hello, Molly Haywood speaking!' Molly's voice had the same tone she used when talking to the parish priest, except the volume was much louder. 'Is there anybody there?'

'You're not at a séance, Mam,' Daisy hissed, 'he can hear quite well, without you having to shout.'

Molly wrinkled her nose and listened for a voice at the other end of the line.

'Aunt Molly?' The deep voice sounded a little uncertain, and when Molly confirmed that, yes, it was she who was now speaking, Aiden seemed to let out a relieved sigh before he passed on his mother's good wishes for the coming new year. 'I have a little favour to ask,' Aiden said, 'and please say no if you feel I am taking advantage of your good nature...'

'Go on, lad,' Molly said in her usual pragmatic way. 'If I don't like the idea, I'll soon let you know, so spit it out before it chokes you.'

'Do you still take in lodgers, Aunt Moll?' Aiden asked, and Molly's forehead pleated in confusion. The last she'd heard, Aiden had a particularly good job working for Lord Caraway, the most feared judge in the land, according to most people. She knew Aiden chauffeured Lord Caraway around all over the place when he was not working in the greenhouses at Oakland Hall. Aiden had worked there since he was demobbed from the army back in 1918.

'Aye, lad, I can always find room for my family. Why do you want to move to Beamer Street?'

'The room isn't for me, Aunt Molly,' said Aiden. 'I have a friend, and she...'

'She?' exclaimed Molly and Daisy put her finger to her lips, knowing her mam would be so engrossed in her call she would not be aware she was talking so loudly. Molly wrinkled her nose again, but nevertheless she lowered her tone. 'What kind of *she*?'

'I'll tell you when we get there,' said Aiden. 'I don't want to discuss anything on the telephone.'

'Aye, you never know who's listening,' Molly said twitching the makeshift curtain. Her probing nature was already curious. She'd be like a cat on broken glass, waiting to find out what Aiden had to say. 'I do have a room as it happens.' Molly would never turn her nose up at a bit of extra, knowing the money always came in handy when she had a growing family to feed. 'When do you want to come and see it?'

'Will this evening suit?' Aiden sounded relieved, and Molly

prayed that he had not got a young girl in the family way. It would be like Mary Jane all over again, and Molly didn't want to get herself a reputation for collecting stray girls in trouble, whose family wanted them out of the way. *Perish the thought.*

'She also has the sweetest five-year-old daughter, who will be accompanying her.'

'What about her husband?' Molly could not keep the obvious curiosity from her voice, knowing the chatter had died down in the shop, and she was sure straining ears would be trying to catch every word.

'I'll tell you when I get there,' said Aiden.

'Later today is fine by me, will you be coming in your car?' Molly shouted down the phone, unable to resist a bit of boasting, and when Aiden said he would be in the car, Molly almost jumped for joy. 'I'll look forward to seeing you in your motor, give my love to your mam!' Her voice rose again, to the enjoyment of the long line of customers waiting to collect their New Year's Eve orders, and Molly heard the click on the line as Daisy motioned for her to put the earpiece in its holder. However, Molly wasn't sure where it was.

'I don't think you needed the telephone, Mam,' Daisy laughed as she took the earpiece from her mother and placed it on the brass cradle to cut the call.

'That was your cousin, Aiden.' Molly ignored her eldest daughter's remark.

'Really?' Daisy smiled, knowing her mother sometimes found new-fangled inventions, like telephones, and the gas ovens in the shop, strange and confusing contraptions, but once she got over the newness, she was eager to try them out.

'He's coming for a visit this evening,' Molly whispered to Daisy, 'and he's bringing a lady friend.'

'Maybe he has good news.' Daisy was excited at the thought of her cousin finding himself a lady friend. 'After all, he's twenty-six, getting on a bit, it's about time he settled down.' She liked her cousin, who was not only a war hero for saving his whole platoon when he picked up a live grenade and threw it out of their trench, but a very handsome one too. 'Any woman would be lucky to have him.'

'This one's got a daughter, apparently,' Molly whispered, looking troubled. Although, she kept her troublesome thoughts to herself, fervently hoping their Aiden was not biting off more than he could chew.

'That telephone call,' Ina King said before Molly left the shop, 'was it bad news?'

Molly gave her a look that could wither a weed at forty paces. 'I thought you needed to buy bread,' Molly said, noticing Ina was about to leave the shop empty-handed. 'I can't linger, I've to get a pan of scouse on the go.'

Her attempt to let her neighbour know she was in a hurry was futile as Ina hurried alongside, forcing Molly to stop a while in the shop doorway.

'Is there anything I can get for you, Ina?' Molly could never intentionally ignore anybody.

Ina suddenly seemed a bit furtive, checking to make sure she could not be overheard from the shop. 'I was wondering,' Ina whispered, 'if you had such a thing as a couple of coppers to lend me for the gas meter. I can pay you back when our Charlie gets home with his wages. I thought he would be home by now, it being dinnertime, but...'

Ina had eight children, and the Good Lord alone knew how many she had lost over the years. Like most people around here, she waged a constant battle to keep her family fed and warm. But sometimes to hear Ina talk, she was the only woman in the street to have a problem keeping body and soul together, her house clean, and enough money to pay the rent.

'Here,' Molly said, opening her coat. Scrabbling around in the purse she took from her apron pocket, she removed a silver sixpence. 'I've only got a tanner to spare, but at least it'll get you some gas and enough for a loaf. You can't go without bread and gas at New Year.'

Nor could she afford her neighbour's begging bowl all year, thought Molly, knowing Ina's husband was a docker who worked only when there was plenty of ships in, but the casual labour on the docks was notoriously hard to come by, some weeks. And she knew that meant Ina's family wage was often irregular and sometimes non-existent, giving her neighbour cause to go cap in hand to anybody who would lend her a copper or two, including the parish priest, upon whose altar she lit a candle every morning.

'Thanks ever so, Moll, your blood's worth bottling.' Ina showed her appreciation by nudging Molly with her elbow. 'I don't know what I'd do without friends like you.'

Me neither. Molly did not voice her thoughts, knowing she had been in the same boat herself, before her eldest two started work and subsidised her meagre pension from the railway, after her beloved Bert was killed.

'I reckon the weather will turn before the day's out.' Ina looked up to the low, stone-coloured clouds, heavy with the promise of snow, and Molly did likewise. 'Fancy your relation having a telephone.' Ina was not satisfied she had heard all of Molly's news and was sure she was keeping something back.

'He works for a Peer of the Realm and has full autonomy to use His Lordship's telephone.' Whether Aiden had full *authority* to use the private telephone, Molly couldn't be truly sure, but Ina didn't need to know that. 'I suppose your lot are waiting for their dinner?' Molly said, eager to be inside out of the cold weather.

'That's if they're up yet,' Ina answered, giving Molly cause to think she was too soft with her kids.

'I don't take with the idea of letting my lot lie in bed all day, while I'm up at the crack of dawn.' Molly shrugged.

'There's no point in getting out of a warm bed to sit in front of a dead fire.' Ina's gratitude for the sixpence dissolved like the first flakes of snow landing in a puddle between the cobbles.

'I suppose you're right.' No wonder Ina's thin features were haggard, given she usually had one of her young'uns hanging off the hem of her skirts. Molly knew Ina had once been quite a beauty, but Paddy King had been the ruin of her.

'D'you know if the coalman's been, yet?'

'He knocked earlier, but got no answer at your house, so he dropped a couple of hundredweight down the coalhole,' Molly answered, nodding to a round steel plate, situated in the centre of a narrow pathway, and lifted by the coalman who dropped the coal out of a hessian sack perched on his shoulder, into the cellar.

'I went to Strand Road,' Ina said as Molly eyed her neighbour's wicker shopping basket, which held a couple of small parcels. Everybody had hard times at some stage, thought Molly, but Ina and her brood, which was not as large as some families round about, seemed to have more than most. 'I've been up all through the night listening to our Liz's chest – it's wheezing like a pair of bellows.'

'I'm sorry to hear that, Ina.' Molly was genuinely sad to hear Ina's news but wasn't surprised. In this built-up, back-to-back, industrialised area dominated by the nearby docks, consumptive chests were common. 'I hope she's better soon.'

'Me too,' Ina said, 'it's costing me a bliddy fortune in linctus, but it's doing no good.' Molly knew that even though Ina had her faults, she did her best for her offspring. 'If she doesn't buck up soon, I don't know what I'll do.'

'Why don't you take her along to the dispensary?' Molly said, and Ina gave her a look that left Molly in no doubt that she had said the wrong thing.

'I'm not taking her there!' Ina, like many dockside people, refused to be taken to the workhouse infirmary, the fear wasn't so much about going in – 'You only ever get out of there, feet first in a wooden box.'

'The coalman said he'll call this afternoon for the money,' Molly said, needing to get a move on if she was going to get her pan of scouse on the hob.

'I'm sure he will too.' Ina gave a hollow laugh, but the humour did not reach her eyes. 'I'll have to hide behind the sofa again. Thanks for the sixpence.' She looked down into her palm at the silver coin. 'I'd better go and get that fire lit.' Ina did not make a move and Molly got the feeling her neighbour wanted to say something else. Then, in the blink of an eye, Ina was back to her usual feisty self as she said, 'He'd better not have dropped coal dust all over my step if he knows what's good fer him. I only scrubbed it this morning.'

'There should be a bit of work going tomorrow, on the docks, for your Paddy?' Molly said, moving to one side to allow another customer out of the bakery, knowing Ina's husband was having a hard time finding work, likely due to the fact that he was a bit of an instigator, who didn't know when to keep his mouth shut, and was passed over for many a job. And when he did have the good luck to land something, it didn't take much for Paddy King to down tools if he thought he had a grievance, or wasn't getting his fair share. 'I can't see many turning in on New Year's Day.'

'Like I say,' Ina answered, as if they had already had the conversation, 'he's had a few hours here and there, but not enough to keep a family the size of ours going. I mean, it's a good thing our Charlie got that job in the dry goods warehouse.'

'Well, if I hear of any more work going spare down the docks, I'll be sure to let you know,' said Molly, glad her own misfortunes were behind her. 'I got some lovely neck ends of lamb and some pot herbs for the pan of scouse if you fancy a bowlful,' Molly said, gratified of the fact she could afford to do her neighbour a good turn, since her two eldest were working full-time. And what with a new lodger on the way, life was looking good.

'I won't if you don't mind, Mol. I've just got a nice piece of gammon from Liggett's,' Ina said, not to be outdone as she pulled the cotton cover over her measly groceries. 'I've always got split peas in for the pan of pea whack.'

Molly nodded and said, with a generosity of knowing there was not a cat-in-hell's chance Ina had a gammon ham in that basket, 'That's what you need on a day like this, a nice big pan of pea soup, full of meat and veg, so thick it'll stick to your ribs and keep the cold weather out.'

'Aye, or a lovely bowl of scouse with lots of meat, and pot herbs, and potatoes,' Ina concurred, and Molly felt so sorry for her neighbour who did her best, but never seemed to get any better for it.

'Of course,' Molly said, her all-seeing eyes had spied the thin package in Ina's basket, and suspected the 'nice gammon ham' was nothing more than half a pound of bacon scraps to make the soup. Which was no shame, especially when there was plenty of veg, split peas, red lentils, or pearl barley, which were never in short supply now that Charlie was working in the dry foods warehouse along the dock road.

Molly recalled days in the past when she could barely afford *blind scouse*, a meatless stew consisting only of potatoes, and hopefully some pot herbs, anything that would pass as a meal for her children. But, thankfully, those days were behind her now, since Daisy was working in Mary Jane's Kitchen, and their Davey was working in Simpsons cardboard and paper bag factory – one of the many factories on the dock road.

A small town in the north end of Liverpool, Bootle was one of the most important districts in the country with regard to the many industries connecting to freight, transportation, cargo and shipping. The area employed thousands of men in the processing of imported raw materials, as well as ship repairs, animal food-stuffs, sugar refining and tobacco warehouses. Timber yards abutted flour mills, while abattoirs and margarine factories were just a portion of a whole host of manufacturers.

But the people of the area weren't flush with money, nor was the area of back-to-back houses indicative of an affluent district, but Molly knew everybody looked out for their own and up to now, as far as she knew, nobody had starved to death since the 'great starvation' swelled the population with Irish immigrants, who came over in the 1840s, in search of work on the docks, and settled in the warren of back-to-back courts and terraced houses that had sprung up as rapidly as the docks.

She recognised most streets had a mixture of good and bad, but most people had that community spirit, where everybody 'knew' everybody else and if they could, they would help anybody in trouble. Nevertheless, poor days and bad luck seemed to cling with magnet-strength tenacity to poor Ina and her brood, as Ina's husband joined the hundreds of men in the hiring pens each morning, and each afternoon, hoping to get work.

'We'd better get out of the doorway before our Daisy comes out with the sweeping brush and gives us a job,' Molly laughed.

'Have you seen anything of Mary Jane?' Ina asked.

'She said that this baby's got no intentions of showing itself this year.' Molly shrugged further down into the woollen coat her offspring had clubbed together to buy her for Christmas.

'My last one was like that; he was due in the winter, and I

swear he wanted to stay there till the weather warmed up a bit.'
Ina hunched her thin shoulders and made an exaggerated show of
looking up and down the cobbled street. 'As I say, I've an inkling
he's the last, because I haven't seen me visitors since he were born.'

'Your visitors?' Molly asked, thinking herself a worldly kind of
woman, but Ina's *visitors* were a mystery to her.

'You know,' Ina's eyes travelled southward as she mouthed the
words, '*the change*.'

'What change?' Molly repeated the phrase as a question as
they slowly urged themselves from the relative warmth of the
bakery doorway.

'You know,' Ina sighed, 'when your visitors don't come no
more, and you don't have no more babies.'

Molly's eyes widened. 'Respectable women don't talk about
womanly things in the street, Ina.' Obviously, her neighbour had
not heard about that piece of female etiquette. Having been a
lady's maid before marrying her beloved and much-missed Albert,
Molly would never dream of talking about something so personal.

'As I said, eighteen months old he is, and I've usually kicked off
again by now,' Ina continued, unabashed. 'So,' Ina said, cheering a
little, 'I reckon I should be in the clear by now.'

'Have you been to the doctor?' said Molly, who shivered as the
west wind blew keenly from the river, and she saw Ina's eyes
widen.

'If I had any spare money, I wouldn't be throwing it away on a
ruddy doctor.' Ina folded her arms and pursed her lips, her head
bobbing in time with every word. 'I won't be sharing such private
things with the likes of him when I won't even tell my own
husband.'

Molly wished Ina had not shared it with her either. 'Well then,
be hopes you are in the clear. You don't want any mishaps next
year. Now I must be off.'

'There's Mary Jane now.' Ina waved her hand over Molly's shoulder. 'Coooeee, Mary Jane!'

Molly turned to see her best friend waddling like a huge duck down her own steps. Without acknowledging Ina's strident greeting, Mary Jane opened Molly's gate.

'That's odd, she didn't even let on,' said Ina. 'D'you think everything's all right?'

'Well, with this wind blowing a gale, it's whipping the words from your mouth, she probably didn't hear you,' Molly answered.

Ina, craning her neck, pulled her thick black shawl around her shoulders as a stream of horse traffic turned the Beamer Street corner and made its way down Beamer Terrace, the main thoroughfare towards the docks. 'I wonder why Mary Jane looks so flummoxed?'

'Well, don't let me keep you, Ina. I'll just go and find out,' Molly said knowing she wasn't getting anywhere fast, and she still had a bedroom to prepare for her new lodger.

'Shall I come with you?' Ina asked, not wanting to miss anything.

'No, you have your little one to see to, and a pan of pea whack to make.'

'I suppose I should be getting back.' Ina sounded disappointed. 'Ta-ra, well,' she said, not moving, 'if you need a hand, be sure to let me know.'

'You'll be the first, Ina.' Molly knew that as well as being one of the most inquisitive people in the street, Ina was always there if she was needed, mainly because she didn't want to miss anything.

7

'I was just on my way to the market, Mary Jane. Is everything all right? You look as pale as an uncooked pie,' Molly said as she climbed up the steps to where Mary Jane was standing, her voice echoing in the stillness of the frost-covered street.

'Molly, thank God you're here!' Mary Jane gasped. 'I'm going out of my mind with worry.'

'Let's get inside,' Molly said, knowing Ina was earwigging every word. 'What's the matter?' She took a deep breath to calm herself. 'Are you poorly, have your pains started, shall I run for the midwife?'

Molly knew Mary Jane was as nervous as any mother would be at this stage, and even though she had been advised not to, she had worked right up until Christmas Eve in the shop. She had even been baking up until yesterday, telling everyone she was not ill, she was just having a baby.

'Oh Molly, I think I'm going to die!' Mary Jane cried, and Molly's heart skipped a beat, clearly remembering that Mary Jane lost her last baby, shortly after she and her family moved into the house next door. She did not have an easy time of it when she had little Hollie either, and Molly feared the worst.

'Mary Jane don't you conk out on me.' She was trying to ease the tense situation, even though her own heart began pounding against her ribs like a jackhammer. 'Now, what's the trouble?'

'Oh Molly, I am so scared.' Mary Jane waddled into the back kitchen. 'I've had a terrible fright.'

'All right, let me make you a cup of tea, not everything is as bad as it seems,' said Molly, easing Mary Jane into a straight-backed chair and giving her friend a motherly inspection. Mary Jane's colour was a bit flushed, but she wasn't clammy. Nor was she wincing in pain.

'I've had some kind of accident.'

'Have you hurt yourself? Shall I call the doctor?' Molly's heart was in her throat and the questions fell over themselves in their haste to be out of her mouth.

'I don't know.' Mary Jane rarely broke down. 'I went to the bathroom,' she looked anywhere except at Molly, 'and when I finished...' Mary Jane lowered her voice and mouthed the words, 'you know... having a tinkle... I saw something terrible.'

'What kind of terrible?' asked Molly, seriously worried now.

'Like a jellyfish, only smaller, all pink and disgusting... Oh Molly, I'm going to die, aren't I?' Mary Jane's voice rose to a squeak and her hands trembled.

'Oh, darling girl.' Molly heaved a sigh of relief and hugged her best friend. 'What you saw is perfectly normal, if a bit alarming, but you are not dying, well, not today anyway.'

Mary Jane looked up to Molly from her place at the kitchen table and gave a wobbly smile. She felt safe with Molly, knowing if anybody else had spoken the words, she might have been shocked, but Molly was a fount of all knowledge and the mother she didn't have growing up.

She had been brought up by her three brothers after her parents were drowned when the *Titanic* sank. If anybody should know anything about babies, it was Molly, who looked after her three-year-old daughter, Hollie when she was busy in the shop.

Hollie had thrived into a strong, robust child under Molly's watchful eyes. And when Mary Jane had lost her second child when she moved from the flat to the house next door after marrying Cal, Molly looked after her like the most wonderful mother.

Many women lost at least one child in this tough area, but her loss was not because of hunger or being poor, for she was neither. The doctor Cal had obtained had told them sometimes there was no reason.

But this time, Mary Jane, although in the best of health, had been forbidden by Cal and the doctor to overdo her work.

'It's quite normal,' Molly said as she bustled about the cosy kitchen setting out cups and saucers, waiting for the kettle to boil.

'What do you mean?' Mary Jane asked.

'You've had what we women know as...' she lowered her voice to a whisper and looked to the door to make sure there weren't any sudden visitors, '...a show.'

'A show, what does that mean?' asked the younger woman. 'Is it serious?' Mary Jane's mother did not get the chance to tell her daughter the facts of life.

'It means your baby is on his way.' Molly beamed, she couldn't be prouder. 'It's a sign your body is doing what comes naturally, and it's time to start getting ready to bring a new life into the world.'

'I'll have to send someone for Cal, he's been called to the new dock, and what about the midwife!' Mary Jane stood up and rushed to the door when Molly stopped her.

'I'll send our Freddy if Cal's not home soon,' Molly said reassuringly. 'Do you have any pains?'

'Not even a twinge.' Mary Jane had never felt better.

'It could be hours – or even days,' Molly said, then she laughed. 'If it's as lazy as our Bridie, it might take weeks.'

'Weeks?' Mary Jane gasped. 'I don't think I can go another few weeks, I'll pop!' They both laughed and Mary Jane held her swollen stomach.

'Your baby will come when it's ready,' Molly said in that pragmatic way she had about her. 'I'm sure you wouldn't take a loaf out of the oven before it's cooked, now, would you?'

'Oh Molly, I am so glad you are only next door.' Mary Jane put her hand on her neighbour's arm, she loved Molly Haywood and her lively brood, who had been like family since she had lodged here, having eloped from Ireland in 1921. 'At least one of us knows what to do.'

'Be off with you.' Molly half laughing, glowed with unabashed pleasure. 'Just call me if you need me, day or night. I surmise it could be a while yet.' Molly lifted the brown earthenware teapot and refilled their cups. 'But don't go too far or stretch or carry anything heavy or...'

'I promise,' Mary Jane said. 'I've told Daisy to put a notice in the window of the bakery, telling everyone we will be closing early today. I'm sure you need her at home to help out with chores.'

'Pfff.' Molly allowed a sharp breath of air to escape her lips 'Everything's done. Our Bridie was a good help, and she peeled all the spuds for tea while I got the clean bedding on all the beds.'

'D'you think I should shut the bakery and the teashop tomorrow?' Mary Jane knew she certainly didn't need the money. 'Give the staff a day off.'

'There'll be ructions if you don't have the teashop open for breakfast at least, it's not a bank holiday, and the docks will continue – in a fashion – imagine all those New Year hangovers.'

'Aye,' said Mary Jane, knowing New Year's Day breakfast was one of the busiest for the dock workers who actually turned up for work after a new year skinful.

'Our Daisy will open up, have no fear on that score,' Molly reassured her.

'I loved that first morning of New Year trading, the sights you see when you haven't got your gun.'

'Some of the men looked like they'd been ravaged by a grizzly bear, the morning after the New Year hoolie.' Molly was glad Mary Jane looked a little more relaxed after her scare.

'They'd frighten the living daylights out of you when they dragged themselves into the tea shop, still half-drunk, begging for a cup of extra-strong coffee to get them through the first shift on the dock.'

'I remember Bert going to work on the railway the next day too,' Molly laughed. 'The night before he would be full of good cheer wishing everybody *all the best*, then the next morning he would be cursing everybody who offered him another tot of whisky or rum.'

'It's the same all over,' said Mary Jane, rubbing the side of her stomach, 'they never think of the consequences for the next day.'

'I could give you a dose of castor oil to move things along a bit if you like?' Molly thought poor Mary Jane looked so uncomfortable, hardly able to sit still for long.

'No thank you, I'm having none of that stuff, thanks all the same.' She would bide her time. 'Let nature take her course.'

'I don't blame you,' Molly laughed, 'awful stuff.'

'I'd better let you get on, to put those spuds in the scouse,' Mary Jane said, standing up and moving towards the door.

'I like to let it bubble away for as long as possible,' Molly said.

'I'll send a bowl in for you and Cal when it's ready, or you could always come here.'

'Cal likes us all to eat together,' Mary Jane answered, and so did she. As they both worked, tea time was their family time to catch up on their day. Just her, Cal, and Hollie.

'Of course.' Molly understood. 'Well, if you need anything at all just give me a shout.'

'Don't worry.' Mary Jane was more reassured than she had been as she walked to the front door with Molly. 'You'll hear me calling.'

When she went back into her own home next door, Mary Jane was relieved her baby would not be born any minute, she wanted Cal in the house when the baby came.

8

LAVENDER GREEN, NEW YEAR'S EVE, 1924

The air was icy, but Aiden didn't notice. He was thankful Elodie had finally made the break and left Silas Caraway after he had telephoned his mother's sister, Aunt Molly, who lived near the docks in North Liverpool. Glad she confirmed she had a room for Elodie and Melissa. Elodie had retrieved the suitcases she had packed previously, and it didn't take long for them to be on their way. Aunt Molly's home would be a safe haven for both Elodie and Melissa.

'If only I had known how much you suffered after I left for France.' Aiden caught her hand in his and he held it for a long time. 'I wish I knew what you were going through, I wrote every chance I got,' he said, keeping his eye on the icy road and longing to take her in his arms.

'Maybe it is better that you didn't know,' Elodie answered, sure he would have gone absent without leave to help her. 'But your letters never reached me.'

'Nor your letters to me. I didn't know you were pressured into marrying Lord Caraway. It was a shock, when I finally got to Oakland Hall, to find you living there – with him.'

'Ma was gone – and so were you...' Tears rolled freely down Elodie's cheeks, and she savagely wiped them away with the pad of her hand. 'I thought you were dead. I went to visit your mother not knowing the post office boy had already been with the telegram.' Elodie was glad she could finally tell him what really happened. 'Missing presumed dead. Even now, those words send a chill right through me.'

'Nobody expected me to survive,' Aiden said, 'I was tagged *unknown* because my identity tags had been ripped from me in the chaos of the battle. I was left on the ground of the operating tent – too injured to survive, they said.' Aiden squeezed her hand and Elodie suspected *they* were the medics, and she could only imagine the horror he had been through. 'I was in and out of consciousness for weeks.'

'On the ground...?' Elodie could hardly imagine the hectic scene, but she felt anger well up inside of her at the thought of her poor darling being disregarded, lying in a pool of his own blood.

'I don't know how long I had been lying there, unconscious and out of it,' Aiden said tenderly, 'then I was being moved and all these people were around me. I didn't know where I was or who I was.'

'Oh, my poor darling,' Elodie whispered, tears flowing down her cheeks.

'The medics didn't know what to do for me, and they moved me to a hospital, then another,' Aiden explained, silently telling himself he would divulge the horror of that day only once, and only to Elodie. 'At one point, I was taken to the central hospital, in the hope there was a surgeon, who would attempt to remove the shards of bomb fragments that had ripped through my scalp, and lodged in my skull.'

'Good Lord!' Elodie gasped. 'I didn't know you had shrapnel in your head... only about your leg.'

'That bomb was certainly on a mission to infiltrate as many parts of my body as it could.'

'No wonder you were so ill.' Elodie felt fresh tears run down her cheeks. 'How you have suffered.'

Aiden gave a half-hearted smile. 'Not half as much as when I found out about you marrying that old tyrant.'

'Let's not waste time talking about him.' Elodie looked to Aiden and her heart swelled with love. Even though he returned from war six years ago, they had never been able to talk freely or in depth about their feelings, as Elodie was watched very carefully by Soames, her husband's butler, who reported everything she did back to his master.

Being here next to him was the closest they had been since that day she took him for a walk in the grounds of Oakland Hall, after Aiden had been brought home to recover. That day was the most special of her life. She squeezed his hand and the action seemed to bring his thoughts to the fore.

'Nobody could heal the severe infection in my leg, and I begged them to let me come home. I knew you would work your magic and get rid of the poison that was hampering my recovery, but they said the journey might kill me.'

'Good heavens, you certainly were in a terrible state.' There was a catch in her voice. 'I would have done everything in my power to help you.'

'In the end, the powers-that-be had no choice, but to send me home.'

'I couldn't believe it was you,' answered Elodie, remembering back, to when Aiden was brought into the ballroom of Oakland Hall that October day six years ago. 'I thought I was seeing a ghost.' Even now she felt her heart beat faster. Aiden's homecoming was not something she would ever forget. 'I can't recall if it was the shock of seeing you again, or the exhaustion of work that caused me to faint.'

'I spent long months in a Belgian hospital after being blown up at Passchendaele. But I wasn't the only one who suffered.'

'There were so many injured and killed,' Elodie said, knowing he was being modest about his own suffering.

'I meant *your* suffering,' he said and Elodie lowered her eyes to the floor of the car, she had been going through mental torture, unable to tell anybody. Not even Aiden.

'Why didn't you tell me what you were going through for all these years?' Aiden asked, taking his eyes off the road for a second.

'I felt ashamed, I couldn't tell anybody,' Elodie answered. 'The servants knew, obviously. To Silas they are invisible. But they were not invisible to me when he would rant and belittle me in front of them.'

As he expertly steered the car down the steep Lancashire hills, Aiden knew exactly why he had kept his distance and the knowledge made him cringe. He had been angry that Elodie had been fool enough to marry His Lordship, but now that he knew the truth he too felt ashamed.

'I couldn't tell you I had married Silas when you were recovering,' Elodie explained, 'being with you again wiped his very existence from my mind, all I could think about was you, that you were alive.'

'All I could think about on the journey home was how I was going to ask you to marry me.' Aiden felt as if he had been blown up all over again when he found out she had married.

'It was only after we...' Elodie could not voice the truth even now. 'I felt so ashamed of my deception – not to Silas!' she said quickly. 'In the years since then, I felt as though I was cheating on you.'

'It was a blow finding out the way I did, I can tell you.' Aiden's recovery in the Belgian hospital had been long and complicated. For much of it, he didn't even know his own name, and he found out later his mother had received a telegram saying he was missing, presumed dead. And, by the time he was identified, and sent home, still gravely injured from the trenches, his wonderful Elodie, his sole reason for fighting so hard to live, had already married Lord Silas Caraway. The shocking realisation was as painful and sudden as the shrapnel that had ripped into his skull and shattered his body.

The Blighty wounds were enough to kill him the surgeons said, and they didn't know how he survived. 'I am hoping to live long enough to see my girl,' he told them, 'even if only for one last time.'

'Don't say that.' Elodie couldn't bear to think of the months she had to try and continue to live a normal existence without him.

'My wounds had become septic by the time I got back to Oakland as you know, and I could no longer serve.'

'I feared you may even lose your foot,' Elodie said, recalling the day they brought in the only man she had ever loved. 'You were drifting in and out of consciousness, which gave you some respite from the pain.'

'I kept imagining seeing pals who had copped it, never to return home. I was totally unaware of how long I'd been in Flanders and I didn't really care...' he slowed the car down to a crawl halfway down the hill '...until I heard your familiar voice.'

'That's when I fainted.' Elodie could feel the heat rising to her cheeks.

Aiden's voice had barely been a whisper when he had said her name, and at first he had thought he may have already died and was now in heaven.

He had only a hazy memory of being brought home in a Red

Cross ambulance. It was October 1918 and the whole village had turned out to greet him with banners declaring he was their hero.

'I was beside you every day to bathe and dress your wounds. Silas had no say in what I did by that time, he spent so much time in London, while I had the backing of the hospital staff and the war office who encouraged the making up of the herbal medicines.'

'I know, you did a sterling job.' Aiden knew her presence was a double-edged sword. He wished she did not come each day, but he knew he could not live a day without seeing her. 'Your ma would have been so proud of you,' Aiden told her. 'Even my own mother said you are a natural healer.'

After a painful convalescence, the infection that had threatened Aiden's life had begun to wane. But nothing could replace the flesh that had been eaten away by the poison in his leg. The calf of his left leg dipped like the crater in which he had been found, exhausted and half dead. The left leg would always be weaker than the other, giving him a slight limp, which Aiden strived to overcome.

'Do you remember me asking you not to make me better too quickly?' Aiden gave a gentle laugh. His whole being felt lighter now she was moving further away from Oakland Hall.

'I do remember,' Elodie answered, 'seeing as it was me who wrote the daily report for your officers.' Elodie knew leg ulcers were notoriously difficult to heal, and Aiden bravely bore the daily binding with fortitude, even though she knew the pain must be excruciating. He grew a little stronger every day. This most handsome man she had ever seen, and if Elodie was honest with herself, she had dragged out the treatment far longer than she should have done. 'The last thing I wanted was to see your leg healing enough to send you right back to war and put yourself in the firing line again.' All she was concerned about was that Aiden survived.

Then, as he grew stronger, the strangest thing happened. Lord Caraway returned to visit him and to offer Aiden his old job, working as a gardener at Oakland Hall. And as part of his duties had been to drive the officers in France, Aiden was given the role as his chauffeur as soon as he was fit enough to work, after being discharged from the army on medical grounds.

'The wages he pays are a pittance,' Aiden had told her when she came to tend his leg the following day, 'I'd be better off going back to fight.'

'Don't say that, Aiden,' she had begged him, 'I don't know what I'd do if...'

Elodie knew she should never have said such a thing when she saw the light of love in his eyes. Her being a married woman. But she could not help herself.

The war had ended before Aiden's leg healed well enough for him to be sent home, but his presence strengthened the flame inside her that had never died, and taking Aiden out to the gardens in the hospital wheelchair on that chilly, sunny afternoon, Elodie was unable to resist his kisses.

'If it hadn't been for your gentle care, I would never have survived,' Aiden said, looking straight ahead. Her calm intensity to her work gave him the strength he needed. The only thing that frightened him more than war, or death, was the thought of living the rest of his days without her.

'I only took the job so I could see Elodie every day, that is the only consolation of working for Lord Caraway,' he told his pal Will Birch, who had been picked up from the same trench, half-blinded when a trench mortar bomb blew up near his face.

'He can't be as bad as that ugly sprout of a corporal,' Will, a usually quiet lad, chuckled.

'Don't you believe it,' Aiden had replied.

The nursing staff were full of joy and merriment when they brought the news the armistice had been signed at 11 a.m. on the eleventh day of the eleventh month. Aiden was quiet now, remembering that wonderful day when the guns of war had fallen silent, and there was a national and international sigh of relief, the carnage was over.

Aiden had seen Elodie coming into the ward. She was her usual sunny self, nodding and smiling to the other patients, stopping to have a little chat, her friendly exchange cheering them up no end, especially when she confirmed the news that the war was over.

A loud whoop went up in the rows of single iron beds that lined the white-tiled walls of the ward and Aiden's heart sang when he watched her giggle at their response. She was the most beautiful, caring human being he had ever seen.

Damn that bloody war! If it hadn't been for his call-up, Aiden would have been the one to marry Elodie. Not Lord Caraway. He would have been her husband now.

Watching her, his heart had swelled, and he'd wondered how he could ever tell her the terrible truth about her husband, and what he had done. Aiden had tried not to stare as she went to every bed, giving out cups of calming chamomile tea with words of encouragement and comfort, he knew her sensitivity to the plight of others came as naturally as breathing. Elodie would help anybody, even though she had been through so much herself. Especially after her poor mother had taken her own life.

Aiden knew he would never forgive himself for going to war without even saying goodbye. It might have been easier for him to do so, but now he realised she must so badly have needed a friend.

So, what did he expect? The news he came home to, that she had married Lord Caraway was a kick in the guts, and almost finished him off. But after long weeks of gentle attention at the hospital, where she spent nights mopping his brow with cool compresses, binding his wounds in strong echinacea-soaked dressings – to draw out the infection, she said – and staying with him until she could barely hold open her own eyes, the wounds began to heal. And when he was on the mend, aware of his surroundings and looking forward to her coming onto the ward, he discovered she was married.

At that moment, Aiden had wished he could have died. He would be no wiser then and could have passed out of this life an ignorant but less devastated man.

'You look much brighter this morning, Aiden,' Elodie had said with a smile as wide as the ocean as she finally approached him, and his heart did that little flip, which he had no control over.

'All the better for seeing you, my dear,' he'd said in a mock big-bad-wolf voice, and even though he was shattered by what he had learned, her presence did do him the power of good.

'You had me worried last night,' Elodie had said, sitting on the chair beside his bed, and when his eyebrows had pleated in an unasked question, she had enlightened him. 'You were shouting in your sleep, thrashing your arms and legs – I thought you were going to burst your stitches.'

'What was I shouting?' Aiden had asked, intrigued; he didn't know he shouted in his sleep, but it was nothing unusual given the circumstances, most soldiers did the same. His curiosity had got the better of him and he took hold of her hand, surprised when she didn't pull away as a married woman should.

'I can't say.' She had given a low, embarrassed laugh and her face had grown adorably pink. 'It would sound conceited.'

'I tell you what, Nurse,' Will had called from the next bed, 'I might not be able to see much, but I do know he's got his eye on a beautiful nurse in here – her name's Elodie, would that be you by any chance?'

'Aiden,' Elodie had sounded shocked even though she could not hide her smile, 'you shouldn't say things like that, someone will hear you.'

'I don't care who hears me,' Aiden had told her, 'it's true, you are the most beautiful girl I ever met, and I rue the day I ever left Lavender Green without making you my wife.'

'Oh, Aiden, that is the nicest thing I have ever heard.' There was a happy tear in Elodie's eye. She had never been one to hide her feelings. She found it impossible to disguise her happiness, in much the same way she could not hide her sadness. Even if somebody else fell over, Elodie felt their pain. 'Would you like me to take you out into the garden,' she had asked, her eyes never leaving his. 'If you are well wrapped up, I can't see Matron refusing – after all, she is always saying the fresh air is as good as any tonic.'

'Lead the way,' Aiden had whispered, his heart pounding at the thought of being alone with his favourite girl.

'I'll go and fetch a wheelchair,' Elodie had said, and he'd put his hand on her arm to stay her a moment, his touch as light as a feather.

'You know you're the only girl I will ever love. If it was the right time of year, I would have picked you some flowers,' he'd said, and she had laughed.

'Matron would have had your guts for stitches,' she had answered. Then, halfway around the huge lawn, they felt the first spots of rain begin to fall. 'I'll have to get you back inside.'

'It's only a shower,' he'd said, not knowing if it was going to ease off or if it would turn into an all-day event, 'let's take refuge in the summer house.' He had an uncontrollable urge to kiss her...

'I wrote to you every day,' she'd said as they headed towards the summer house, 'I even thought I might have had a letter or two from you.'

'But I did write,' Aiden had said, as she closed the door of the summer house behind them, and he stepped out of the wheelchair and put his arms around her, looking deep into her eyes, 'every chance I got.'

Elodie had believed him. Aiden had never let her down before. She recalled going to the cottage every day to check for his letters, until one day it was in flames. There was nothing but a charred shell when the fire was eventually put out. All her memories destroyed.

'When Silas took me in, to Oakland Hall, I went to the post office every day to see if there was any post for me from you and they told me nothing had been delivered.'

'Let me guess,' Aiden had said, 'that's when Lord Caraway asked you to marry him?'

'He said I would have a good life, no worries or cares, a fine house... but none of it meant anything to me...' She had paused momentarily. 'He was so kind to me, making sure I was comfortable, cared for. He even allowed me to make my cures without any hindrance.'

'He didn't *allow* it; he would have been *requested* to allow the use of his premises for a dispensary,' Aiden had told her, and she had nodded.

'I was stupid to believe he had my interest at heart,' she'd said, and Aiden had lifted her hands to his lips and returned the kiss.

'You weren't stupid at all. You were bereft, cajoled, and duped by a man who should have known better. He needed a young wife to give him the son he wanted.'

'I'm sure he could have found someone better than me.' Elodie had noticed that Aiden's expression had changed immediately.

'Don't ever say that again,' he'd whispered, 'you are worth a hundred of him. He should kiss the ground you walk on.' Aiden had lowered his head and closed his eyes. 'Your mother was gone. Your home, too. You had nothing. He had you exactly where he wanted you, my darling. I am so sorry.'

'It's not your fault.' Elodie had taken hold of his hands in hers and kissed them. 'I could not bear the thought I would never see you again. I prayed every day and night that I would.'

'I didn't know who I was or where I was for a long time, but I always knew there was a girl back home waiting for me. I was certain of it.' His voice had been quiet, his expression so gentle, his manner relaxed, making her relax.

'Oh, my love, it is me who should be sorry, I...' Elodie had never got to finish what she was about to say as he took her in his arms, his lips meeting hers. They could no longer deny the love they felt for each other, and she did not resist him when he pulled her towards him. Nor when his hand caught and lifted the hem of her Voluntary Aid Detachment uniform...

When they left the summer house that afternoon, they knew intimately more about each other than they had ever done before, and Aiden knew for certain, he would never love any woman like he loved Elodie Kirrin.

* * *

'Melissa is mine, isn't she?' Aiden said, on the long journey to Liverpool, and Elodie nodded.

'Of course, she's yours. And if Silas ever asked me, I would have told him and taken the consequences.' She had known the moment the ring was on her finger that she was tied to Silas for life. How many times she longed to tell him the truth. But it was not herself she feared for, it was Melissa. 'I would have told him with pleasure because I would have been proud to tell him you were her father. And not just to wipe the superior scorn from his face either. She gives me the strength to face each day, knowing she is part of you.'

'If I had known, I would have...'

'I know, and that is why I didn't tell you. I wanted to tell you when I discovered I was expecting.' All through the long months ahead when she saw Aiden working in the gardens, she had longed to tell him, but knew he would confront Silas with the news, and bring unbelievable trouble upon himself and his family, so she had stayed silent.

'I would see him walking in the gardens with you, his arm around your waist, and I wanted to lay him out, put him flat on his back.'

'I dared not even look your way in case he caught sight of the love I had for you, because I am sure it was as plain as day.'

'He didn't know how lucky he was.' Aiden stared straight ahead, concentrating on the icy road. 'I loved it when Melissa would come down to the greenhouses. I can still see her pretty little face, beaming with pleasure that day I gave her the small potting table I had made so she could help me plant up the herbs.'

'That is her favourite pastime,' said Elodie with a smile. 'It looks like the horticultural gift has been passed on from both parents.'

'Well, she won't go far wrong,' Aiden said proudly, looking into the mirror to check his daughter was still asleep, safely cocooned in blankets on the back seat.

'When I presented him with Melissa,' Elodie sighed, her shoulders slumped, 'only minutes old, I told him I had given birth to a daughter.' Elodie's chin trembled at the memory. 'He didn't even look at her. Then he slammed out of the room without a word. He went back to London for six weeks.'

'The man's a bloody fool,' said Aiden. 'Excuse my language in front of our daughter.' He swelled with pride, longing to let that prig of a man know who her real father was. He was unable to understand what kind of cold-hearted man could deny a child he believed to be his.

Elodie knew Silas's offer of marriage did not come with a happy-ever-after, but it was not as nightmarish as it became after Melissa was born. But there was nothing she could do about it. He had dropped the kind-and-gentle façade, letting her know in no uncertain terms she was dependent upon him, believing she had nothing of her own. But Elodie was never that stupid. She had been through tough times for most of her life, her mother had taught her there were canny ways to survive, and it was a lesson well learned.

His proposal had been like an exchange of business contracts, and he had responded to his wedding vows like he was passing sentence. Thinking about it now, that was exactly what he had done. He had sentenced her to a life of abject misery. In his eyes, she would never compare to his first wife who died giving birth to his angelic son. He had told her so many times, and she had longed to tell him that child was not his either, but where would that have got her? Nowhere, except on the streets.

'I knew what I had done, loving you as I did that day,' Elodie said, 'and I do not regret one moment of it.'

Aiden took her hand again as he drove through the streets of Liverpool.

'My emotions had shut down completely and, except for the love of our daughter, my desire for happiness was as fragile as a dandelion in a hurricane.' Her lack of emotion had been a much-needed balm of self-preservation in the last seven years.

What Silas had put her through could never be called love. He had never *made love* to her. He had degraded her. Forced himself on her, and then left her humiliated without a backward glance.

His ability to inflict torment and shame knew no bounds, and she would curl up like a shaded flower, turning in on herself, promising that one day she would get away from him.

However, it was only when the maid had brought a bundle of letters that morning, and Elodie saw one that was addressed to her husband. It bore the discreet hallmark of a first-rate Harley Street physician and her curiosity had been aroused.

As soon as Elodie had seen the address, she'd suspected it contained the results of the many examinations Silas had made her undergo in his determination to find out why she had not conceived the son he craved.

The letter had arrived in the second post, and Elodie had no compunction about carefully steaming it open, making sure the servants could not see her. As her eyes rapidly zigzagged the words on the page, she was horrified to learn the letter contained evidence he had spent the last seven years trying to conceal. Silas had been made infertile by the venereal disease he had contracted years earlier. Proof of what Lady Felicia had believed, when Elodie had overheard her talking to her mother all those years ago was there in black and white. The letter confirmed what Elodie had always suspected, Silas Caraway was not Melissa's father – and what's more, he never could be. He was barren.

Gripping the earphone of the candlestick telephone, Elodie's hand had shaken so much, she could hardly keep hold of it. Silas had installed a telephone so Aiden could be on hand at any hour of the day or night.

Conflicting emotions had run parallel through her body. One was fear of his punishment when Silas discovered he was incapable of fathering a child. And she knew she would pay the price of the revelation. The other emotion was elation, knowing he could not spread the poison he carried within him.

Melissa is not his daughter. Her mother's voice had come into

Elodie's head as clearly as if she were standing next to her. 'Thank God,' Elodie had whispered, feeling relieved. Melissa had nothing to connect her to him. This was Elodie's sign to leave.

With a shaking hand, she had carefully dialled the number to the head gardener's cottage. The telephone had been answered almost immediately, and Elodie had raised the mouthpiece to her lips.

'I'm ready.'

'I'll pick you up at the edge of the woods, near the gate. Can you manage Melissa?'

Elodie had assured him she could. Aiden Newman was her only ally.

Her tread had been light, silent, and dressed in warm, expensive clothes against the freezing temperature, Elodie had urged her daughter to remain quiet, so as not to alert the servants.

'We mustn't make a sound,' she had whispered, making sure her daughter put on her thick woollen gloves before they reached the walled garden.

Even though Silas wanted nothing to do with her or Melissa, he would move heaven and earth to get her back. A flutter had risen in her chest. Silas had no rights over Melissa whatsoever. But Elodie knew the only way she could protect herself and her child was to get as far away from Oakland Hall as she could, forever.

'Our new beginning,' Elodie had whispered to Melissa. Freedom. A chance to breathe.

In the years she had been his wife, Elodie had not visited any friends of Silas's, or socialised with women in her societal setting, as she was expected to do. She had never been included in the communal circles, the village fetes, which other women of means were so practised in. Silas would never allow her jiggery-pokery, her herbal concoctions, to be spoken of in polite society. Her balms and tinctures were never discussed within hearing distance of his precious inner circle. Heaven forbid.

One thing Elodie was proud of was the fact she had amassed a small fortune of her own from selling potions she secretly made to his rich friend's wives. Tonics to pep up their flagging love life, or calmatives to cool a rampaging longing. Balms to enhance their beauty. The higher echelon sought her discreet expertise through a post office number, or by word of mouth. The women who refused to talk openly to her proved her best clientele.

She was also leaving behind her beloved mother's remains in an unmarked grave. The plot she visited daily, attempting to seek answers as to why her mother had left her to the bear pit that was Oakland Hall and the cruellest of men. But she had to go somewhere Silas would never think to find her, get as far away as possible before he got back from London. Because, without any doubt, this was one fight she would never win.

Simply burning the physician's letter was not enough, leaving nothing to chance, the doctor would make a follow-up telephone call to Silas at his chambers, or even visit him at his club. Elodie's heart had pounded so loudly, she could hear it thrashing in her ears. Clenching her jaw, she had wrapped her arms around Melissa's shoulders, holding her close, knowing she would die in the gutter before she would allow any harm to come to her darling child.

It being New Year's Eve, Elodie knew Silas would be heading to the station to get the next train home. If the physician had already spoken to him, Silas would demand answers she was no longer prepared to give. She shivered, knowing she had suffered seven cruel years of marriage to a man who despised her. Now, nothing was going to stop her from living the life she was meant to live, as determination coursed through her veins. She had taken seven long years to gather enough money to enable her to lead the independent life she dreamed of, free from her husband's tyrannical outbursts. She would have done it long ago. But he had his spies, servants watching her every move. Agreeing to marry Silas Caraway was the worst mistake she had ever made.

Elodie knew she should have trusted her mother's warning never to have anything to do with him and attempted to block out the awful pictures in her mind. But the memories would always be here in Lavender Green. The vicious criticisms. The sly insults...

The creaking rafters.

Elodie knew her mother's tragic demise on her sixteenth birthday would stay with her for the rest of her life. The memory could not be healed until she found out the truth... But what Elodie wanted most of all was to use the incredible legacy of her mother's gift of healing, which would enable her to make a living helping others.

9

Elodie leaned over her seat to where Melissa was lying on the plush upholstery and reached for her daughter's small gloved hand, knowing she must do everything in her power to safeguard her.

She was taking Melissa to a place where nobody knew them, and where she could sell her herbal remedies without fear of being ridiculed by Silas, knowing her husband had tried to destroy everything *the wise women*, her female ancestors, had taught her.

Silas had razed the cottage to the ground, all her possessions and memories destroyed. That was the day she had come to the unshakeable conclusion, she could never love such a cruel man. And she was right.

The freezing winter air had already caused frost crystals to form on the windows of the car, and Elodie did not want her daughter to catch a chill. Memories of the influenza pandemic after the war was over, which had killed as many people as the war had done, was still fresh in her mind.

The child shuffled and Elodie gently shushed her, leaning

from her seat at the front of the car and tenderly stroking her daughter's cheek. Melissa was the focus of Elodie's life, her world, her everything. As Elodie, herself, had once been to her own mother, who would have adored this beautiful child had she lived long enough to see her. Whereas Silas barely glanced at Melissa. She was a girl. Not the son he wanted.

It was wrong to bring Melissa out in such terrible weather, but Elodie had had no choice. She had no intentions of spending another night in that mausoleum with Silas, who would head straight back to Oakland Hall when he discovered the truth. A New Year would mean nothing to him. She knew she would endure the most of his evil anger and frustration and could withstand that up to a point, but she would never allow Silas to aim his vitriolic hatred towards her young, innocent daughter.

Any choice Elodie thought she had was quickly taken from her when she married Silas.

Every day, he had reminded her of the great honour he had bestowed upon her, allowing her to live in his huge house, giving her clothes she could never possibly afford, buying her jewels and furs she rarely wore. It was all a sham.

When they were alone, the situation was vastly different.

'Your kind should only be allowed in by the servants entrance,' he would tell her, 'so don't get above yourself.'

She was not allowed to speak to the servants unless she was giving an order. And only then if he was not at home. Silas forbade Elodie to go outside the surrounding walls of Oakland Hall without him.

Even when he was away, he paid servants to spy on her and make sure she stayed within the confines of the grounds. He had spies everywhere and they did everything they could to curry favour, because by being useful to him through word or deed, Silas secured their place in his employment.

Loyalty to their own kind meant nothing to the staff. They wanted as much power as they could muster, and if that meant telling tales to Lord Caraway about his young wife spending hours in the greenhouses with the gardener, then so be it. Even though she was only growing the herbs she needed for the balms, and tinctures. But still, Elodie was forced to vehemently defend herself and Aiden.

'We'll soon be there,' Aiden said offering Elodie a reassuring smile, and she silently smiled back, wondering what Aiden's aunt was going to think when she saw her and Melissa turning up in a new motor car. What was she going to say when his Aunt Molly asked about her husband? Questions were firing inside her head so fast she could hardly keep up with them, let alone find a solution.

10

'Is there any news?' Ina asked, jumping the queue in the shop, after telling Daisy she had seen Mary Jane going into Molly's house.

'Not that I've heard, Ina,' said Daisy, a little distracted when she saw that handsome young reporter from the *Herald* going into the teashop at the back of the bakery, and realising she could not go and serve him his daily cuppa because she had a queue and Mavis, her assistant, had hurried out back instead. She could not wait for this day to be over; they had been rushed off their feet all day, and she was dying for a cup of tea.

'As I say,' Ina said, in her usual way of starting a conversation in the middle and expecting everybody else to catch up, 'I thought something must have happened.' She leant against the counter like she had all the time in the world, unlike most of the Beamer Street women, who were busy making sure their houses were scrubbed clean for New Year and their cookers were in full swing.

'Not as far as I know,' Daisy said, serving a customer and still feeling a bit peeved at Mavis rushing to serve Max.

'I wouldn't be surprised if she goes in the next few hours,' Ina told the women in the queue, who nodded in agreement.

'It'll come when it's ready and not before,' said Peggy Tenant, making the sign of the cross.

'Like I say, she won't want the same trouble she had last time.' Ina, with her tendency to avoid the bright side if at all possible, was never one to let a touch of drama go to waste, as she reminded the women that Mary Jane had developed toxaemia before giving birth to her young daughter, Hollie, and afterwards had temporarily lost her sight due to the condition. 'I was called upon to save little Hollie's life, if you remember,' Ina reminded Daisy.

'Hardly saved her life, Ina, the child could have got by with a little evaporated milk for a few days,' said Daisy. 'And from what I remember you were very well paid.'

'Aye, but not by Mary Jane!' Ina retorted.

'She could hardly pay you when she was out for the count.' Daisy served another customer, realising Ina could be here all day if she had an audience. 'She didn't see the light of day for the first week.'

'It was himself who paid me to keep that babby alive.' Then, turning to the other women in the queue, she said, 'You do know Mr Everdine is Mary Jane's *second* husband?' Ina nodded when Peggy, who had moved into Beamer Street not long after the child was born, showed some interest.

'I didn't know,' said Peggy.

'As I say, some girls couldn't get one man after the war, and Mary Jane managed to bag herself two – so what does that tell ye?' Ina looked suitably pleased when she saw surprise register on Peggy's face. 'Cal Everdine visited Mary Jane every day after that babby was born, I can tell you. Every day, mind. If you ask me...'

'Nobody did ask you,' Daisy said under her breath, giving the local gossip a cautionary glare of her dark eyes. 'I know something, there would be no such conversation if Mary Jane was here in the shop.'

'It's like I said,' Ina ignored Daisy, knowing she had a captive audience now, 'with him not being the father of the child.'

At the collective gasp, Daisy had heard enough.

'Your tongue is like a runaway horse, once it starts there's no stopping it. It's nobody else's business but theirs.' Daisy's warning tone did nothing to stop Ina now she was in full flow.

'Mary Jane's first husband did a flit back to Ireland before the child was due, if you please.' Ina's Irish brogue filled the shop. 'As I said, what kind of man does that? I ask you...'

'What happened to her husband?' Peggy asked, her curiosity getting the better of her.

'He died in a mountain-climbing accident back home in Ireland. Although,' Ina lowered her voice a tad more, 'I heard his death *might* not have been an accident. He owed money to some fierce, bad men who you wouldn't want to upset, if you get my drift.'

'When you've finished shredding Mary Jane's good character, Ina.' Daisy glared, showing her deep displeasure. 'Mr Everdine is the love of Mary Jane's life, and he has made no secret of the fact he adores the very ground she walks on, too.' Daisy had a romantic heart and liked nothing more than to see two people who were so in love. 'And will you be paying for this week's provisions, or will they stay on the book till Friday?' Daisy was not going to stand here and allow this two-faced madam to malign her employer and friend, who was not here to defend herself, knowing if it weren't for Mary Jane, Ina's family, and many in Beamer Street would have gone hungry many a time.

11

Silas had evicted more families and sent more people to the gallows than any other judge in the British Isles. To his way of thinking, Elodie was merely a strong, healthy young woman who would bear him a son. But eviction would not be enough for Lord Caraway when he found out about the letter.

Elodie had suffered physical and emotional cruelty from her marriage and now she knew she deserved better, a man who loved and respected her. A man like Aiden, and if she were truthful, Aiden was the only man she had ever loved, or would ever love.

He was attentive at first, but the novelty soon wore off and Silas swiftly let her know he loved nobody and nothing except power. He grew more bitter as time went by, subjecting Elodie to painful medical examinations to find out why she had not conceived since she had Melissa. But the tests proved there was nothing wrong with her. He warned Elodie that Melissa would not inherit his wealth. He would bequeath it to a cattery before he would give Melissa a penny.

* * *

'We should be in Beamer Street in about half an hour,' said Aiden, his voice jolting Elodie out of her thoughts.

He loved her before he knew Melissa was his daughter, and now he loved her even more if that were possible. Elodie and Melissa were going to have a fresh start. And he was going to do all he could to help them.

'The day I found out I was expecting your child was the happiest day of my life,' Elodie told Aiden. At last, she had someone she could call her own for the first time since her mother had died. And now they were heading to safety, away from the abuse and mental torment, a place where she would not be a prisoner in her own home.

Aiden was quiet, and Elodie could tell he was mulling something over.

'Is everything all right?' she asked.

'Yes, of course,' Aiden said quickly. There was something he must tell her, but he didn't know how to. For the second time in his life, he was keeping something important from her and he was uneasy at the prospect. Look what had happened last time. He went off to war and came back when it was too late.

This time he wasn't going to war – but he knew something that was going to blow her life apart when she found out.

But this time you will be here to see her through, he told himself. The notion gave him a small crumb of comfort. But, he thought, she had to know her husband had killed her mother. Deborah had not committed suicide.

His thoughts travelled back to the talk he had with Will in the greenhouse that morning.

'How's it going?' young Will had asked. He had bagged himself a job as part-time gardener when his eyesight had improved. 'I've put all the herbs in the boxes ready.'

'Good man,' Aiden had said to Will.

'Did I ever tell you, I used to collect the medicines from the pharmaceuticals?' Will stopped suddenly and thought for a moment. 'It took me ages to learn how to say such a long word. Anyway, I used to collect the herbal tonics and balms from Ma Kirrin's cottage and bring them back here to the dispensary.' He lowered his voice to a conspiratorial level and looked around before continuing. 'I 'appened over there one day when Elodie was out collecting. And you'll never guess what I saw?'

'Well, I won't until you tell me.'

'I rang the bell at the gate as usual,' Will had said, 'but there were no answer and I knew the missus would be inside the cottage, she never went out while there was work to be done for the hospital, which was real busy.'

'Don't take the scenic route, Will.' Aiden was also busy, and he needed Will to get to the point.

'I opened the gate, 'cause the missus usually left the cures in a box in the back, like, if she were too busy to chat...'

'I get the picture,' Aiden had muttered, stacking boxes onto a cart while Will casually filled a cigarette paper with tobacco.

'Lord Caraway 'isself were there, in the cottage, I could hear 'im. And 'e didn't sound too sociable neither. He was saying something about Elodie.'

'What did he say about Elodie?' Aiden was suddenly attentive to what Will had to say. 'When was this?'

'It were the day the missus committed hari-kari. 'Cept, as far as I could see, she weren't in no hari-kari mood, she were givin' back as good as she got. She gave His Lordship a right tongue-lashin'.'

Aiden's mouth had dried and fell open. He'd put down the trays he had been collecting and they were quickly forgotten when he went over to Will's bench.

'Did you see anything else?' Aiden had asked.

'He landed her a back'ander that sent 'er flying across the

room, I heard the crack as her head hit the hearth from outside, I was sickened I can tell you,' Will had said. 'If I'd have been braver, I would 'ave confronted 'im, but he'd 'ave evicted my whole family.'

'Are you saying what I think you're saying?' Aiden's thoughts had been well ahead of Will's words and a chill had run down his spine. 'Do you think her death might not have been suicide?'

'I'd swear to it,' Will had answered.

'Elodie said Lord Caraway signed her mother's death certificate himself.' Aiden had sat down on the edge of Will's bench. His voice was equally low.

'He were there, in the cottage, tellin' the missus 'e would 'ave Elodie any time he liked, saying the missus promised him, when his first wife died,' Will said. '"You promised me I could have her," Lord Caraway shouted, then he moved across the room, and I couldn't see no more for a while, but I heard Ma Kirrin telling him he wasn't going to have her. She said she'd done nothing wrong and nor had Elodie.'

Deborah was not the type to do herself in, thought Aiden. 'She loved life and would never put her daughter through such heartache no matter how bad things got.' She knew the villagers would shun Elodie. Aiden was quiet for a long time, mulling things over. Everything was beginning to slot into place. Deborah's death. Elodie's marriage to a man who could give her anything except love, and respect.

'Why didn't you tell somebody?' Aiden had asked, aware there was little they could have done about it even if Will had told him what he saw. Who was going to believe two working-class lads over a high court judge and member of parliament?

'We were going to war if you hadn't noticed. And anyway, would you say something against Lord Caraway?' Will had put the unlit cigarette into his mouth and pushed back the peak of his flat cap. 'To be honest I was glad to get my call-up papers and get the hell out of there.'

'Jesus wept!' Aiden could not believe what he had heard, and yet, if he thought about it, he could believe every word... Silas Caraway had killed Elodie's mother.

12

'This is going to be a feisty one.' Mary Jane gave a wan smile as she paced the length of the front parlour, refusing to describe it as *the drawing room*, like Cissy Stone had called it, rubbing the side of her swollen stomach with the flat of her hand. She chuckled to ease her husband's worried face.

'Are you in pain, sweetheart?' Cal, nervous as a cat in a dog pound, got up and began pacing with her. 'Is there anything I can do?' He had never felt so useless, Mary Jane had lost a baby, the day after they moved into this house eighteen months ago, and Cal had been worried since she'd told him nine months ago that she was in the family way again. He did not want anything bad to happen this time and was eager to do something, anything, to ease his beloved wife's discomfort.

'You can sit down for a start.' Mary Jane sounded irritated, and Cal knew it was better to leave her be when he saw that impatient flash in her marine-coloured eyes.

'I'm sure you have the situation covered, sweetheart. I'll make you a nice cup of tea.'

'I'm sorry, Cal,' Mary Jane's voice was softer now, her emotions all over the place, 'I didn't mean to be so tetchy with you.'

'You be as tetchy as you like, sweetheart.' Cal, who had worked as an engineer in the Canadian silver mines, was now involved in the construction of a new dock in the north end of the seven miles of dockland, spoke in a soothing manner that still carried more than a hint of an American accent.

Mary Jane smiled, thanking every saint in heaven she could think of, for the day she had met her wonderful husband – even though he did nearly run her over when she arrived off the boat from Ireland. But she did not dwell on those days. Now she was Mrs Mary Jane Everdine, wife of the most handsome, caring man in the world.

Mother of three-year-old Hollie, she was almost ready to give birth to Cal's child, if the Good Lord spared it, knowing Cal already considered himself to be Hollie's father. He had been part of Hollie's life since the day she was born, in fact he had held her before Mary Jane had.

'Is everything all right, do you think?' Cal's voice was tinged with ill-disguised anxiety. 'Shall I go and fetch the doctor, the midwife?'

'No, my darling.' Mary Jane fought to keep her own worry in check. 'I'm just feeling restless, that's all.' She had scrubbed and polished the house from top to bottom, had crocheted cot blankets, pram blankets, knitted enough cardigans, booties, tiny hats, and matinee jackets to clothe an army of babies, anything to keep herself busy. 'Molly said I'm *nesting*. It's my body's way of preparing for the arrival of our baby.' She did not tell Cal about her scare earlier. Some things were better for men not to know, she thought. 'I'm not in pain, Cal. I just feel more comfortable walking than sitting.'

Mary Jane didn't remember anything about her daughter

Hollie's birth. Motherhood and large families were commonplace along the dockside, and the women who shopped in Mary Jane's Kitchen bakery shop, had given her chapter and verse about every aspect of what was to come. Some of which was beautiful and some, like Ina's recollections, were downright terrifying. But, she decided, she wasn't going to dwell on those. Each birth was different, so Molly said, even in the same family.

'Right now, it's doing the Charleston.'

'What is the Charleston?' asked her husband, his eyebrows pleating.

'It's the latest dance craze. Daisy showed me after an American sailor came into the shop and showed her how to do it,' said Mary Jane.

'Show me how it's done.' Cal loved nothing better than to take his beautiful wife in his arms and dance.

However, Mary Jane shook her head. 'You will have to wait until this one's born,' she said, 'otherwise I'll give birth right here. That dance is so fast, I've never seen anything like it.'

'Sounds like my kinda dance,' Cal had mischief in his eyes, 'but I wouldn't want you doing anything that would hurt you or our child.'

'I know, my love.' Recalling the danger of her first pregnancy, when she contracted toxaemia just before she gave birth to Hollie, she wasn't going to take any chances this time around.

13

'I have never seen so many people in my life.' Elodie was in awe of the crowded pavements and huge busy shops.

'Liverpool doesn't have the same manufacturing interests as, say, Manchester or Sheffield,' Aiden told her as they travelled towards his maternal aunt's home in Beamer Street at the north end of dockside Liverpool. He knew Elodie's nerves were in shreds, she had told him the whole sorry tale of her marriage on the way here, and he was so glad she had made the move she needed to get away.

All these people rushing around like ants. New Year's Eve ants going about their business. Elodie plucked at the skin on her fingers. Then she removed her wedding, engagement, and eternity rings. Something to fall back on if money began to run out. *No. That would not happen.*

'You never know,' Aiden said cheerfully, 'one of these days you might see your name over the door of one of these fine shops.'

He had longed to see her set free for years, but there was nothing he could do to rescue her from the tyranny of a cruel marriage, not then. But times had changed, and now that she needed his help, he made sure he would always be there for her, no matter what the cost to him personally.

'None of the industrial towns would be able to operate without Liverpool importing the raw materials.' Aiden felt the need to keep some kind of conversation going, if only to stop his thoughts, dwelling on the terrible consequences of what could happen, if Elodie was ever found by Lord Caraway. They were unthinkable. 'Her importance is being a seaport.'

'You sound so pleased with your family's native city,' said Elodie.

'Liverpool's not like anywhere else in the world,' Aiden said. 'For a start, her commercial wealth increases from overseeing the produce of faraway countries.'

'I have never seen anything like it,' said Elodie, who would never have been able to imagine the size and magnitude of the place she had just entered.

'But while her docks are crowded with ships from all parts of the world, making the city one of the most prosperous in England,' Aiden informed her, 'those wealthy streets and boulevards lie cheek by jowl with some of the poorest people in the country. You've never seen such poverty as you will see here.'

'Now I feel nervous.' In the years since her marriage to Silas Caraway, she had become even less worldly-wise. The maze of Liverpool streets were filled with swift-footed people of all shapes, sizes, and colours. 'I've never seen so many different nationalities.'

'The same as in most seaports, I should imagine,' said Aiden.

Elodie's eyes were never still as she viewed the hawkers selling fish and fruit from baskets at the roadside, large horses pulling heavily laden carts from the docks, omnibuses filled with commuters going about their business, some women in furs, window-shopping, others in dark, woollen shawls, huddling their babies to their breast. There were male and female down-and-outs begging on street corners, while barefoot youngsters fleetingly criss-crossed the busy roads, and wove their way through crowded streets. Her eyes nearly popped out of their sockets when she saw dark-skinned sailors from hotter countries promenading along London Road clothed in numerous coats and hats to keep warm, as they made their way from the market to their ships lying at anchor in the dock.

'I didn't know this many people existed.' Elodie was in awe.

'Some would give you the shirt off their back,' Aiden told her, 'while others would pinch it while you weren't looking, so be careful.'

'I don't think I would dare wander these streets alone,' she said. The city streets were amazingly fast-moving, albeit exciting, in contrast to the sleepy village she had left a few hours ago. The picture palaces, theatres, and music halls with their dazzling electric lights, advertising the latest films, plays, and concerts all flew past the motorcar.

When the whistle of a passing steam train sounded as they crossed a bridge, Elodie almost shot out of her seat.

The early-evening's grey gauze, casting its shadow over the city, was eliminated by the glow of the gas lamps, and the lights shining from shop windows. All gave the streets a golden luminosity that reflected on the damp slush-covered pavements.

Aiden drove the car onto the dock road, then turned into a narrow back street; there were no trees, no grass, the only green she could see was the verdigris patina that covered the damp walls and gable ends of the red-brick buildings. A ship's horn sounded on the misty river and Elodie, although not expecting the splendour of Oakland Hall, doubted she would ever get used to the noise and the bustle of a place like this.

* * *

Pulling the net curtain to one side, Mary Jane felt that unmistakable surge of joy when she saw the flakes of snow flutter down, illuminated in the golden glow of the gaslight from lamps on the opposite side of the street, where the smaller three-up, three-down terraced houses combined with a variety of shops, including her bakery. She saw Daisy, Molly's eldest, turn out the lights in the shop.

Daisy was her mainstay in the days of her confinement, and she was doing a sterling job managing the shop. The Haywood family were people who would stand by somebody through thick and thin. Salt of the earth, they were, and Molly was the mother Mary Jane had never known.

'If I could, I'd have the child myself,' Cal said, breaking into her thoughts, and Mary Jane smiled in answer to her husband, whom she loved with all her heart. He had made such a difference to her life and, unbeknown to the residents, he owned every property in Beamer Street, something she didn't know when she moved into the street. And that's the way he wanted it to stay.

'If you could have the child, you'd be in the circus, as a living breathing curiosity,' she answered before turning around and putting her arms around his slim waist. Cal, at thirty-five, had been through so much. Before she'd met him, he had drunk his way from North to South America, almost killing himself in the process after losing his first wife and unborn child in a fire. He then cleaned up his act and joined up to fight in the trenches. A bomb blast had caused terrible injuries that even now left him with a slight limp. Although, he did not let it hinder him in any way. The properties, left to him by his late father, were managed by one of the property agencies in the business quarter of the city overlooking the River Mersey, and nobody, apart from Molly and her family, were any the wiser. As far as the neighbours were concerned, Cal Everdine was an industrious man who did his best to look out for his family.

Although Cal was friendly enough, he liked to keep his private life to himself. He didn't want anybody to know he was wealthy and owned a lot of dockside properties. He just wanted to be a family man.

Having never experienced a true family after being sent away to Canada to learn his profession, his beloved mother had died, and his father had quickly remarried without even telling him. Nobody, least of all his haughty young wife, was more surprised when his father's will was read out and Cal had inherited everything. His father obviously knew his new wife was a gold digger. Leaving Cal well off and secure was the only thing his father had ever done for him. But Cal was loath to spend the inheritance, preferring instead to work hard and provide for his family himself.

'Would you like some toast, a biscuit maybe?' He knew that his incessant fussing was beginning to wear on his darling wife's nerves.

'Molly is bringing us some of her lovely stew,' Mary Jane said, knowing nobody made a good pan of scouse like Molly.

'I could go and get it,' Cal said. Popping in next door to Molly's house was a pleasure he never tired of. Passing the time of day with the family and enjoying their relay race to fill him in on all the local news.

'Molly will bring it when she's ready, surely we can wait until then?' Mary Jane smiled.

'We can and we will, Mrs Everdine,' said Cal, making Mary Jane's heart jump like a mad thing when he called her by his name. 'Then, later on, we can lie in our cosy bed and listen to the church bells and ships' horns celebrating a brand-new year.'

14

Silas must never find out where she and Melissa, named after the sweet-scented herbal lemon balm, were staying, because sure as hens laid eggs he would have her daughter taken from her and made a ward of court.

Then he would make sure Elodie never saw her daughter again. He would start the rumours of black magic, which he had always threatened to do, to keep her in her place.

The accusations would ensure she never saw her darling daughter again. But she was determined she and Melissa would no longer live under such a threat. When he discovered it was not possible to father an heir, he would blame everything on her. Not himself.

He would return to Oakland Hall in the knowledge that what he wanted as much as life itself was never going to come to fruition and no herbs, lotions, potions, or medicine was going to change that.

It was imperative she and the child reach safety before Silas forced the truth from her about Aiden, which she had kept secret for so long. Because if that should happen, she and Melissa were not the only ones in danger.

'Aunt Molly is the salt of the earth,' Aiden reassured her. 'You will really like her.'

'We're here now,' Elodie whispered to her daughter, cute as a button in her red tam-o'-shanter, carrying her rag doll by one arm, which she'd got for Christmas.

'I'll make sure he never finds you.' Aiden's voice was full of the warmth she needed, happy with the news she would be lodging with his aunt and her family. Thinking about it now, Aiden knew he should have tried to persuade her to move to Liverpool years ago, when he was demobbed from the army. But he did not have the means to support her back then and, if truth be told, he could not bear the thought of being separated from her again whilst he worked back at Oakland Hall to save enough money to set them up.

'My only regret about leaving is that I won't be able to put flowers on my mother's grave.' There was a catch in Elodie's voice, which finished on a whisper.

'I will make sure your mother has fresh flowers every single day,' Aiden assured her.

'Thank you,' Elodie said. She knew Aiden was doing all he could to make things right. Although he was putting himself in danger by helping her.

'I am in awe of your bravery, starting over again in a new place with people you don't know.'

'Call it my spirit of adventure.' Elodie gave him a wide smile and Aiden knew she was just as courageous as any of the nurses or ambulance drivers he had come across in France. Elodie had a new life ahead of her. New challenges. New goals.

Elodie's eyes took in the place she would now call home. The upper classes who had once occupied these properties had moved to more salubrious areas years ago and some of the larger houses were now turned into lodging houses or homes for the large families.

'She's exhausted from the long journey,' said Aiden who loved the child every bit as much as her mother did and enjoyed the time Melissa had spent in the greenhouses tending the plants he grew or helping him with little chores in the garden.

A short while later the car glided silently down Beamer Street, but it still caused a stir from the drinkers singing to a lively piano tune, enjoying the run-up to 1925, in the public house at the top of the street, to the residents who had been busy cleaning and cooking all day in readiness for the coming new year.

'Flash,' said Ina King with withering accuracy, her ever-watching eyes peering from outside the bakery, watching with the interest of a predatory cat about to pounce, as every child in the street, her own included, ran alongside the shiny motorcar, their mucky faces alight with glee. A posh motor was a rare thing in Beamer Street.

'Look, it's our Aiden,' said Daisy who had finished work for the day, when the car stopped outside her house and saw her mam come out to greet the visitors. Molly's eyes were as wide as side plates. The inhabitants of the street craning their necks to get a glimpse of the new arrivals.

Molly had never seen a car like this one in Beamer Street, nor a woman in a coat so obviously expensive. Oh, and that hat, Molly thought, what she would give for a hat like that. And the child was wearing a real fur coat. A child – in a fur coat! She had never seen the like around here.

'Would you look at that coat.' Ina's eyes were as round as Molly's. No woman or child dressed in those kinds of clothes, unless they were someone of importance, and never around here. Ina crossed the road to Molly in a flash.

'So, this is your nephew, Molly?' Ina said as if she had been invited.

'This is our Aiden,' Molly answered, put out at her neighbour's intrusion.

Aiden lifted Melissa with ease from the back seat of the motor-car, and she awoke, reluctant to be put down to shake Ina's hand.

'And isn't that a pretty hat,' Ina said addressing Melissa who peeped out at them from behind her mother.

'These people are never relations of yours, Molly?' Ina, aghast, whispered from the side of her mouth as Molly straightened her back and raised her chin. She liked the idea that Ina, who often boasted she had come from 'money', thought Molly had a rich relative.

'That would be telling, Ina,' said Molly. 'Well, let's get inside we don't want to be standing out here catching our death of cold in the snow.'

Aiden's voice was low and tender as he encouraged Melissa from behind her mother, to let him cocoon her in the thick travel-ling blanket as Molly led the way up the steps to the front door.

'I do wish you could stay, Aiden,' Elodie said, following closely, but there was no time to say any more as Molly ushered them into the house.

Molly knew Ina's eyes would be out on stalks, along with the rest of the neighbours as she closed the vestibule door.

'How ya, Aunty Molly?' said Aiden, her sister's lad.

'I'm fit as a flea, lad,' Molly laughed. He was hardly a lad any more. He was a strapping young man who'd fought in the war in France and had come home an injured hero who saved a lot of men with his bravery. She was full of pride for all her relatives, but this one held a special place in her heart. 'You're looking grand, I must say.' Molly's beaming smile lit up her face. 'How's the leg?'

'A lot better than it was,' he said, and his warm dark eyes

turned towards Elodie standing by his side, 'and it's all thanks to this wonderful woman here. She's a magic touch with those healing hands of hers.' Aiden's ambling vocabulary was so different to the people who lived around here, where the machine-gun, hundred-words-a-minute vocabulary was more commonly heard. Molly gave Elodie a welcoming smile. So this was the girl her sister had spoken about, who had nursed Aiden back to health after the war.

'How's your mam?' asked Molly bustling them into the cosy front room where a roaring fire was burning brightly. She hadn't seen her sister since her niece was wed; Molly had made the special journey back to her Lancashire countryside home on a steam train, with her four kids.

'She's in the pink, Aunt Moll,' Aiden said, knowing his mother was the only person who knew he was coming to Beamer Street. 'She sent you this,' he said, handing over a basket of provisions. 'She said you must come back home and see her again, soon.'

'That's nice of her,' said Molly, thrilled at the gift of fresh eggs, butter and cream. 'Tell her, thank you, I will certainly make good use of these.' Nothing ever went to waste food-wise in Molly's busy household. 'And who have we here?' Molly gave her visitor her friendliest smile. Never one to stand on ceremony, she took to folk as she found them, and could usually tell if she would get on with them in the first moments of meeting. But there was something about this woman. She reminded Molly so much of Mary Jane when she had met her for the first time three and a half years ago. *It's the eyes*, thought Molly. Although not the same colour, they seemed only a blink away from a tear, even though her smile was as wide as the River Mersey.

This woman certainly looked well-to-do, in her burgundy silk-velour coat and that coveted hat, with its deep, softly pleating crown and narrow brim turned up at the back. Those rosettes on the side were real pink silk with a burgundy ribbon, matching her stylish winter coat, which fastened at low waist level with a large pink mother-of-pearl. And if Molly wasn't mistaken, the brindle-coloured stand-up collar and cuffs were real rabbit fur.

Taking in the fabulous attire in one swoop of her observant eyes, Molly knew she could never afford such clothes, and although she would have given her eye teeth for a hat like that, she didn't begrudge anybody else having them. She wouldn't mind a pair of those ox-blood leather shoes with a matching strap and button across the instep either. Those leather-covered Louis heels would stay in her dreams forever.

'My name is Elodie Cara... Kirrin.' Elodie held out her leather-gloved hand, reverting quickly to her maiden name. Silas must not have any inkling of her whereabouts and Mrs Kirrin seemed more in keeping in a street like this. Lady Elodie Caraway was far too grand, and she had never felt comfortable with the name.

Molly took her hand, giving it a friendly shake. It had not escaped her notice that the girl was going to call herself by another name and quickly changed her mind.

Something was going on here, she thought, silently wondering what it was. Although, she wouldn't embarrass the woman by prying. There was plenty of time for that.

'Take us as you find us, Ellie, love,' Molly said in her usual friendly manner. Then, as her curiosity got the better of her, Molly was urged to say, 'So, Elodie, that's a lovely name?'

'Thank you. I was named after my great-great-grandmother,' she said. 'She was a healer, what the villagers would call a wise woman in days when such a practice was frowned upon.'

'She never was...' Molly stopped talking when she saw Aiden give a little shake of his head. She'd grown up in Lavender Green and knew the stories of the Pendle witches nearby. She would have liked to talk about it, but Aiden's swift warning to say no more, stopped her in her tracks. Molly heard Ellie laugh.

'My great-great-grandma wasn't a witch; she was a healer who used natures cures to heal the infirm. Like I do. But, unlike my ancestors, I am not afraid of being persecuted.'

'Aye,' said Molly, 'I remember hearing about the witch-finder in the schoolroom.'

'Yes, those terrible days when women were drowned on the ducking stool by Matthew Hopkins, who tried to curry favour with King James, terrified of the things he knew nothing about.'

'I see you know your history.' Molly nodded and smiled. 'I like a girl to have a bit of nous about her, an inquisitive brain is a wonderful thing. I encourage it in both my daughters, Daisy, and Bridie.' Molly believed that a time would come when women would hold their own, like they did during the war, when they kept the country going while the men were away fighting for the country.

'How lovely that you have two daughters,' Elodie remarked.

'Our Daisy earns her living over the road, there, in Mary Jane's bakery.' Molly pointed to the bakery across the street. 'Mary Jane made sure our Daisy wasn't stuck in a factory, slaving away for buttons all week.' Molly stretched to her full five feet two inches. 'She manages the baker's shop now the owner is indisposed.' Molly would not go into detail of her neighbour's private business. 'If more girls took notice of women's fight for independence, they wouldn't be so eager to run up the aisle with the first bloke who showed them a bit of consideration.'

'I suppose you're right,' Elodie said, knowing she had done that very same thing. She had only married to keep a roof over her head, but she would keep that information private.

'Elodie is a widow,' Aiden said before Molly had time to ask questions. He and Elodie had agreed the story on the journey

here. 'Her husband was killed at the Somme.' The story Aiden had
conjured, quickly endeared Elodie to Molly, whose own husband
had been killed too.

'Come on, lass, let's get a nice hot cup of tea to thaw you out,'
Molly said, ushering.

Elodie was warming to this woman she had only just met yet
felt she had known for years. But even so, she was not inclined to
share her secrets. There was a moment's silence and then Molly
said, quite unexpectedly, harking back to their earlier conversation, 'Fancy such a powerful man as the king, believing in such
things as witches, just because a woman had the know-how to
heal people.' Long silences made her nervous, so she did her best
not to allow them into her conversations.

'Thankfully, such superstitious nonsense has long since been
ignored,' Elodie said.

'Not everywhere.' Molly's eyes lost their twinkle momentarily
and her voice held a cautionary note. Superstition and myth went
hand in hand in some places, especially around the dockside,
where lack of funds could lead to all kinds of beliefs. 'You'll find
people choose to believe what suits them.'

Molly looked across the street through the window to where
Ina was putting her milk bottles out earlier than usual. She
knew her neighbour might appear to be taking no notice of what
was going on at this side of the street, but Ina would be
chomping at the bit to come over and find out all about her
well-to-do visitor.

'Clear off out of it, you lot.' Molly banged on the window and
called to the street children gazing in awe at the fabulous, shiny
motorcar, and in seconds the street was cleared of children who
ran to the horse and cart coming up Beamer Terrace from the
docks. She knew that growing up in the north end of the docklands could be hard for the large families who resided here, espe-

cially when money was scarce, and the children would make their own, sometimes dangerous, fun.

Beamer Terrace, a main thoroughfare leading up from the docks, was always busy with passing carts. Some were commandeered by the street urchins, who, as the laden carts turned into Beamer Street, would jump on the back for a ride, or even take their mother's bread knife and slit open the sacks while their pals raced behind, collecting the 'spoils' in their upturned jerseys, especially when the carts were carrying sacks of raw sugar cane, which the locals called *togy*. Or another favourite, sweet chewy 'locusts' – the carob beans used for cattle food. Molly had warned their Bridie, if she ever caught her swinging on the back of a cart she would not be able to sit down for a week. A group of young girls collected the coke that had fallen off the back of a high-sided lorry as it came out of the gas works. Climbing the steep slope, the girls would collect whatever fell off the back and put it in their buckets. In some families, that was the only fuel they could afford.

'Here, let me hang up your coat,' Molly said, knowing she was better off than some these days.

'This is a lovely room,' said Elodie, turning from the window.

Molly waved her hand towards the chair by the blazing fire, which she had lit in readiness for her visitor. 'Let me get you a bite to eat, you must be starving.'

Molly smiled when she gazed at the exhausted child now sleeping once more, after Aiden had settled her on the sofa, covering her tenderly with the travelling rug.

Melissa reminded her of her own children when they were young, and she used to settle them in here for their afternoon nap when they were much younger. She was sure Elodie and Melissa would fit in with her family very nicely. Bridie was going to love having a younger child to entertain.

'I'm sorry to put you to all this trouble,' Elodie said, as the delicious aroma of meaty scouse filled the room and made her stomach grumble. The front room was well-furnished and comfortable. The last thing she wanted was grandeur of any kind. A kind word or a well-meaning gesture was all she needed right now.

Looking out of the wide bay window, she could see the long street leading up from the dock road towards Beamer Street. On one corner was the bakery, and on the other was empty premises.

'I'll go and make that tea, while you thaw out a bit,' Molly said, bustling towards the door undoing the buttons of her coat.

After a moment, the sound of crockery being laid out in the kitchen encouraged Elodie to speak. 'Do you think he would ever think of looking for me in a place like this?' she asked Aiden, watching the cart-pulling horses clamber up the steep, cobble-stoned, rise from the docks known as *the brew*. But her attention was caught by a group of boys and, it seemed, the thrill of the motorcar had waned when another horse and cart came to a standstill before turning left into Beamer Street, and a young lad, unable to resist the urge, clambered onto the back of the cart and pulled out a wad of cotton.

'That's Ina King's lad,' said Molly, bringing in the tray of tea and sandwiches. 'He's always up to something, and she won't say no to some polishing cloths.'

When they were settled, the niceties out of the way, and the plate of ham sandwiches, which she had intended to put out for her new year table, had been eaten, while the pan of scouse bubbled away on the stove in the back kitchen. Molly waited to hear what Aiden had to tell her.

'It's like this Aunt Molly, you see, Elodie... Mrs Kirrin...' Aiden began, and Molly was a little surprised to see her put her hand on his arm to silence him.

'Let me, Aiden,' Elodie said, and Molly admired her immediately, any woman who had the gumption to speak up for herself was all right by her. She liked a woman to have her own say, it had been a long time coming. This young woman didn't seem like she was the kind to be pushed around by anybody. 'What Aiden is trying to say, Mrs Haywood...'

'Molly, please, everybody calls me Molly.'

'And you must call me Elodie,' she said. 'Aiden tells me you have a room I can rent, is that right?'

This woman looked like she could afford to purchase a whole house. Even one of the better-off houses along Merton Road, thought Molly, never mind a room, and not just a rented room in the backstreets.

'If you don't mind me asking,' Molly said, leaning forward and lowering her voice in case her youngest daughter, Bridie, came barging into the front room wondering why there had been a posh car outside their house. 'Why do you want a room around here?'

'I want to open an apothecary,' Elodie said, knowing she couldn't tell Molly the truth about her disastrous marriage and the fact that she had run away for her own safety. 'I feel this is the kind of area I can do some good.' Elodie was thinking on her feet, and she surprised herself by the speed of her thoughts. 'I'm not sure how long I will need the room – but I want to get started as soon as possible and I am quite able to pay the going rate.'

'Well.' Molly became a little flummoxed and started clearing the cups and saucers onto the wooden tray, which Daisy had 'borrowed' from the bakery. 'I don't doubt you can pay,' Molly's words tripped over themselves in their haste to be out of her mouth, 'but I doubt the empty rooms upstairs will be up to the standard you are obviously accustomed to.'

Then, wherever the notion came from she would never know, her gaze shifted from her nephew to the woman sitting beside him, and in the next breath she said, 'Are you two...?' She left the question hanging in the air.

'No! Nothing like that.' However, Elodie's colour rose, when she said quickly, 'The room is for me and my little Melissa – we do not mind sharing.'

'There'll be no need for that, lass.' Molly was relieved that her nephew and this woman were not going to parade as a married couple because her conscience would not allow that to happen. Imagine what the parish priest would say! He'd have her excommunicated from the church as soon as look at her. 'I have two spare rooms, at the top of the house, right next to each other. Mind you,' said Molly, putting the tray of crockery back on the side table, 'if you want the use of the small room for the child, I will need to buy a single bed.' Although, how she was going to afford to buy a bed, at such short notice, was anybody's guess.

'I don't want you to go to any expense on my behalf,' said Elodie, as the child woke and placed one small hand in her mother's and one in Aiden's.

'You can have the use of this room too, if that suits,' Molly interrupted, 'we only use it at Christmas, anyway.'

'That's very kind of you.' Elodie knew she would be very cosy in this room, filled with a solid, highly polished three-piece suite, a table in the bay window holding a huge aspidistra, and a piano at the far wall near the door. 'I will not forget your generous hospitality.'

Molly smiled, thinking Elodie's softly spoken words, although low, sounded sincere and – what was that word her Daisy had said this morning? – cultured. That was it, she thought. Elodie was cultured.

'And please don't worry about buying the bed, I will purchase one forthwith.'

'Forthwith.' Molly silently mouthed the word. She didn't know anybody, apart from Mary Jane and Cal, who could afford to go out and buy a bed – forthwith.

"S'cuse me a minute,' Molly said standing up, 'I'll have to go and check on the scouse, I don't want the pan to boil dry, and, if you don't mind, I've just got to make a bit of shortcrust pastry, there would be ructions if my lot didn't have a nice thick crust to go with their meal. I won't be long.'

When Molly reached the parlour door she turned to Aiden. 'Do me a favour, lad, and pull those curtains across, otherwise we'll have every bugger nosing in.'

Elodie suspecting Molly was leaving her and Aiden alone to have a private talk got up from the chair. 'Here, let me,' she said. Before she closed the curtains, she looked out at the fluttering snow illuminated in the gaslights, covering the cobbles and the roof tops, and thought how different her, and Melissa's, life was about to become.

'What do you think?' Aiden asked, seeming nervous about her opinion.

'I think this will do very nicely,' Elodie answered, and she meant it. 'This room is bigger than the one Ma and me shared back at the cottage.'

'It's not Oakland Hall, though, is it?'

'You're right, it's not,' Elodie said, pulling the curtains across the wire over the bay windows. Nevertheless, Elodie had seen more life in this street in the short time since she had arrived than she had seen for years. 'But home is where you make it, I say, and I meant it when I told Molly that I intend to open my own apothecary.'

'What about the plants and roots you'll need?' Aiden asked as she ambled gracefully back to her seat by the fire.

Elodie thought for a moment. 'I doubt there will be as much growing space, but I will work with what I've got.' She had made her move and it had taken all the courage she could muster, and she wasn't going to let anything stop her now.

'I'm more likely to smell smoke from household and manufacturing chimneys than the sweet scent of freshly mown grass, or the perfume of beautiful plants and flowers. But I will adjust.' It was a case of having to, she thought.

This was a down-to-earth hard-working maritime port, and from what she had seen so far, by the look of some of its ill-clad inhabitants, flowers were a luxury a lot of people could not afford. But everybody needed to be healed at some time or other.

'That empty shop across the road is in an ideal spot for an apothecary,' Elodie said, her mind racing with ideas for her and Melissa's future. 'I'll find out who the landlord is and get things moving.'

'She's been here five minutes and already she's taking over the dock road,' Aiden laughed, his pride at her suggestion obvious. Glancing at the clock, he said reluctantly, 'I'll have to get back before he returns from London. There'll be hell to pay if I'm not there to pick him up from the station.'

A rush of trepidation shot through Elodie, and not for the first time since she left Oakland Hall, she wondered what she would do without him.

'Don't worry, Aunt Molly will look after you,' Aiden said when he saw the look of something akin to panic flash in her eyes as the parlour door opened and Molly came in.

'Oh,' Molly said, 'you're not staying for your tea?'

'I have to get back to pick up my boss from the London train.'

'London, is it?' Molly said with a nod of her head. 'My, how the other half live.'

'Aye,' Aiden said, looking to Elodie, his eyes tender. 'The snow may become heavy, and I don't want to be stuck on the hills.'

Molly could see as plain as day the look of love between them and remembered her Albert looking at her like that many moons ago.

'I'll ring you tomorrow morning, say nine o'clock, at the bakery. Is that all right?' Not wanting to leave Elodie, yet knowing he must, there was a silent agreement between the two of them. 'I'll let you know when I can bring supplies.' Aiden's words, although short and simple, carried a multitude of meaning and Elodie understood the look in his eyes. That look told her Aiden would be back as soon as Silas had gone back to London. 'Take care of yourself and Melissa.'

'I will. And thank you.' There was a lump forming in Elodie's throat even as she tried to speak. What would he be going back to? Silas was not going to take kindly to her leaving, nor about her taking Melissa. When she spoke again her words were barely a whisper. 'Safe journey.'

15

'Will it do, Ellie?' Molly asked as she stood on the wooden step leading down into one of the bedrooms, and Elodie's dark eyes took in every inch of the comfortable room, with a queen-sized bed between two sash windows, a wardrobe in the alcove by the side of the fire, with a matching chest of drawers in the other alcove, and a bedside table. A straight-backed chair with Queen Anne legs was situated beside the bed at the far window, which had a wonderful array of opaque patterns from the ice on the glass.

'It will do very nicely,' said Elodie, knowing she would have to get used to being called by the name only Aiden had ever called her. She liked the room, and she liked the name. All she had to do now was explain to Melissa why they would not be going back to Lavender Green or to Oakland Hall. The days of indulged imprisonment were over.

'I'll get our Freddy to come up and light the fire,' said Molly, looking towards the Victorian cast-iron fireplace with its narrow mantlepiece over the unlit fire. 'The coalman only came today so there's plenty of coal to make a good glow, all nice and cosy.'

'Don't go wasting your coal,' said Elodie, 'the room won't be used until bedtime. I'm sure I will spend most of my time downstairs.'

'That's very considerate of you, lass,' said Molly. 'I'll fill the coal scuttle for the parlour.'

This room was not much smaller than her bedroom back at Oakland Hall, but it was a good deal bigger than the room she had once shared with her mother in the cottage. This would suit her and Melissa perfectly, she thought, moving over to the window.

The snow was coming down harder now and, rubbing the window, Elodie could make out the busy street below seething with children throwing snowballs and building snowmen with coal-black eyes and a twig-like nose. No carrots, she mused, suspecting the vegetables would be put to better use.

The children did not seem to notice the cold, she thought, even those who were dressed in clothes that were most unsuitable for weather like this, the proof was in the orange-mottled glow of their cheeks as they gathered snow, their hands covered only by the sopping wet cuffs of their jerseys, or even old socks.

Although the street was close to the docks, it was respectable enough, with its polished doorknobs and lion's head knockers, scrubbed steps, and polished windows. Beamer Street was lined on this side with grand, soot-covered, apex-fronted residences with high ceilings and large bay windows that let in plenty of light, while on the other side of the cobbled road were smaller, less grand but well-kept. The red-brick terraced houses had smaller bay windows with narrow pathways leading to one step and then the front door, unlike these houses, with their three wide steps. And while the gates on this side were decorative wrought-iron, there were wooden gates on the other side, with an ankle-high sandstone wall separating every pathway.

There was a shop of some description on every corner, and

there was also a small variety of assorted retail premises sitting side by side – a butcher's shop, a greengrocer's, a grocer's, a chandler's as well as the bakery on the corner, where Molly's daughter worked. And across the cobbled street on the other corner was the empty premises that had caught her attention earlier.

Her heart leapt. For the first time since she left Oakland Hall, Elodie felt a lightness in her chest, her pulse quickening, and her mind beginning to fizz, knowing she may be looking at the answer to her prayers.

'So, you're a healer?' Molly said, conversationally, knowing there must be more to Ellie than met the eye. There was certainly money in this healing lark if, as a war widow like herself, she could afford clothes like these.

'I was a nurse during the war, herbal healing has been in my family for centuries.'

'Well, how about that, then.' Molly could not imagine being responsible for healing injured soldiers. 'I'd have been the tea lady, making a cuppa for the patients.' Molly laughed. 'That must have been interesting.'

'Don't get me started,' Elodie laughed, 'I'll have you here all day.'

'Have you lived in Lavender Green all your life?' Molly asked, and Elodie gave a cautionary nod. She would much rather talk about her herbs than about her private life, but felt Molly, who had been so kind, deserved some kind of explanation.

'All my life.' Elodie tried to steer the conversation in another direction, 'I've been surrounded by herbs, making balms, ointments, tinctures, and teas. Doctors are all well and good, but herbs are just as healing.'

'Well,' said Molly, 'there's plenty 'round here, respectable people, mind, who may not always have money for the likes of doctors.'

'I can imagine,' said Elodie, who knew doctors could cost a great deal, when only a good tonic was needed.

'Look at the likes of Ina King,' Molly confided, 'she can't even afford to get the doctor for her daughter, who has a terrible cough, and there are many of the older folk who don't trust them at all, remembering the tales of the workhouse infirmary, and preferring the old remedies.'

'I'm sure there is something we can do to put that right,' said Elodie, her thoughts beginning to run away with themselves.

Molly liked the way Ellie said, 'we', like she was going to be of some help too.

'Almost every house has someone who works on the docks, when they can get taken on, that is.' Molly knew she was luckier than most, not having to find rent money since Cal let her and her family live here rent free. 'A lot of dock work is casual, and with the best will in the world, there isn't enough work to go around for every man who needs it.' She paused before saying, 'Usually, medicine comes low down on the list and only when it's desperately needed.'

Elodie, who was never happier than when she was helping those less fortunate, experienced the same stirring of excitement she felt when healing wounded heroes.

'Well, I'll leave you to get settled,' Molly said, leaving the room. She liked this woman on sight, and she was never wrong when it came to knowing what someone was genuinely like on the first meeting. And she knew Ellie had a tale to tell. Why else would she be here in the backstreets of the Liverpool Dockland? 'Melissa will be fine on the couch, I'll keep my eye on her, come down when you're ready.'

Elodie could hear Molly's nimble tread on the stairs and, looking out across the street, she read the words, *Mary Jane's Kitchen, delicious pies, and cakes, enjoyed by Kings*. The gold lettering, sprawled across the shop window, caught in the flickering light from a nearby gas lamp as shopkeepers pushed back the striped awnings with a long pole. She had never seen anything like this place. Back in the village, people made their own bread. Nobody bought it from a shop. If the villagers needed milk, they went to one of the nearby farms with a jug. There was the village shop, of course, but it was not stocked with anything like the amount of food shops around here. The sight of gas-lit, well-stocked grocery shops was a novelty, and the street lamps mesmerised her.

In Lavender Green, people carried a paraffin lamp to light their way, there were no street lamps. Strangers were in danger of falling down a ditch or getting run down by a horse. Food, although plain, was filling, nourishing and there were no external walls lined with advertisements for Oxo cubes, or Ovaltine malted milk drinks like there were here.

She had not seen one blade of grass. Nor were there any trees. It was nothing like the clean, fresh countryside back at Lavender Green.

But, she thought, beggars can't be choosers.

* * *

'I'm just going to take some of this stew into Mary Jane and Cal who live next door,' said Molly, carrying a large, covered bowl on a wooden tray, when Elodie came downstairs. 'She's expecting a new arrival, so I offered to make her a bit of tea.'

'Would you like a hand to carry it?' Elodie asked and Molly's eyes lit up.

'I'm sure she'd be made up to meet you. She has a little girl too, Hollie, she's only three, but Melissa might like to meet her now she's awake.'

'That would be lovely,' said Elodie, knowing her daughter had never had much chance to be with other children before. Having a private tutor, Melissa didn't attend the village school.

'Mary Jane's new too, been in Beamer Street since the summer of 1921, but she's made her mark, and she's due to have her baby any time,' Molly lowered her voice, 'her last pregnancy did not go to term, although, we won't go into the whys and wherefores just now.' Molly knew if Mary Jane wanted Ellie to know all her business, she had a good enough tongue in her own head to tell her.

'Can Melissa come and make a snowman?' asked Bridie, hopefully holding the child's hand, wanting to show off their new house guest to the other kids in the street.

'We're just going to see Mary Jane and her daughter,' Elodie answered. Melissa wasn't used to playing with other children, at her husband's behest, and no children were invited to Oakland Hall. Not even on her birthday. Here, in Beamer Street, Elodie had seen children not much older than Melissa carrying their younger siblings on their hip as they 'played' outside.

'If the children aren't helping indoors, they're outside minding younger siblings, even neighbour's children,' Molly said as they descended the steps of her house, 'getting fresh air into their lungs while their mothers clean the house.'

Elodie knew the air around these parts was far from fresh. The smoke from domestic and industrial chimneys took care of that. Although the snow, which was now quickly turning to grey slush, did make the street look picture perfect for a while, like something off a Christmas card.

There was a great deal of excitement as Molly introduced Mary Jane and her family, even the two little girls were excited and immediately swapped dollies, but Molly didn't linger. Making her excuses to get back next door she left the two women to get acquainted, sure they would get on like a house on fire.

'You'll love it here,' said Mary Jane when Molly had left,

'everyone is so friendly – well nearly everyone – you won't have met Ina King yet.' Mary Jane laughed.

'Please, don't stand on my behalf,' Elodie said, noticing that Mary Jane's colour was a bit high, and she was wearing her husband's slippers. 'You must get your rest for the big occasion.'

'The sooner, the better,' said Mary Jane. 'If I go much longer, I'll explode.' She sat down on a straight-backed chair at the table, the only place she could get comfortable. 'Were you like this when you were having your Melissa?' Mary Jane asked, and Elodie smiled, evading the question.

'We all have a different tale to tell when it comes to bringing babies into the world. There are thousands born and none are identical.'

'You can say that again.' Mary Jane's ready laugh filled the room as Cal went out to the kitchen to make a pot of tea and put the stew in the oven to keep warm. 'Have you seen the size of these puddings?' She lifted her feet, letting her husband's slippers dangle. 'I can't even get my own slippers on.'

'How was Hollie's birth?' Elodie asked, and although her query sounded like a conversational question between two mothers, Elodie was trying to determine if she need worry. When Mary Jane told her she contracted toxaemia before Hollie was born, in such dramatic circumstances, Elodie knew she was right to be worried.

'Right then,' Elodie said, 'it's complete bedrest for you. I want you to keep those feet up and you are not to do anything strenuous except breathe, right?' Elodie's dynamic manner was sweetened with a smile.

'I hear you,' Mary Jane said, looking to Cal who put the tea tray on the table and announced he would carry her into the front room, already prepared for Mary Jane's confinement, if she let him. She would not, she told him plainly.

'Right,' said Elodie, helping Mary Jane into the bed in the parlour. She had been helping to deliver babies since she was big enough to accompany her mother. 'If you need anything, you only have to ask.'

'Thank you, I'm thrilled you're here to help.' Mary Jane had welcomed her into her home, and they had an immediate rapport between the two 'outsiders'. 'It may take a while for some of the neighbours to accept you,' Mary Jane said. 'Like Ina, now there's a tough nut to crack, she'll be like headlice if you can enrich her life in some way.'

'Headlice?' Elodie's brow pleated.

'Hard to get rid of,' Mary Jane laughed, and then Elodie laughed too.

'I'm sure I know a cure for that.'

'It won't go to waste around here,' Mary Jane laughed again, and Cal left the talking and went to warm the plates ready for their evening meal. Mary Jane pointed to her swollen abdomen. 'This one's been having conniptions in here.' Her neighbourly chat hid the worry she had been feeling all day. 'Last night I'm sure it was doing the Black Bottom, there were hands and legs all over the place, but today, nothing.'

'He'll be gathering his strength for the final push,' said Elodie.

'He?' Mary Jane looked a little shocked.

'Just a turn of phrase, I don't like calling them "it", do you?'

'No, you're right,' said Mary Jane.

'I'm sure there's nothing to worry about, but I understand your concern.' Elodie's voice softened. 'I hope you don't mind Molly telling me you didn't go full term with your last baby.'

'No.' Mary Jane bit her lip and pulled at the skin on the back of her hand. Usually so sure of herself, she could not help but feel she had failed in some way when she lost her last baby, after Hollie. 'Molly worries about me like I'm one of her own. She knows who she can confide in and who she'd rather keep in the dark,' said Mary Jane who desperately longed to keep this one.

'I had a little girl. I had her christened, only a small ceremony, here in the house, just me and Cal and the priest... I think about her every day.' Her voice trailed, Mary Jane had said much more than she intended, but there was something in Ellie's caring way that drew information from her, a manner she trusted. 'I haven't even told Molly about the christening, and I tell her everything.'

'Your secret's safe with me,' Elodie assured her as she finished her tea, realising people drank a lot of tea around here. In the short time she had been here, she had been offered at least four cups.

'Molly's my best friend, the mother I never knew, she came to my rescue many a time when I first moved into Beamer Street.' She reached out and touched Elodie's arm. 'And as far as I can see, you are cut from the same cloth.' Mary Jane made her mind up quickly about people and was rarely wrong in her assumptions.

'If there is anything I can do to help, even if you only want to share a concern, no matter how big or small,' Elodie said in that calm, soothing way she had about her, 'I'm here to listen, not to pass them on.' Discretion had been her mother's watchword and Elodie knew no other way to be. 'Don't hesitate to call on me.'

Elodie knew that moving to a new place was going to be unsettling at first, but the few people she had met were the kindest, most generous people she had ever known. The acceptance was more readily given than it would have been in Lavender Green, where some people only looked out for themselves. 'Don't forget, if you need anything you just call out, and if you can't call out bang on the wall.'

'Oh, I will.' Mary Jane felt much calmer now.

* * *

'We would love it if you and the little one would come into the kitchen for your tea,' Molly said when Mary Jane and Melissa came back. 'It would be a great opportunity to meet the family.'

'That's very kind of you,' said Elodie. 'Are you sure we won't be intruding?'

'Not at all,' said Molly, 'it will be lovely to have new faces at the table, and there is always plenty. I throw everything into a pan of scouse. Neck ends of lamb, shin beef, good wholesome vegetables, and so many spuds you can stand your spoon up in it.'

'Sounds lovely,' Elodie said, and she meant it. 'Doesn't that sound lovely, Melissa?' She smiled when the child shyly nodded, and when Molly went out of the room, Elodie beckoned her daughter over to her fireside chair and said, 'Don't worry, little one, you will soon get used to this place, we both will.'

At least here they would not be scared of their own shadow or the sound of her husband's key in the front door. 'We will make a new life here. And you can even go to the local school, would you like that?' The child nodded her head with enthusiasm. She had never been to school before.

* * *

Molly introduced the whole family, who were now sitting around the large kitchen table and Elodie, in turn, introduced her daughter and herself.

'So, you want to be an electrician, Freddy?' Elodie asked, genuinely interested in other people's lives, she felt privileged the Haywood family had taken to her and Melissa so readily that they wanted to share their private life.

'He wants to go away to sea,' Molly interrupted, something she did a lot, Elodie noticed, 'but he's a bit young yet and I told him he'll go further with a trade to his name.'

'He certainly will,' said Elodie, 'I've heard that electricity is going to be the thing of the future, in time, everybody will have it in their homes, and in their workplaces.'

'There you go, Fred, tomorrow's a brand-new year. You never know what it will bring,' said Molly, and as if Elodie's words had cemented her decision, she added, 'At least one of my lot will have a trade behind them.'

'Only the one with a trade, Mam?' Daisy asked indignantly. 'What do you think I do all day, paint me nails like one of those flappers?'

'You know I didn't mean you,' said Molly, dismissing Daisy's words with the flick of her hand. 'Us women will always have to bake and cook. It's what we do.'

'Can they make a three-tier wedding cake as well?' Daisy asked, feeling her mam was doing what she always did, taking her for granted. The thought disappeared as quickly as it came. Ma had put up with such a lot over the years, and speaking before she got her thoughts in order was just her way, Daisy knew she didn't mean anything by it.

But Mary Jane had put her through catering college on a three-year, day-release course, and Daisy had passed her examinations with flying colours. Ma could never have afforded to do that, bless her.

'I think it's wonderful that you have a trade,' Elodie told Daisy, who beamed at the compliment. 'It is important that women have the wherewithal to go out and earn their own money. And you will always have something to fall back on, people always need bread.'

'I said that didn't I, Daisy?' said Molly. 'I said get yourself a good trade and you won't be beholden to anybody, didn't I say that, Daisy?'

'Yes, Mam, you said that.' Although, for the life of her, Daisy could not recall a time when she was not her mother's backbone since Pa died. Even if she wanted to go off and do something for herself, Daisy knew she could never leave her mother to look after the family alone. How would she cope?

'I was wondering,' said Elodie, 'that empty shop on the corner...'

'It used to be a chemist before Mister Bull passed away, God rest his miserly soul,' Molly said, making a quick sign of the cross on her chest. 'It's been empty for a couple of months.'

'That shop would be perfect for my apothecary.' Elodie's mind began to race. A new year to look forward, not back.

'What's an apothecary?' asked Daisy, glad of the interruption.

'A dispensary,' Elodie answered. 'Years ago, my ancestors, being herbal healers, were called *wise women*.'

'We used to have a wise woman in our village, before I wed your beloved pa,' Molly told her offspring gathered around the table, her eyes glazed over. 'Her name was Elodie, and you'll never guess?' She paused for a moment. 'She was only Ellie's grandma!' Molly nodded her head to emphasise her words. 'And very respected she was too.'

'She passed everything she learned from her mother down to my mother, and my mother passed it down to me, our healing goes back as far as the sixteenth century, maybe even beyond that.'

'See, didn't I tell you!!' Molly said, her spoon halfway between her bowl and lip. However, she didn't mention that her sister had told her of the rumours that had gone around the village like wildfire, after Lady Felicia died in childbirth under the watch of the healer, Deborah Kirrin... *Oh my goodness! If only her sister lived a bit closer, she might have known more.*

'I didn't see a letting sign over the premises?' Elodie said casually, noticing a meaningful look pass between mother and daughter.

'I'll see what I can find out,' Molly told her whilst her mind was on other things. From what her sister had told her, Molly recalled Deborah Kirrin hung herself because she could not bear the thought of being the cause of Lady Felicia dying. Molly was so deep in thought she hardly caught Ellie's question.

'Is it a big shop?' Elodie asked and Daisy tapped her mother's foot with her own.

'About the same size as the bakery,' Daisy answered. 'It would certainly be big enough for an apothecary.'

16

'Please, Lord, not again. It's too early,' Mary Jane drew her legs up to her swollen belly and wanted to walk. Cal and Hollie were asleep in their own rooms upstairs. The discomfort, for it could never be called a pain, ebbed away and she tried to think happy thoughts of Cal and Hollie and how good her life was now, to take her mind off what might be coming.

Marriage to Cal was the best time of her life, and Mary Jane knew she was in the finest place. She and Cal were two halves of the same soul. They were meant for each other. And, hopefully, tomorrow would be the day she would give him the best gift he could ever dream of, and a new brother or sister for Hollie.

Slipping from under the warm covers, a rising heat took over her body and a slow gathering in her stomach of something unsettling, yet exciting. She felt a pinch of every nerve ending, every muscle contracting into itself until it reached a crescendo of pain she had never known. The tightening shattered any coherent thought from her mind. Doubling over, she gripped the headboard of the bed. 'Jesus, Mary and Joseph!' she gasped, holding on for dear life as her knees almost gave way, but she had no inclination to sit down, or call out for her husband's help. She mustn't wake Hollie, she thought, as the pain loosened its leonine grip and gradually padded away like a feeble kitten.

Taking a deep breath, Mary Jane decided to put a little more coal on the fire and then go to make herself a cup of tea. Creeping out into the hallway, she heard her daughter whimper upstairs and Mary Jane knew she could not leave her.

'Mammy?' Hollie's voice, thick with sleep, was anxious as she held out her arms to her mother, and Mary Jane went to her, lying beside her and holding her close.

'Shh, darling girl, go back to sleep, Mammy's here. It's only the church bells, nothing to worry about.' Mary Jane pulled the covers around Hollie's shoulders and chin so that only her nose and eyes were visible. In seconds, she was fast asleep again.

Holding on to what power she possessed, Mary Jane's inner strength brought her through another spasm, knowing she must not wake Hollie again. The heat she had generated during her last contraction dissipated, and she could feel the bite of the cold midwinter chill.

Silently slipping from her daughter's room and, closing the door behind her, Mary Jane crossed the thick carpeted landing and made her way down the stairs, marvelling at the memory's inability to recall the last pain. She would let Cal sleep on, this might go on for hours and she didn't want him fussing over her.

She remembered Molly telling her about the practice pains, which she experienced before having her own children. Having given birth to four children of her own, Molly would know about such things, and she too could be experiencing the same.

As she reached the bottom stair, Mary Jane could hear the church bells ring in 1925, and the sound of her neighbours singing 'Auld Lang Syne', just as the next pain, stronger this time, gripped her and held her fast. That was too quick! Not yet! She knew she would never get back up those stairs to wake Cal and she didn't want to shout and wake Hollie!

Another pain, more intense this time, ripped through her body and she gasped at its strength. These were not practice pains.

The contraction ebbed, but before it diminished completely, another one took its place.

'God help me!' Mary Jane whispered as the pain died to nothing. 'I can't do this on my own.'

What if there was no time for the midwife to get here and she had to deliver the child herself? What if there were complications, like there had been last time? What if...

'Stop it,' she whispered to herself, 'you are being hysterical, and you have a young daughter who needs her mother to be calm.' Her stomach tightened into a twisted knot, and Mary Jane was sure her time had come.

Gasping for air when the pain subsided, she supported her lower abdomen with both hands, and Mary Jane felt that incapacitating fear surge up inside her once more.

'Not yet, little one,' she whispered, sitting on the stairs, 'just stay there, warm and snug till morning.' Her breathing hitched in her throat. Then became shallow and quick. She felt dizzy. Squeezing her eyes tight shut, she tried to will away the pain that was moving her baby closer to birth. Then, as quickly as the pain came, it dissolved to nothing. Like it never happened.

Pushing one foot in front of the other, Mary Jane crossed the hallway and headed towards the front door. She could hear voices, and she prayed. Pushing the bolt back from the lock, she managed to open the front door before the next overwhelming pain.

It had been snowing hard and the whole street was white. People were singing. The church bells were ringing. The ships were sounding their horns on the River Mersey. The combined sounds were welcoming the brand-new year. New opportunities.

New life. Mary Jane heard the midnight revellers gathered in Beamer Street, thankful when she saw Molly wishing Ina King all the best for the coming year, in that strange light that only came when snow was lying on the ground.

She tried to speak, but no sound came. Then she saw her friend looking her way and the expression of panic was plain to see on Molly's face. A small pop between her legs was the only indication Mary Jane's waters had broken, and she looked down. To her horror, she could see a puddle forming around her slippered feet. There was no stopping this now, she thought. The child was on its way.

'Get inside, Mary Jane, get in!' Molly, Ellie, and Peggy Tenant cried in unison, hurrying across the cobbled street to Mary Jane's side and alerting Ina King to her plight. Hushing and shushing, they managed to help her back inside her home.

'Ina, get the hot water going,' said Molly, glad that Ellie was with her, 'we'll need clean towels and newspapers.'

'I do know what's needed, thank you, Sergeant Major,' Ina grumbled. Having enjoyed a couple of large tots of mother's ruin to let in the new year, she was in the mood for a singsong, not a birthing. 'I've had a few babies of me own if you hadn't noticed.'

'We couldn't help but notice,' said Molly, who was not known to intentionally keep her opinions to herself.

'Mrs Cavanagh's having jars out,' said Ina. 'I was enjoying a good old singsong at her piano.'

'We heard,' Peggy Tenant said, taking off her coat and rolling up her sleeves. 'You were doing a fair impression of a strangled cat.'

'I'm sure Mary Jane is sorry to be missing the party but has her mind on other things just now.'

Molly wondered where Ina got the energy from to dance the night away, having given birth to many more than the eight surviving children she had reared. Another gasp brought the women's attention back to Mary Jane. And Molly summoned Ellie.

'Come on, lass,' Elodie's soothing tone gave Mary Jane courage as they helped her into the parlour, 'let's get you settled.'

'In... The... Front... Room,' Mary Jane gasped as another pain robbed her of her ability to speak in full sentences.

'Save your strength, Mary Jane, you're going to need it,' said Elodie while the other women hovered in the background making soothing noises. Molly was separating broadsheet newspaper pages and spreading them across the bed that Cal, and Molly's eldest lad Davey, had brought downstairs from the spare bedroom. Mary Jane had insisted she would not have every woman in Beamer Street traipsing up and down her stairs to welcome the newborn. So, the parlour had been prepared since before Christmas in readiness for the new arrival.

'It's about bloody time,' said Ina King, 'I thought you were going to keep hold of that child until summer.'

Mary Jane gave her neighbour a glowering look that told Ina she was in no mood for funny comments right now. She was prevented from speaking when she had an uncontrollable urge to push.

'Get her on the bed,' Elodie whispered urgently when she saw the streaks of meconium on the back of Mary Jane's legs after her waters broke. She knew the baby was in trouble.

'Best get her drawers off,' said Ina, and noticed Molly give her a look that could wither a rose. None of the women voiced their thoughts. But Molly suspected she and Peggy were both of the same mind, knowing Ina was well versed in getting her drawers off.

'Shouldn't we let her walk, until she's ready to drop, it'll be quicker that way,' Ina said as Mary Jane, kneeling, gripped the headboard of the bed.

'She delivers quick,' Molly said, 'but Ellie knows what she is doing.' Neither she nor her sister believed the village rumours that Ellie's ma had been to blame for Lady Felicia's death. If the girl was anywhere near as good, Molly knew Mary Jane was in the best of hands. 'It doesn't look like we'll have time to send for Martha.' Martha was the local unofficial midwife, who brought the babies into the world and prepared the oldies when the time came to lay them out.

'It wouldn't do no good anyway,' said Ina, 'she was well in her cups when I saw her at the hoolie, she was sliding down the wall, pie-eyed she was.'

Another pain gripped Mary Jane. All three women stopped what they were doing and watched the youngest in the room crawl onto the bed on her hands and knees.

'We don't need Martha.' Elodie's voice was deceptively calm as she handed Mary Jane a rolled-up towel to bite on, her words hiding the panic she felt when she saw the yellow dregs of residue on Mary Jane's pale Gaelic skin. 'Don't push, Mary Jane, you must not push. Let your own body do the work. That's it, good girl.' She could feel the baby's head advancing. 'Your baby is on its way. It won't be long now.' She knew the birth might be too quick for this poor mite to survive. But she was going to do everything in her power to save the child and the mother. 'Mary Jane, pant for me.' Elodie's face was solemn as Mary Jane did as she was told, but Elodie strongly suspected the umbilical cord was wrapped around the baby's neck. Although, in some cases the unborn child may come to no harm, this situation was not straightforward and would become critical if the cord tightened around the infant's neck. 'You are doing a wonderful job, Mary Jane, small puffs now, pretend you are blowing out the candles on your birthday cake.'

Elodie gave Molly a worrying look and Molly, who was

mopping Mary Jane's brow rolled her eyes to the heavens, saying a silent prayer.

Ina, bringing in a bowl of hot water and clean towels, put down the bowl and said to Peggy, 'Feel them.' She pushed the towels to Peggy. 'Have you ever felt anything so soft in your life?' The random comment brought a few smiles and Mary Jane lifted her head and gasped out her words.

'Take one home with you, Ina – don't mind me.'

'I was only saying,' Ina pursed her lips and rolled her eyes, 'but I don't mind if I do.' The room fell silent.

Elodie was giving all her attention to Mary Jane. 'Come on, lass,' she said in the Lancashire enunciation, which Molly knew so well, 'I know you're exhausted, but you can do this.'

Molly's hands flew to her lips to stop the anguished cry that threatened to alert her good friend she was in trouble.

'She doesn't do things the easy way,' Molly whispered.

'Mary Jane, I want you to give me a really good cough,' Elodie said soothingly.

'A good cough?' Ina glared at Elodie like she had just insulted the parish priest. 'I've never heard the likes in all my life.'

'And another one,' said Elodie, ignoring her neighbour as she slipped her finger underneath the umbilical cord and eased it over the baby's head, gently setting the child free. 'Just one more cough, Mary Jane, you can do it...'

When Ina realised what Elodie was doing she understood.

'Give it all you've got, girl!' cried Ina and the emotional scene brought tears to her eyes. 'Go on, lass, clear your lungs!'

The women held their breath for the final push, and before anybody could utter a word, a slippery little human shot into the world onto the sports pages of the *Liverpool Daily Post*.

'Well, would you look at that!' Ina blew her nose and wiped her eyes on one of the new towels as Elodie deftly held the child by its ankles and gave its bottom a sharp slap, enraging the child into taking its first breath and giving the women cause to surge forward in unison while the newborn yelled fit to raise the roof.

'Well, will you listen to the temper on him,' Molly laughed as Elodie cut and tied the cord, wrapping the newborn's umbilical stump in a clean bandage, before swaddling him in a clean sheet and handing the child to Mary Jane.

'I'll go and make a nice cup of tea. I think we've all earned it,' Molly told her tired friend, who was unable to take her eyes off her new son.

All the women gathered to admire and make sure the new baby boy had everything he should have, and then Mary Jane's face crumpled into a contorted grimace.

'Let me see what's going on here,' said Elodie, moving the others out of the way while Molly, Peggy and Ina looked to each other and silently shrugged.

'Shall I put the kettle on?' asked Molly and then she saw Elodie's expression change to one of concern.

'I may need you to go and fetch the doctor,' she said, examining Mary Jane, who was by now exhausted.

'What's up?' Molly whispered and her jaw dropped when Elodie told her there was another one on the way.

'Another one?!' Molly and Ina said in unison.

'Okay, my lovely,' said Elodie, 'you are doing just fine, a wonderful job.' She was silent for a moment, and all held their breath. 'That's it, little one, I need to turn you just a little, now don't be furious with me, it's for the best.' Elodie spoke as if the child were already here and a moment later she told Mary Jane to give one more push. 'Here we go!' Elodie forgot her calm composure as a brand-new baby girl came screaming into the world, and she laughed with pleasure. 'Well, if you think he's got a temper it's nothing as fierce as this one.'

'Two?!' Mary Jane could hardly believe what she had just been through.

'No wonder you looked like a barrage balloon!' Ina said. 'Well, you never do things by halves, Mary Jane, and that's a fact.'

'I'll stay with her till morning,' Elodie said.

'There's no need,' Mary Jane said, 'you've done enough. I just want Cal.' Mary Jane was drop dead tired but doubted she would sleep a wink, thrilled when the parlour door opened, and Cal filled the doorway with his solid presence.

'Has something happened?' he asked, and the four women laughed.

'You could say so, my darling,' Mary Jane whispered. 'Come and meet your son – and your daughter.'

'Two?' Cal's eyes lit up and the smile on his face went from ear to ear. 'You clever girl, Mary Jane! I was afraid the child might not be fit and healthy, but the power of their determined yells told me we have nothing to fear on that score.'

'They're both little fighters, like their mam,' Molly said, shocked when Mary Jane gave a weak laugh, closed her eyes, and passed out.

'Go and fetch Doctor Harvey!' Cal ordered. 'Mary Jane! Mary Jane, stay with me. Come on, our babies need you!' His heart was in his throat, thundering like a runaway train. He didn't know what he would do if history repeated itself and he lost Mary Jane. He would never get over it.

'Will you keep that bliddy noise down,' Mary Jane grumbled, still holding on to her newborn babies in both arms, after her exhaustion had caused her to faint momentarily, 'you'll wake Hollie.'

'I'm already awake.' Hollie was standing in the doorway, rubbing her sleepy eyes, and holding on to her teddy bear. 'Did

Mister Stork bring me a new baby sister?' she asked, edging shyly towards the bed.

'He did, and he also brought you a little brother.' Pride shone from Cal's eyes as he took the children from Mary Jane and sat down on the easy chair beside the bed, holding both babies in his big strong arms.

'But I wanted one I can play with.' Hollie sounded a little disappointed, but not for long. She bent to give her new brother a welcome home kiss, then her sister.

Cal let Hollie climb onto his knee. 'Now you have a brand-new brother, what shall we call him?'

'Rudolph,' said Hollie, leaning over once more to kiss the velvet cheek of the new addition to the family. 'Are we going to keep him?'

'Of course, we will keep him,' Mary Jane smiled sleepily, 'but let's think of another name. And your little sister, what's her name?'

'She's Neave,' Hollie said without hesitation, 'just like my dolly.'

Mary Jane gave Cal a sleepy smile and gently closed her eyes.

'I am so grateful for everything you have done for Mary Jane,' Cal said to Molly and the other women.

'Oh, it had nowt to do wi' me, lad,' Molly said. 'I was just the messenger.' She looked to Elodie and smiled. 'It's this one you've got to thank. She took over with the confidence of a fully qualified midwife,' Molly lowered her voice and leaned towards Cal, 'I'll even go so far as to say, if she hadn't been here, poor Mary Jane could have lost her first-born.'

Cal stood rigid, his mouth falling open. 'Really?!' he whispered.

Molly nodded. 'This one,' she said, jerking her thumb towards Elodie, 'she knew before the babe was even born that he was in distress, and she made sure she did everything she could to bring that little mite into the world alive.' Molly smiled, proud of the young woman. 'The other one was a bit easier but determined to come into the world arse-first, but Ellie turned her and that was it, Bob's your uncle and Fanny's your aunt.'

'I don't know what to say,' Cal addressed Elodie, who shook her head.

'Anybody would have done the same thing,' Elodie said, and everybody was surprised when Ina King put her two pennorth into the conversation.

'Well, I'm telling you something for free,' said Ina, 'I've had eight of me own, and if it was up to me to deliver them little ones, I'd have run screaming in the street for the nearest midwife, because I would not have had a clue about how to untangle the cord from around one baby's neck to stop him strangling himself, and to turn the other one so it came out the right way.'

Cal's face drained of colour. 'I didn't know…'

'Well, with you being a man, like,' Ina was getting into her stride now, 'you're not supposed to know about these things, but we women, well, it's second nature to us.'

'When you get back from screaming the street down, is it?' Molly could not help herself. 'Ellie's one of the best, a trained healer, she is.' Molly could not help singing Ellie's praises, realising she wasn't going to do it herself.

'Well, if there is anything I can do in return, you only have to say,' Cal said, taking hold of the hands that saved the life of his children, 'I mean it, anything at all. Just let me know and it's yours.'

'Thank you, but there's no need.' Elodie felt a mixture of embarrassment at all the fuss.

'You don't want to go saying that,' said Ina, affronted, 'you don't go looking a gift horse in the eye.'

The women were all talking in hushed tones at once, the excitement of the New Year twins was going to be the topic of conversation for a long time to come.

'Now, let's leave this lovely, happy family to get acquainted with their new arrivals,' said Molly.

17

Molly was just going to her bed when Daisy hurried from the middle bedroom she shared with her younger sister, Bridie. Melissa, who was thrilled to have a 'big sister' in Bridie, nodded eagerly when Bridie offered to let her sleep in her room while waiting for her new bed to arrive.

'You'll never guess in a hundred years!' Molly said gleefully. 'She's only gone and had twins!'

'Twins?'

Molly answered with a nod of her head. 'Boy and a girl.'

'Well, I'll be...' Daisy was shocked and thrilled. 'Are they all...?'

'Fighting fit and rearing to get on with it, thanks to Ellie,' Molly assured her daughter. 'If it hadn't been for her the news might not have been so happy. She was marvellous.'

'Oh, that is good news.' Daisy was truly awake now.

'Well, I'm away to my bed,' Molly yawned, 'I've to be up in two and a half hours to get our Davey to work.'

The house was silent, save for Daisy's light tread on the stair runner, secured with brass rods to keep the carpet in place, which she polished every Sunday before nine o'clock mass. She liked Sunday mornings, when she had a lie-in until seven o'clock.

Daisy did not want to wake anybody at this unearthly hour when most people were still asleep. She lit the gas mantle in the back-kitchen and put a flame to the gas oven, to take the chill off the room. Opening the curtains just a little, Daisy saw that it had snowed heavily overnight.

'Hello 1925,' she said, eyeing the cob of black coal, a saucer of salt, an uncut loaf of bread, and a few coppers on the kitchen table, which her mother had set out to welcome the new year in the belief her household would prosper all year if she was in possession of such things at midnight. 'Let's hope you're a good one.'

Moments later, sipping her hot tea near the open door of the cooker, Daisy knew that even though there were many midnight celebrations last night, the bakery would still be busy this morning, as time and toast waited for no working man.

Even though Mary Jane's bakery and tea shop was only across the road, Daisy still wrapped up in a warm woollen coat her mam had bought her for Christmas with a cheque, which she paid off weekly, from the clubman at Ruby's Emporium along the dock road.

Daisy always liked to look smart and never let the lack of money give her cause to slop around in any old tat. Her clothes were of better quality now she was earning, and she had even taken up buying some patterns from Woolworths and having a go at making her own clothes. She was also saving for a treadle sewing machine. Daisy had always been handy with a needle and thread and liked to keep her hands busy in the evening, so after scouring jumble sales in the more affluent areas of Crosby or Formby, she would buy decent-quality clothing to reshape or take apart and recreate a dress or skirt in one of her own modern styles. She had even made a loose-fitting jacket from an old coat, although she would not be able to wear it until the weather warmed up a bit.

Hemlines had lifted dramatically, and she loved the new length, while corsets, thankfully, had been abandoned by young women, and Daisy would be ever grateful the ant-shaped silhouette that almost cut a woman in half, which some of the older generation favoured, had been abandoned by the bright young things.

Not that she could see herself as a flapper, Daisy thought, looking into the oval mirror above the mantlepiece as she combed the sleek bob, which had been cropped short to the nape of her neck before Christmas, so her new cloche hat fitted close to her head like a helmet.

Even though she could not contemplate the heady lifestyle of a flapper, she loved the clothes they wore, and the make-up they used, wondering if she dare try a bit of lipstick and rouge when she had somewhere special to go – whenever that may be.

Winding a long woollen scarf several times around her neck, Daisy was satisfied with her appearance, and after pulling on a pair of home-made mittens that matched her bright scarf, she picked up her oversized handbag, very much resembling a doctor's medical bag, and made her way out of the house to work.

She must go to Strand Road in her dinnertime, she thought quietly closing the front door behind her, and buy something blue for Cal and Mary Jane's new baby boy and something pink for their little girl.

The snow-covered street was silent at such an early hour when even the dockworkers were still in their beds, and the navy-blue sky twinkled with thousands of scattered stars. Daisy made her way across the cobbled road towards the bakery. She loved this tranquil time of day, when everybody was tucked up warmly, and she felt the street belonged to her, alone.

The snow cast an ethereal glow, which hovered over the usually sooty buildings, making everything look perfect. Even the pigeons and sparrows were still abed. Taking a deep breath of crisp air, Daisy knew that, even the smell was different. Clean, as yet uncluttered by fumes from the docks and chimneys.

The loud honk of a motor horn behind her made Daisy almost jump out of her skin, wrenching her out of her reverie. She had not been expecting to see or hear anybody at this time of the day, especially a dark-coloured, soft-topped Vauxhall Tourer careering down Beamer Street, causing a snake-like imprint on the virginal snow-covered cobbles, proof, if any were needed, that Jeremiah Swift, owner of Beamer's Electricals, singing at the top of his voice, was apparently drunk as a lord and obviously incapable of driving in a straight line.

'Stupid man!' Daisy said under her breath, knowing if she had been a bit slower, she could have been the one making an imprint in the snow.

She unlocked the shop door and headed behind the counter, then made her way to the bakery at the back, knowing Percy, one of the other bakers, would be in soon, and, as she did every morning, Daisy put the kettle on the gas stove to boil.

Percy was like a father to Daisy, and even though he had lost an eye in France during the war, he never mentioned how or when. Although he did tell Daisy that the months he spent recovering, instead of being invalided out of the army, he learned to bake in the hospital kitchen.

Percy was around the same age as her own da would have been, as far as Daisy could tell, and was always cheerful. Teasing her unmercifully, he was as wise and kind-hearted as her own father had been, from what she could remember. Percy's determination to count his blessings never wavered, and his positivity never ceased to amaze her. Percy, in his resolve not to become one of the disappointed ex-servicemen who returned home from the carnage and trauma of the Western Front and join the ranks of the mass unemployed, refused to allow his affliction to define him. Nor was he going to succumb to the familiar scene of men hopeful for a day, or even a morning's work, around the dockside, where dole queues lengthened by the day.

'Morning, Dais, two sugars in mine,' called Percy, who had a quick smile and a quip for every occasion. He had an extra-special smile for her mam, she noticed, and he whistled a lively tune whenever Molly was in the shop.

'You ever heard the word "please"?' Daisy called back. Percy was a tonic and no mistake, and even though his wife died years ago leaving him childless, he never seemed lonely. Always off to play bowls in the local park, or darts in the pub, and football – he never shut up about football. What with Percy regaling their Freddy, another football-mad supporter, about going to Wembley to see Newcastle United beat Aston Villa 2–0, Daisy felt as if she had been there too. But he was everybody's friend, was Percy, and he would make some woman a lovely husband.

'Sorry, little'n,' Percy said, taking off his flat cap, muffler and overcoat, and hanging them on the hook behind the door, before hauling a fifty-pound bag of strong flour from the pile by the door. 'Two sugars, *please*, *Your Majesty*.'

'That's better.' Daisy smiled. She had already poured the tea and was thrilled to pass on the latest news. 'You'll never guess, Mary Jane gave birth to twins on the stroke of midnight!'

'So does that mean one was born in 1924 and the other in 1925?'

'No, definitely 1925,' said Daisy thoughtfully. 'According to me mam, the bells had already finished ringing.' She did not intend to go into detail about something as delicate as the actual births because she didn't know all the details yet.

'Well, what do you know,' Percy said, scratching his head. 'Your mam is a very shrewd woman, Dais, she would know. Fancy Mrs Everdine deciding New Year was the time to bring new lives into the world. Two lives at that.'

'I don't reckon she had much say in the matter, Percy.' Daisy smiled, proud of the woman who was not only her employer, but her good friend too. 'One day I'm going to be like Mary Jane.'

'I thought you said you would never marry,' said Percy, covering yeast with sugar, and allowing it to ferment, before scooping flour into a large white tin bowl.

'I said I'm not getting married until I'm thirty,' Daisy answered.

'Well, you'd better get a move on,' Percy laughed, 'you haven't got much time left.'

'Cheeky blighter,' said Daisy, only half joking, 'I've only just turned eighteen.'

'You must have had a very hard life, Dais,' Percy quipped, and his smile froze when he saw her pour his cup of hot tea down the sink. 'Oh, come on, Dais, you know I didn't mean it. I wouldn't upset you for the world.'

'And I didn't mean to pour your tea down the sink – but I still did it,' she answered, knowing there was another cup in the pot. 'Here,' she said, handing him another freshly poured cup of tea, 'we'll say no more about it.'

'You're ever so kind, miss.' Percy gave her a broad smile, tugging his forelock. 'Here, what do you say we make a celebration birthday cake for the new babies?'

'That's a wonderful idea. A slice of cake for every customer.'

'We'll be overrun when word gets round.' Percy had the kind of open face that always appeared cheerful. 'I'm not sure I was thinking straight when I suggested a birthday cake, and certainly not a slice for every customer.'

'Only the ones who come in to buy, Perc,' said Daisy, tapping the side of her nose.

'We'll be run off our feet,' he laughed, 'we must send out the cavalry for more supplies.'

'You do talk daft sometimes,' Daisy laughed, comically batting her sooty lashes like Clara Bow, ducking when he threw a tea towel in her direction.

'We mustn't forget to send your mam a piece of cake too.' Percy smiled along with Daisy, who suspected Percy had a soft spot for her mam.

18

'Daisy.' A customer who looked cold and hungry leaned over the teashop counter. 'Can I have a word, luv?'

Fish slice in hand, she manoeuvred past another waitress who was frying bacon and when she reached the counter, she leaned forward. 'Hiya, Mister Brookes, is everything all right?' Daisy knew some of her customers did not have the wherewithal to purchase a full breakfast, and that was before the dock strike denied them a chance of a day's work and pay.

'I don't like to ask you this but...' he looked around to make sure nobody could hear him, his words barely audible, 'well, you see, my missus had a baby girl last night and...'

'That's wonderful news, Mister Brookes, the same day as Mary Jane.' Daisy's genuine enthusiasm showed in the twinkle of her eyes, and she began moving sausages around a frying pan on the stove at the side of the counter, then began filling a plain white serviceable plate with bacon and egg, straining the sausages and putting them on too. Quickly buttering a couple of rounds of toast as thick as doorsteps, she could not fail to see the longing in

Mister Brookes eyes. 'I bet you're dead on your feet being up all night, what did she call her?'

'Emily,' said Mister Brookes, unable to drag his hungry eyes from the plate.

'Here, no charge,' she whispered, sliding the plate towards him, knowing Mary Jane would do the same herself if she saw a man in need. 'It's hungry work having a baby. You need to keep your strength up to help Mrs Brookes.' She smiled at the look of gratitude in his sunken eyes. 'I do hope that dock strike is over soon, don't you?' She stopped talking, saying suddenly, 'Listen to me rattling on, Mister Brookes, what was it you wanted to say to me?'

'I've forgotten.' Mister Brookes' eyes filled with gratitude as he gazed at the feast before him. He had not eaten for two days and the thought of standing on the picket line filled him with dread, but it had to be done, if the workers were to be listened to in a serious way.

'Call it a welcome to the world breakfast.' Daisy smiled, knowing a lot of families were precariously placed when there was a dock dispute. 'And could you get one of your kids to pick up Mrs Brookes' bread, I'm sure she'll be famished too.'

'I didn't know she—'

'Yes, she ordered it yesterday,' Daisy innocently cut off his words, knowing even though they didn't have much, the families around the dockside had their pride. Mrs Brookes was a regular customer who had a clutch of children all under five. 'She must have had an inkling, aye?'

'Thank you, Daisy, I won't forget this.' His look of gratitude swelled her heart and Daisy wished she could feed everybody who went without on the first day of the new year.

'You take your breakfast over to the table and I'll bring you a mug of tea.' The teashop at the back of Mary Jane's Kitchen supplied simple things like fried egg on toast, bacon on toast, or sausage on toast and if the customers could not pay on the day, Mary Jane allowed the names to go into the *canape book*, a play on words between herself and Daisy. Knowing the customers who *can-na-pay* would do so when they could.

Daisy knew this would be their first stop to settle up when the strike was over, and they went back to work. Nobody in the area was going to suffer the indignity of having their name and their debt advertised in the shop window.

The people may be poor, but they had their pride, and although they may be soft-hearted when the need arose, neither Mary Jane nor Daisy had a soft head. Both shrewd business-women, they knew there were some things of vital importance around the dockside, a clean bed – preferably shared by a loving wife – a good name, and a full belly.

Daisy's breakfasts were top notch, albeit cheap and cheerful. Nothing fancy, but they set a body up for the day's gruelling work ahead. It didn't take her long to realise that the customers were not just dock workers who ate in the café. Office workers, factory workers, warehousemen and railway workers, carters and black-smiths, draymen, and all manner of employees along the dock road popped in for a carry-out, a parcel of toasted sandwiches wrapped in brown paper and tied with string. But there were still some who liked to eat inside and in no time Mary Jane and Daisy had had to open the rooms upstairs and lay on more staff.

The café was run very efficiently, and Daisy was in her element. Her cheerful smile and sunny disposition made her a natural confidante with the customers, who ribbed and bantered their way to a smile. The male customers loved her, and she was never short of offers from admirers to go to the pictures or to the music hall.

Nevertheless, Daisy only had eyes for one customer, the

cheeky young reporter, Max, who worked on the local newspaper and came in looking for interesting stories for the *Daily Herald*.

'Cuppa char and one of your dazzling smiles please, lovely Daisy,' he quipped that morning in that bold way he had about him, his flat cap pushed to the back of his head, showing off a shock of thick black curly hair and vibrant blue eyes. But then he stopped midway between the door and the counter, dramatically raising his hands in the air. 'What have you done to your hair?' His jaw dropped, and he looked around as if trying to find something. 'Where has it gone!'

Daisy giggled. He always had that effect on her, and she reached for a thick white cup and saucer. 'Have you seen the actress, Colleen Moore?' Daisy asked and Max shook his head.

'Can't say I have. Does she live around here?'

'No. You twit,' said Daisy, pouring steaming tea into the cup. 'Well, have you missed a treat? She has her hair cut like this – it's called a shingled bob; do you like it?' Daisy patted her new hairstyle, tapered into the back of her head, exposing the hairline at the neck like a boy.

Mesmerised by her audacity, Max would never tell Daisy he thought women should not be allowed to cut their hair so short, because she would never speak to him again. He did know the longer hair at the sides flicked perfectly under her beautiful high cheekbones. 'It's lovely,' he said simply.

'Why thank you, kind sir,' Daisy said in a mocking tone, feeling giddy as a kipper. 'Mind, I don't need any man's permission to have my hair cut short. It's all the rage.'

'I don't know about that, Dais,' Max loved her long hair, 'it's more like an outrage.'

'I'm thinking of wearing a headband, like the flappers.'

'Lord, love a duck.' Max sighed under his breath. 'You don't need a headband to make you look pretty.'

'What was that?' asked Daisy, visibly shocked, waiting to take his usual order of a round of toast, well done and slathered in 'best' butter.

'I was wondering what ya doing tonight, Dais?' Max thought for a moment. He quite liked the idea of an independent-thinking girl who had a mind of her own. And now he looked at it properly, in the light of the electric bulb, he didn't really mind about her hair being short either. 'Only a beautiful face can carry off a style like that,' he said smiling, 'it suits you, Dais.' He was thrilled she looked pleased. 'So, d'you fancy going to the pictures with me? There's a good film on at the Excelsior.'

'I wouldn't be caught dead in that fleapit.' Daisy threw her hands in the air, and Max let out that infectious laugh that always made her giggle. She couldn't help herself. No matter how much she wanted to tell him he was the cheekiest boy she had ever come across, he always made her laugh.

'I thought you'd say that very thing,' Max said with a grin, 'so, out of the goodness of my heart and from the depth of my very deep pockets...' He brought out two tickets and flicked them with his fingernail, 'I purchased two, not one, but two rare specimens, namely tickets for the Variety Theatre in town. How about that?'

'The Variety Theatre?' Daisy's jaw dropped; she had always wanted to go to the theatre. 'Who's on?'

'Harry Lauder, no less!' Max said and went on to give a rendition of 'Roamin' in the Gloamin''. Daisy's eyes lit up and her face went bright pink. He knew how much she loved music and was always humming one tune or another. 'So, whadayasay?'

'I don't know why you talk in such a common way,' Daisy said. 'I know you don't live around the dockside.' It was true, Max was born and raised in one of the large, well-to-do houses that looked out onto the golden shore overlooking the wider waters of the River Mersey.

'The men talk more freely if they think I'm one of them.' Max looked around and lowered his voice, his blue eyes twinkling. Then he winked at her.

'You are such a cheeky so-and-so,' Daisy said, feigning shock, 'there is no doubt about that.'

'Go on, Dais, be a sport.' His bottom lip pouted in an upside-down smile.

'Now don't you go giving me those Buster Keaton eyes. I have to be up early every morning.' Daisy did not want to sound too eager. She pushed the cup and saucer across the counter.

'All work and no play, Dais,' Max said, handing her the money and blowing onto the hot tea before taking a sip. 'It'll be a night to remember.'

'Oh, go on then,' she said, and when he finished his tea, Daisy came from behind the counter as the breakfast session was over, and the other girls could manage without her. Descending the two wooden stairs to the shop at the front of the bakery, Max followed closely behind. 'Seeing as tomorrow is my day off.'

'I'll pick you up at half past six,' he said, not daring to wink again in case she changed her mind and clocked him with the flour sack she was holding. 'You're gonna love it.'

'We'll see about that, shall we?' Daisy smiled, watching him stride out of the café with his flat cap tilted at a jaunty angle, and hop on his bicycle and ride down the street, without even holding onto the handlebars. 'Cocky so-and-so,' she said, unable to hide her admiration.

The telephone rang and Daisy went to answer it.

'Mary Jane's Kitchen, bakery and confectioners,' she said in her best telephone voice, 'how may I help you?'

'Hello, Daisy, Aiden here, is it possible you could fetch Elodie for me please?'

'Hello, Aiden,' Daisy said, thankful Mary Jane wasn't here to witness all these telephone calls. 'I'll go and fetch her.'

'You look like you've lost a tanner and found a ten-bob note,' said Ina King as she came into the shop, making a beeline for the bargain basket, where a couple of yesterday's loaves were still available.

'I don't know what you mean.' Daisy's face flushed pink, knowing, for the rest of the day she would be walking on air.

'Hello, Daisy love,' said her mother, Molly, who had followed Ina into the shop. 'I've just been in to see Mary Jane and her new babies.'

'Will you tell Ellie she's wanted on the telephone,' Daisy lowered her voice to a whisper, 'it's our Aiden, he'll ring her back in half an hour.'

'Really?' Molly's eyebrows lifted. There was a lot going on today with telephone calls and new babies.

'Has Mary Jane thought of any names yet?' asked Daisy when Molly came back from telling Ellie about the phone call. 'Everybody who has come into the shop today has been asking; it's all they can talk about.'

'I'm sure she'll let us know as soon as she's decided,' said Molly, and very soon there was a buzz of maternal conversation from the women of Beamer Street.

'Ellie did a fine job from what Peggy said earlier,' said Daisy as Elodie came into the shop to await the call.

'She was marvellous,' said Ina, and all the women gaped. Ina King did not give compliments, especially not to newcomers to Beamer Street.

'She certainly was,' said Molly, but something was niggling at her. Ellie wasn't short of money, and her child was better educated than most children her age. To her credit, Ellie wanted to open the shop across the road and had the means to do so. But Molly had the feeling she was running from something. But was it something to do with Aiden? she wondered. A small cloud of dread, the first of the new year, hovered over Molly's head. What had she let herself in for?

* * *

Daisy checked her appearance in the full-length mirror that formed an oval on her mother's wardrobe door. The pleated skirt and twinset looked smart and serviceable, thought Daisy, who longed to wear the kind of fancy chiffons and silks she drooled over in women's magazines. But what good were chiffons and such when she hardly ever went anywhere to show off such creations. Given the early hour she had to be up each morning it did not bode well for nights out at the theatre. So, tonight was particularly special. Daisy's stomach did a giddy little flip when she imagined what the night had in store for her. But she never imagined she would be left sitting on her own to watch the show whilst Max went for ice creams and did not come back for the whole of the second half. Nor did she expect to walk home on her own after Max did a disappearing trick that would have made Harry Houdini proud.

'Did you have a nice time, lovey?' asked Molly when Daisy got home, shocked when Daisy said she didn't want to talk about it and she would be going into work tomorrow, then hurried off to bed without even waiting for her nightly cocoa.

* * *

'Newman, get in here. Now!' The last was more than a command, it was a threat, and Aiden knew what was coming. It was the first day of the new year and Aiden understood it wasn't beyond the realms of possibility for Lord Caraway to lash out at the nearest person to him when he was in this mood. Although Aiden was more than a match, if it came to it, knowing he was well able to defend himself if the old goat wanted to try it on.

In fact, thought Aiden, he wouldn't mind putting his pompous employer on his arse. Silas Caraway might have got away with flogging him when he was a nipper, and he might be handy with his fists when it came to using them on his wife, but Aiden was a grown man now, and a strong one at that.

'You wanted me, sir?' Aiden stood, legs apart, hands clasped in front of him, his strong chin held high. He had been the tallest man in his regiment and had often joked that he would be the first to get a bullet in his head, until his jocular portent turned out to be true, but he had been luckier than most.

A sergeant in the King's Fusiliers, his stance was that of a man who knew his place but would not be intimidated by this over-bearing bully. Aiden kowtowed to no man. He had done his duty for King and country, and he did it with pride. Which was more than this jumped-up excuse of a man had done.

'Do you have any idea what this is all about?' Lord Caraway waved a piece of paper in the air. 'Soames has just brought it to me as I got home very late last night.'

'I did wonder why you had not telephoned for the car, my lord. I thought you must be staying in London for the New Year celebrations.' Aiden had heard from Will that Lord Caraway had been as drunk as a skunk even before he'd got to the village pub in a hansom cab and then was brought back to the hall on the preacher's mule. 'I can't say I have any knowledge of the letter, sir,' Aiden answered truthfully, knowing Elodie had not mentioned leaving a letter, although he did have his suspicions. Although why she would want to do so was beyond Aiden, given that this man had treated her so badly.

'Read it!' Caraway thrust the letter into Aiden's hand.

'This looks like a private correspondence from Lady Elodie.' Aiden refused to call Ellie by her husband's surname.

'You know where she is. You must do.' Silas shot a venomous glance, holding Aiden's unflinching glare. 'You will tell me, Newman, or I will have you horsewhipped.'

'The letter says she has taken the child away to build up her strength after her winter cold.' Aiden shrugged, playing innocent, and he could tell His Lordship didn't believe a word he said. Nevertheless, Aiden decided there was no way he was going to give this bombastic excuse of a man one iota of information.

Aiden had spent many long hours in mud-filled trenches while bullets flew around him in all directions, rats the size of cats grazed on decaying soldiers lying dead beside him. Sick with hunger, he would still summon the strength to fire his gun at the enemy in freezing-wet clothes during a snowstorm, while this impotent cowardly man hid behind the formality, power, and undue respect of a judge's gavel.

'Where has she gone?' Silas Caraway growled. 'And who the hell in their right mind would do such a thing in this weather? She has everything she could ever wish for here. I want the truth.' Lord Caraway spat out the instruction. Frustration, and disdain wrapped his words.

Aiden said nothing. Instead, he returned the high-court judge's glare, feeling nothing but contempt.

'Now, you listen to me—' Lord Caraway said, emphasising each of his three last words.

'I am sorry, sir, but I have no idea.' Aiden interrupted the demonic flow of words. He had no qualms about lying to save his beloved Ellie, and certainly had no intentions of giving this man any information of her whereabouts.

He never had and he never would put Ellie or the child in

danger, and if this overblown oaf wanted to know his true feelings, Aiden would be obliged to let him know in no uncertain terms. Especially if he continued shouting at him like he was still that young boy he had once terrified.

The shrill ring of the telephone put any further enquiries on hold for the time being.

'Get out,' Silas dismissed him with a commanding gesture, 'but be warned, this is not the end to the matter.'

Closing the door quietly behind him, Aiden knew he had done the right thing by biding his time. He loved Ellie far too much to demand she left her husband. She had given him the critical care he needed to survive, and to gain the strength he needed when he was brought home from the trenches on a stretcher. And in the quiet hours, when the only thing he had for company were his thoughts, Aiden promised himself that one day Ellie would take her rightful place by his side, and he would care for her and their daughter to the end of his days.

Without Ellie's love and gentle care, he would never have survived the knowledge she had married another man when he went away to fight.

So now it was his turn to repay her.

19

Mary Jane's new arrivals were the talk of Beamer Street for days, as neighbours and customers alike came into her front room with little gifts of baby mittens, booties, matinee jackets, and cardigans that they had knitted especially, and Mary Jane was thrilled with every single one of them. But today she suddenly felt as if dark clouds were pressing down upon her, and she could not shake the feeling. Only this morning she had burst into tears for no good reason whilst trying to feed her son, who didn't seem particularly keen on taking his mother's milk.

'How are you feeling this morning?' Elodie asked. She popped in every morning and afternoon. It was a few days since Mary Jane had given birth, and while Cal was as proud as any man could be over his bonny babies, Mary Jane was feeling a bit teary, which was so unlike her. 'You will have days like this,' Elodie said when Mary Jane did not answer. 'How's the feeding coming on?' Ellie asked Mary Jane, who was sitting up in bed attempting to feed her son.

Mary Jane's chin gave a little wobble. 'Useless. That's how I feel.'

Elodie understood the problem. Mary Jane's son was screaming the place down and his sister was getting upset, making Mary Jane feel even more inadequate.

'I longed for this time. I imagined being all serene, accepting visitors with a smile, happy to feed my babies,' Mary Jane cried. 'I dreamt about lying here, just me and the two of them, getting to know each other, stroking their downy hair, and brushing my finger across peachy cheeks while they lay contented, but the little beggars hate me!'

'It's not your fault.' Elodie knew Mary Jane was a good mother.

'Isn't it the most natural thing any mother can do for her child,' cried Mary Jane, 'but how can I do that when my breasts are so hard and painful, they look like those barrage balloons Ina talked about, and feel like they will burst.' Tears were now rolling freely down her cheeks. 'I've tried and tried to feed them, but the milk won't come. I am terrified I will starve the two of them.'

'I doubt that.' Elodie tilted her head to make eye contact, calmly sitting in the chair beside the bed, nodding and listening while Mary Jane poured out her failings as a mother. 'They have enough power in their little bodies to make that ear-splitting noise,' Elodie gave a little smile, 'which tells me they are not wasting away.' She never once raised her voice over their harsh cacophony, instead she remained calm and took control. 'Here, let me get you a pillow, put it under your elbow.' Elodie made Mary Jane more comfortable. 'Now, I don't want you to think this is going to be a battle.' Elodie could see Mary Jane was suffering from painful mastitis, her breasts were engorged.

'But my breasts are so sore, I don't think I can do it. My nipples are so flat they can't attach, and when they do it is so painful, I could cry.'

'Like everything else about babies,' Elodie assured her, 'it just takes a bit of practice. I helped many new mothers in the village when their milk was a bit sluggish,' she gave a little laugh, 'even some who weren't new mothers. So do not fret, I know just the thing.' Elodie took off her coat and rolled up her sleeves. 'Do you have a cabbage?'

'A cabbage?' said Mary Jane, her brow creasing, then after a pause, her eyes widened. 'I remember the mammies using that very thing back home. I used to think to myself, surely they are not feeding that child cabbage leaves.'

Elodie laughed, but in a kind way. 'The leaves will absorb some of the fluid from the glands and reduce the pain and the hardness of your engorged breasts and help you feed for longer. Just slip the cold cabbage leaf against your breasts.'

'How long for?'

'Until the cabbage leaf has wilted for today. But as this can dry up your milk, only use the cabbage leaf about three times a day for twenty minutes, until you start to feel some relief, then you can start to breastfeed again. And while you are doing that I will give you some powdered willow bark for the pain.'

'Willow bark?' asked Mary Jane.

'You may know it as aspirin,' Elodie said, 'but in contrast to synthetic aspirin, willow bark will not harm your insides. You won't want me going into all that now, but if you, do just ask.'

'Believe me, I trust you.' Mary Jane smiled. 'I've got my own personal doctor living right next door. So, the cabbage must be cold?'

'All cabbage is cold at this time of year,' said Elodie, confident her friend would feel the benefit soon, 'or maybe you could hire a wet nurse.'

'I am not sending for Ina King again,' Mary Jane sounded suddenly resolute, 'that woman still reminds me that my Hollie would not be here if it wasn't for her coming to the rescue, and me lying there blind and useless for three weeks. I won't be beholden to that woman, she'd take such pleasure in letting everybody know I am not able to feed my own children, and I'm not having that.'

'Well then, let's get you some relief with the cabbage leaves,' said Elodie. 'I'll just nip over to the greengrocer's and buy a cabbage.'

'Here, let me give you the money,' said Mary Jane, reaching under her pillow for her purse. But Elodie was out of the front room in a flash, and a few minutes later she was back again with a cold cabbage.

'We will do this three times a day for twenty minutes,' said Elodie, 'any longer might reduce the flow of your milk, but this will certainly help to reduce the engorgement.'

'Even the word sounds painful.' Mary Jane laughed for the first time, relieved to feel the coldness of the cabbage leaf ease her.

'I will bathe the babies,' Elodie said, 'so you just lie back and relax, then I will do a warm compress, which should do the trick.'

Mary Jane was grateful to this unassuming young woman.

'It's summat I've done since I was knee-high to my mother,' Elodie laughed when she saw Mary Jane's wide-eyed response.

'Are you settling in with Molly and her brood?' Mary Jane asked, the cold cabbage leaf soothing and cooling her, making her less anxious, as Elodie dipped her elbow in the baby bath.

'The salt of the earth,' Elodie said, 'to be honest, I like most of the people in Beamer Street. Everybody's in the same boat.' Except Mary Jane – and herself.

'She lost her husband in the war,' Mary Jane confided, wondering if that was when Elodie had lost her husband. 'But like most, she's done a wonderful job raising her family.'

Taking the wet little body from the large bowl, Elodie placed the baby on a warmed towel on her knee, wrapping the slippery baby and drying her.

'Aye, many lost a husband in the war,' said Mary Jane, 'and

those who saw their other half coming home safely began popping babies out again every year.'

'I feel so sorry for those women,' said Elodie, making sure every nook and cranny had been talcum powdered, 'if only something could be done.'

'The problem is,' said Mary Jane, 'the authorities – men – won't allow working-class women access to information about birth control, only those who can afford to pay for such knowledge. That is why there are more children in poor families, who can ill afford the luxury of so many mouths to feed.'

'But the demand for such knowledge is rapidly growing,' Elodie answered, glad she had found somebody else who spoke her language. The circles her husband often frequented, where there was plenty of money to pay a physician who would give such information, were certainly not available to the likes of the people around the dockside, where it was most needed.

'People around here don't even have the money to pay the doctor most of the time, so they would not dream of wasting their hard-earned coppers on finding out how to stop having babies – I doubt they even know there is such information available.'

'I suppose so,' said Elodie, 'but what if that information was available to them?'

'In what way?' asked Mary Jane, interested in what Elodie had to say.

'I know the authorities would not countenance such a thing, nor the Catholic church, but women should be spared the yearly battering their body must endure to procreate, when they cannot afford to feed the children they already have.' Elodie had always felt passionate about women being given a choice, but how could they do so when they had so much worry about where the next meal was coming from or if their old man could find work.

'I like the way you're thinking,' said Mary Jane. This girl had her head screwed on and a zest for life that was denied many her age around here.

'I was wondering if anybody knew the address of the landlord of that corner shop across the road?' Elodie said as she dressed the baby in a fresh vest, nappy, white flannel nightgown, and a beautiful shawl Mary Jane had made for both her twins.

'You want to open the shop?' Mary Jane answered the question with a query of her own. She loved the idea, of seeing history repeating itself, when Elodie explained.

'I want to help people who cannot help themselves. It's what I've always done, as my mother did before me.' Elodie passed the contented bundle back to her mother. 'I could give some poor women discreet advice on maternal as well as child welfare,' she told Mary Jane.

'That's if they are ready to listen.' Mary Jane knew some girls listened only to their mothers. 'Some of the superstitions would make your hair curl. I have always felt sorry for those women who have more mouths to feed than money.'

'Not to mention the childhood diseases some families cannot afford to have treated – boils, nits, bronchial and chest complaints.'

'You'll have plenty of customers,' Mary Jane said, contentedly stroking her adored baby's cheek, as she slept contentedly in her arms.

'I'm not looking to make money,' Elodie said. 'I want to ease their burden where I can.' Caring for those less fortunate was as natural as breathing. 'I only need to make enough money to keep the business going after I've stocked it.'

'That's very generous of you,' said Mary Jane, 'and it will prevent the snake-oil merchants from robbing these poor people blind with their coloured water that does nothing to help cure their ills.'

'All I need to do is find out who the landlord is and how much they want to rent the shop.'

'I might be able to help you out there.' Mary Jane smiled as the cold cabbage leaf did its work. 'Let me have a word with someone I know.'

'That would be splendid,' said Elodie, immediately feeling a warm glow. 'I'll call in after dinner to see how you are feeling.'

* * *

Elodie called to see Mary Jane that afternoon as promised and was thrilled to discover Mary Jane was feeling much brighter. Their conversation had given Mary Jane something to think about. She understood burning ambition. And if the local people were to benefit then that was more to the good.

'I've been in touch with the landlord,' said Mary Jane, and Elodie's jaw dropped.

'But how?' she asked, knowing Mary Jane was confined to bed for ten days after giving birth.

'He brought me my lunch,' she laughed. 'Between me and you,' Mary Jane confided, 'Cal owns that corner shop – in fact, he owns many of the houses and buildings around here – and he said you can have it as a thank you for safely delivering our babies. There is just one condition,' Mary Jane said lowering her voice, 'you must tell nobody about our little arrangement. Cal likes to keep his private business just that. Private.'

'Mister Everdine is the landlord?' Elodie was amazed.

'He is,' said Mary Jane, 'and I trust you won't breathe a word.'

'Of course,' said Elodie. She had enough secrets of her own to keep quiet about. 'You have my word.'

'Well, that's good enough for me,' Mary Jane answered. 'The keys are on the table over there, along with the deeds to the shop, all you have to do is sign them and it's all yours, lock, stock, and the flat upstairs.'

Elodie was so thrilled, she kissed Mary Jane and went to find Cal, who was out in the kitchen washing cabbage leaves.

'You don't know how much this means to me,' Elodie said carrying the tray of tea and biscuits, which Cal had organised, into the parlour. When the babies had been settled, they sat down to drink their tea and chat over the details of the shop. Picking up the deeds, Elodie read them. 'But I can pay, I have the means.'

'I don't doubt it,' said Mary Jane, as Cal busied himself, carrying the baby's bath out to the scullery not wanting to get involved in the business side of things, which he left up to Mary Jane. 'Your clothes alone would fetch a pretty penny, and I don't doubt you have come from more salubrious surroundings – but what I can't fathom is why you would want to come and live in a place like this, near the docks.'

'If what I've heard is true,' Elodie said, 'I am here for the same reason you came to Beamer Street. There is someone I need to get away from,' Elodie offered, knowing she could trust Mary Jane and Cal. 'But I am not here to pry into your private affairs.'

'I didn't think you were,' Mary Jane answered, feeling much better since the cabbage leaf began to work its magic, easing the ache in her breasts. 'You remind me of the girl I was, a few years ago, when I nearly made the biggest mistake of my life.'

'I fear I did make the biggest mistake of my life,' Elodie confessed.

'Let's just leave it at that for now.' Mary Jane smiled and Elodie agreed.

'You should feel some ease soon,' said Elodie, 'then you, *her,* and *his nibs* will be the picture of serenity.'

'I am already feeling the benefit.' Mary Jane was feeling sleepy for the first time in ages.

20

'Did I hear your lodger is opening that empty shop to sell twigs and weeds?' Ina, next in the queue at the bakery, asked Daisy, who wondered when Ina was going to start carping about their new arrival.

'No, you did not hear that,' Molly answered at the front of the queue, knowing Ellie wanted the news kept quiet, and Daisy did her best not to crack a smile. She knew her mother was more than a match for Ina, one of the fastest gossipmongers in the northwest.

'Am I the only one who gets a whiff of the sea when she's around?' Ina asked and the other women in the queue looked puzzled.

'What's that supposed to mean?' asked Molly, who was never afraid to challenge Ina, unlike some of the women in Beamer Street.

'I think she means there's something fishy about your mam's lodger,' said Peggy Tenant.

'Mrs Kirrin is not one for advertising her daily doings, as you well know,' said Molly, 'and I don't keep track of the ins and outs of her business.' Molly was apt to tell a trivial lie if the occasion called for it, but in this instance, she felt Ellie was entitled to her privacy.

'What about her family? Where did she say she was from?' Ina was in no rush while there were some customers who might have something she had not yet discovered. She knew that Ellie received a lot of telephone calls from Molly's nephew, who came from a Lancashire village, and wondered what the link was. 'I saw your Aiden bringing boxes of plants to the shop.'

'It's none of my business,' Molly said, with an air of exasperation 'She may not have any family for all I know, and don't ask me anything else, because I'm not so nosey as some I could mention.'

'That's a surprise, Molly,' Ina sniffed, 'you're usually one of the first with a bit of jangle.'

'I don't know, Ina, you're not usually far behind me.' Molly had no intentions of letting this one get the better of her.

'All I know, is Ellie has come to help those who can't help themselves.' Daisy did not want a war of words in the shop between her mother and Ina King.

'Like I say, how is she supposed to help sick people with just a few plants and twigs, I ask you?' Ina pursed her lips, and, like a dog with a bone, Daisy knew she would not leave the subject alone until she was satisfied she had every detail. 'It's all a load of tosh if you ask me. How can you heal someone, who's at death's door, with a weed?'

'Your Paddy's finger was as green as a cabbage caterpillar,' said Daisy, who didn't like to hear her friend who had become more than just a lodger, being criticised, 'and swollen fit to burst before Ellie put a warm bread poultice on it.'

The women in the long queue were agog, momentarily putting to one side the notion they had to get back home to their chores. A bit of local argy-bargy was always source for their undivided attention.

'Don't you think I know about poultices?' Ina, shifting one leg behind the other, hitched her shopping basket up her arm, while the other customers held their breath in anticipation of young Daisy's feisty retort. Daisy was proving she was as much in charge as Mary Jane.

'She's really come out of her shell since she's been managing this shop,' one customer said to another, complimenting Daisy, while the rest murmured their agreement. 'Good for her,' they said.

'Well, why didn't you put a poultice on his finger, Ina?' Daisy answered without a shadow of self-doubt, knowing if Mary Jane were here she would have said exactly the same thing. Daisy had learned a lot from Mary Jane, the most important thing was how to manage awkward customers like Ina, who wasn't voicing her thoughts so freely now.

'She never lets her daughter out of her sight.' Ina half turned to the next customer on her right, not inclined to tell the whole shop she rarely had spare bread to use for a poultice. Daisy had become a proper little madam since she had taken over from Mary Jane. Not that she would say so in front of Molly. To hear Molly talk, she'd never seen a poor day in her life, now that she had two offspring working and one doing his apprenticeship at Beamer's, not to mention having a lodger to swell the family coffers. 'You never see her little girl playing in the street like all the other kids,' Ina retorted, trying to entice a little more information from Miss High-and-Mighty here.

But, by the look of it, if Daisy did know anything about Ellie Kirrin, she certainly wasn't going to say.

'I heard her talking to little Melissa when I was cleaning my windows,' said Peggy. 'She sounded like she's talking to another grown-up.'

'Children are more aware than we give them credit for,' Daisy said, expertly twisting a paper bag in a figure eight to tie the corners and secure the contents. 'I like the way Elodie talks to her daughter, asking her opinion, and actually listening to her reply.' She knew there were some mothers who dismissed their offspring as unpaid labour, running messages and minding the younger members of the family. Too busy or too impatient to give the little ones much consideration.

'Well,' Ina huffed, 'you wouldn't get me asking any of mine for advice, they're as thick as two short planks.' You could have heard an egg drop; the shop was so quiet.

'Little Melissa answers her mother in a very confident and respectful manner.' Daisy knew she was goading Ina, but she couldn't resist.

'They speak nice. Educated, like,' Peggy added for good measure.

'Like I said, what good's an education when you've mouths to feed?' Ina asked. 'An education doesn't put bread on your table.'

'Well, not enough for a poultice,' Molly murmured when Ina turned to face her in the queue.

'Will that be all?' Daisy asked, holding her hand out for the bread money.

'A small loaf.' Ina sniffed.

Daisy reached the top shelf for a small loaf, and said haughtily, 'Manners cost nothing, Ina. Not even to us lowly shop girls.' Then, ignoring Ina's wide-eyed outrage at her chastisement, Daisy turned to Peggy.

'Good morning, Mrs Tenant, what can I get you?' Daisy asked knowing that even though Ina had finished her shopping, she was not inclined to move from the front of the counter, slowly adding her supplies to her basket. 'Your back must be aching standing here all this time.' There was no mistaking to whom Daisy aimed the comment.

'Well, if you have any problems in that quarter,' said Ina, 'we now have a resident cure-all who can sort out a bit of backache.' Ina resented the fact that Ellie, being a relative newcomer like Mary Jane, who had only been here a few years too, was the be-all and end-all of conversation because she was opening an apathy! Whatever that was when it was at home.

* * *

'Well, she is opening that shop across the road,' Ina said a few days later when she called into the shop. 'The grocer told me when I went to buy my best butter.'

Daisy raised one eyebrow and doubted Ina's table had ever witnessed the presence of best butter. It would be marge at best or beef dripping.

'Isn't that lovely, Ina,' said a voice from the doorway and all heads turned to see Mary Jane carrying her two new babies into the shop after her first outing to the local church, as all Catholic mothers did after giving birth, to practise the rite of purification and thanksgiving after the birth of their child.

'I feel as right as ninepence by the care Ellie has given me, and after being spoiled rotten by Molly's attention, I'm eager to get on with arrangements for the christening.'

Ina was the only customer who did not hurry forth to get a look at the new arrivals, barely able to remember the night Mary Jane's babies were born, but one thing she did recall was the bouquet of beautiful flowers she received from Cal Everdine. They must have cost a pretty penny at this time of year, Ina thought, knowing the money he paid for them would have been much more gratefully accepted.

'If you ask me,' Ina told Daisy, who was stood behind the counter, 'I'd say Ellie is most certainly a bit odd, who else would want to make healing balms, and potions, when we've got a perfectly good doctor along the road?'

'If I recall,' said Molly, 'some people cannot always afford to call the doctor, and how was your Lizzie's chest after Ellie gave you that syrup?'

'It was getting better anyway,' Ina said sullenly. Trust Molly bliddy Haywood to put her two pennorth in and tell her lodger about their Lizzie's complaint. Mind, the linctus did get rid of the cough, but she wasn't going to tell this lot.

The shop suddenly fell silent. Gone was the happy chatter and appreciative coos of women admiring Mary Jane's baby. And the only sound in the shop was the click of the bakery door as it gently closed.

All eyes were on the door, except Ina who was glad she was being served and not wasting time listening to mindless waffle of these eejit women who believed a blade of grass and the root of a tree could cure all ills. 'A lot of hocus-pocus. Father McBane will have a fit of conniptions when he finds out there's a witch in the parish.'

'Ina!' Daisy whispered sharply, her eyes gazing over Ina's shoulder towards the door and Ina's head twisted on a swivel.

'Hello, Ina.' Elodie had heard every word, but did not seem in the least perturbed, 'Please go on, don't let me disturb your conversation.'

'You don't want to pay any attention to Ina,' said Daisy, desperate to keep the peace and show Mary Jane she was capable of running a harmonious shop in her absence, 'she believes in leprechauns.'

'Just my regular, please Daisy.' Ina, to save face, decided she might as well buy something. 'Put it on the slate. I'll pay on Friday.'

'An attack on the wise woman is an attack on science itself,' said Elodie who had studied her craft all her life, 'so I am not insulted. For thousands of years the only physician of the people was the witch.'

'Go on, now?' a woman from Beamer Terrace said, fascinated. 'You learn something new every time you come in this shop.'

'Emperors, kings, popes, and rich people had doctors, whereas the common population consulted none but the sage – the wise woman.' Elodie directed her explanation to Ina, who looked anywhere but at her. 'In fact, the word "witch" previously indicated a woman of great knowledge. Many women of such wisdom were healers, so in one way you're right, Ina.'

'See!' Ina was visibly relieved. 'Didn't I say? Didn't I?'

'By the way, did you know that the aspirin you buy to cure your headache, or rheumatic pain, or whatever, evolved not only from the bark of the white willow tree, but also from meadowsweet, the herb growing freely in every spring meadow, and is used in many herbal remedies.' Elodie paused. 'The gentlewomen who helped other women through the pain of childbirth and menstruation were brought under the suspicion of the Church, all God-fearing men who felt threatened by the healers.'

A small gasp of shock emanated from Ina's lips. She was a devout Catholic who refused to consider any questioning of the Church, went to early mass every morning, not just Sunday, yet she would call her neighbour fit to burn. 'What's menstru-what's-it?'

'That means your monthly visitors, Ina,' said Molly. 'You know, the one's you don't see any more.' Molly was pleased Ellie had got her point across so expressively.

'I thought that's what it meant,' Ina gave Molly a look of disgust, 'but I don't think Father McBane will see it that way.'

'That's because he will never know a woman's pain.'

'I didn't mean no harm,' Ina said.

'People rarely mean to be malicious,' Elodie's voice was calm and steady, 'but it's the fear of the unknown that keeps women in their place. It's my job to show them I deal only in proven cures, not superstition.'

'Not everybody is so small-minded,' Daisy told Elodie.

Elodie remembered the time the whole village turned against her after her mother's death. Speculation had turned to gospel truth when the cottage, leased by her family from the Caraway family since the seventeenth century, was burned to the ground...

The villagers, like some of the less broad-minded Beamer Street locals, believed she had the power to bewitch because she was a healer. And barely gave her anything except a cursory acknowledgement.

Elodie, taking a long, slow stream of delicious air that smelled of fresh bread and cakes, decided to let those who chose to do so believe what they would.

* * *

'Helping people is my greatest pleasure,' Elodie said later as she sat with Melissa, Molly, and the rest of the lovely Haywood family, at the kitchen table eating their tea, hardly able to contain her excitement.

'Well,' said Daisy with sincerity that was obviously not forced, 'I wish you every success and prosperity.'

'I suspect the business will go from strength to strength,' Molly said with conviction. 'You are just what this area needs. Doctors are expensive to most people who depend on the docks and some medication is prohibitively expensive.'

'I don't expect the business to make me rich,' Elodie answered, 'I just want to help people who need it most.'

'Most men around here work on the docks in some capacity,' Molly said, 'but work is proving harder to come by.'

'If your face doesn't fit, and you don't land a day's work,' Daisy agreed, 'you don't have any money to fall back on.'

'Some men who don't work on the docks, go away to sea,' Molly said looking to her son.

'Aye, many say it's not blood that runs through their veins, but the waters that flow from Liverpool Docks,' said Freddy, knowing the docks played a vital role in the lives of everybody who lived and worked around here.

However, although most of the men in Beamer Street were lucky enough to have some kind of trade, the shipwrights, the joiners, the engineers, and the train drivers, there were also some like Ina's husband, the 'ten-a-penny-workers', whose labour came cheap and who were hired on a casual basis, who were often more out of work than in.

These were the people Elodie wanted to help. Those people, less fortunate, as her mother, her grandmother, and her great-great-grandmother had done before her, and even though Ina was a bitter pill sometimes, Elodie was sure there was a soft heart in there somewhere. Life was hard and had dealt Ina an unfortunate blow, but Elodie could never turn her back on someone. It was not in her nature, as Aiden would say.

She smiled when she thought of him knowing he would be coming to look over the shop today. She missed him so much, but she would never go back to Lavender Green and was determined to help and heal as many people here as she could. Something which Silas had forbidden her to do, and she'd had to practise in secret when work at the hospital ended after the war.

Well, those days are over, she thought with the grit of a woman who was now free to do as she pleased. To see her name, Elodie Kirrin, displayed above the shop door would give her the greatest of pleasure. She would never reveal her married name, knowing she must keep her identity hidden.

'Have you settled in all right?' Aiden asked later that day when he was sizing up the stable at the back of the apothecary, which she intended to use as a potting and work shed for her balms and tinctures. Aiden stretched out both arms horizontally, his arm span, over six feet, was the length of his body from head to toe and gave him an idea of the length of wood needed for the potting tables.

Her arms folded, Elodie leaned her shoulder against the stable door frame watching him measuring and jotting down the figures neatly on the back of a discarded envelope before slipping the pencil behind his ear.

'They're not a quiet family by any means,' Elodie said, giving a low chuckle, content, watching him work without the threat of being spied on by one of the workmen Silas had employed to watch her every move.

'I hope they don't disturb you too much.' Aiden stopped what he was doing and looked over his broad shoulder towards her.

'I love the hustle and bustle of the family, the noise,' she laughed, 'it means there is life in the place, and young Bridie is wonderful with Melissa. They don't disturb me at all,' Elodie answered truthfully. 'The house seems to be in perpetual motion, with everybody coming and going, it is so liberating, without the rigid structure of Oakland Hall.' Where she would have to change her clothes just to sit at the long dining table and silently eat, even when she was alone.

Unlike the Haywoods, who talked non-stop, each one talking louder than the next to be heard. Apart from washing your hands before you sat down to eat, there seemed to be no rules, and she loved it.

'I haven't seen you so alive and enthusiastic for many years,' Aiden told Elodie when she had explained to him that she had acquired the shop across the road. This was the Elodie he had known and loved all her life. Full of ideas and plans for the future. Their future, maybe, one day.

'Would you like to have a look at it?' Elodie had asked and Aiden nodded. 'I haven't got the keys yet, the locks are being changed, but we can look through the window.'

'Won't be long, Aunt Moll, just going to see Elodie's new shop.'

His eyes were warm and tender as he'd followed her out of the house and across the street, seeing immediately what he could do with a place like this.

'There should be plenty of room for a couple of decent-sized greenhouses, if those double gates are anything to go by,' he said, 'it's a pity they are padlocked I would have liked to look around.' He was as enthusiastic as his darling Elodie.

'I'll let you know as soon as I get the keys,' Elodie had said, 'but I don't know who is going to manage all of the plants while I'm working in the apothecary?'

'I could ask Will to call in,' Aiden said, his eyes dancing with mischief when Elodie's jaw dropped, and she began to protest.

'I will do the work,' Aiden said assuring her she would not be on her own. 'I've given in my notice. Will is able to manage the Oakland Hall gardens, and I will be more useful to you here.' He could not bear to be parted from her one more day. Since she had moved into Beamer Street his life felt empty. He had to see her every day.

'That's wonderful news!' Elodie exclaimed, 'and there will be no shortage of custom from what I've been told, or from what I've seen so far.'

'They're a mixed variety, some well fed and clothed, others ill clad and sickly, depending on their breadwinner's work.' But she loved to see the children playing together in the street no matter what the weather.

'From morning till night, you can hear the shouts and the songs. Kids around here love singing sea shanties and little ditties while skipping.' Elodie told him, thrilled that he wanted to make this place his home, too. 'They look after their own, and close ranks when the need arises.'

Elodie realised soon after she arrived in Beamer Street that women in this part of the country were tougher than most through necessity, and they did not give up easily. The women usually dominated families, and it was no surprise to see a child of eight or nine carrying a younger sibling on her hip. Childminding, it seemed, was delegated to the eldest girl, probably while Mam got on with the chores, thought Elodie.

She and Aiden agreed it would be better if he took the flat over the apothecary while the renovations were being done, while she and Melissa would stay with Molly.

'I've never seen her so happy,' said Elodie, 'she has taken to Bridie like a sister and follows her everywhere.'

'Maybe it's for the best if she does stay with the family for a while,' Aiden said, putting his arms around Elodie's slim waist and pulling her towards him. 'She has seen a lot of changes over the past weeks.'

'She loves her new school, too, and has already made friends,' said Elodie, enjoying the muscular outline of his body too much, as he gently pressed against her, and felt she must try to keep the conversation on a more mundane level. Even though she loved him with every beat of her heart, she was still a married woman, even though she wished her situation could be quite different.

* * *

'Ma says she has never seen so much of our Aiden; he's been twice this week.' Daisy said when Elodie called into the bakery to pick up some bread for tea. 'Not that she's complaining of course, it's lovely to see him.'

'He brings me the herbs I will need when I open the apothecary,' Elodie said. 'He grows them for me in his greenhouse.'

She didn't want to tell Daisy that Aiden was going to move into the flat over the apothecary before she told Molly, and thankfully Daisy wasn't one to pry and ask awkward questions.

'It looks like the weather's taken a turn for the better, and spring might soon be here,' said Daisy.

Elodie had been dreading her daughter wanting to play outside with the other children, who might ask questions her daughter was innocent enough to answer truthfully. Knowing how curious the people around here could be, Elodie also knew the children were no different.

While Melissa, as sweet and adorable as the lemon balm she was named after, had been brought up to be honest and polite and would never lie about where she came from, Elodie struggled with the possibility she may have to ask her to lie. Well, not lie exactly, thought Elodie, more like sidestep the truth. Saying nothing at all wasn't lying. Thankfully, the cold weather had prevented her from wanting to go outside, and their true identity was still a well-kept secret, but as the days grew warmer she was eager to be outside with the other children.

And she could not keep her indoors forever. Melissa had friends at school, Elodie reasoned, surely they had asked where she came from? However, now that Aiden had put the idea in her head about moving into Beamer Street, she felt a little more at ease, and the thought of moving on to another place never crossed her mind.

She liked living in this lively, vibrant community, that didn't wallow in self-pity or dwell on its shortcomings, and she got on well with Molly and her family, who kept her entertained with amusing tales about the people who lived around here, and even though some of the larger families struggled to make ends meet, the strong sense of community, especially among local women, meant there was always somebody they could call upon in their hour of need. Even those who seemed a little bitter or unapproachable at first, appeared to have redeeming qualities that were tolerated, even if those, like Ina, were not always pleasant.

Front doors remained open from the moment the inhabitants got up, until it was time to take to their beds. Because most had nothing worth pinching, privacy was almost non-existent, and everybody knew everything about everybody. Whether it be the children playing in the street who talked freely about what they'd heard the grown-ups discussing, or the women socialising at their front doors, nothing, it seemed, was sacred and Elodie decided that it was about time she too put her trust in Molly and came clean about who she really was.

21

Kissing her sleeping daughter goodnight, Elodie knew Melissa was in the best place. She would come to no harm in the lively Haywood household, where everybody looked out for each other. Young Bridie had taken it upon herself to act as 'big sister' and chief minder to Melissa, who loved her company and looked up to her. And since she started at the local infants' school, her true nature was coming to the fore. Elodie believed her daughter's transformation could be thought of as a flower that had been a long time in shade, and now it was feeling the benefit of sunshine and had begun to blossom, and for that Elodie was truly thankful.

If Melissa needed anything, Elodie was confident Molly would be there to make sure she was well looked after. She gazed down on her sleeping daughter, lying contentedly next to Bridie, like two peas in a pod, and doubted Melissa would have time to miss her when she eventually started working in the apothecary. Elodie had come to an arrangement with Molly over looking after Melissa and promised to pay her ten shillings weekly. Molly had stipulated that she didn't want paying for looking after the child, but Elodie had insisted, saying she would feel much better if Molly took the money.

'At least I know Melissa is safe with you.' Molly would let no harm come to her.

She knew Molly was dying to ask what she meant, by her last remark and Elodie knew the time had come when she would tell Molly and Mary Jane the whole story.

Having never lived anywhere except the countryside, Elodie knew this was the last place Silas would ever think of looking for her. He would not give a single thought to her being strong enough to survive the Liverpool dockland backstreets.

Although now she came to think of it, she would never have dreamt she was capable of such a thing either. But, after listening to the strong women of Beamer Street, their views gave her the surge of courage she needed to plough her own furrow. And rather than think she had made her bed and so must lie in it; she relished the challenge to prove she was far more capable of making a good life for herself and her daughter, than she ever thought she could when she lived at Oakland Hall. Since she had moved in with Molly and her family, she felt she had grown. In that short space of time, a few weeks ago, she had become a different person to the one who had married Silas Caraway.

Closing the bedroom door quietly behind her, Elodie reflected on how comfortable she had felt from the moment she stepped foot inside the door. Molly's house had a homely air she had not felt since her mother...

But she mustn't think about that terrible time now. She must be positive and look on the bright side, as her mother would have wanted.

Molly treated her and Melissa like family and she already felt like this was where she belonged. The only thing she missed about being at Lavender Green was Aiden. Darling Aiden, her one true love. But now she could look to the future with renewed hope. Aiden was moving closer, and all her worries would be behind her.

Cal had agreed to let Aiden have the flat above the apothecary, build the greenhouses and turn the stable into a potting shed and workshop. The seedlings she had been nurturing were beginning to show signs of life, and all that was left to do was give the apothecary a good spring clean tomorrow and kit it out ready for business. Elodie couldn't wait. Although she was sure Molly would miss people coming to her door for one of Elodie's cures, and finding out what was ailing them without even having to pry.

She bit her lip the following morning after dropping Melissa off at Saint Patrick's infant school over the bridge and tried not to check the time incessantly, knowing Aiden was moving in today. She had hardly slept at the thought of him coming to Beamer Street and being so close once more, although she had not told Melissa – she wanted it to be a surprise knowing how much her daughter missed him.

She would have to wait another agonising hour or two before he got here, and as the minutes ticked by, she was growing so eager to see him again she felt her heart would burst with anticipation.

Elodie made her way past the large bedrooms, bathroom and indoor lavatory and descended the curving staircase to reach the ground floor. Crossing the wide parquet-floored hallway, she went to the kitchen at the back of the house and put the kettle on to make a pot of tea, unable to eat anything for the excitement of Aiden's arrival. Often silently chastising herself for acting like a lovesick schoolgirl instead of a... Her heart dipped. She was a married woman.

No. She must not think that way. Silas had tricked her into marrying him. He had put her into a situation she could not get out of. If she had refused his offer of marriage, she would have been destitute. Silas would have had no compunction in throwing her out of Oakland Hall, of that she was certain.

She sat in the comfortably furnished front room, which she and Melissa rarely used, preferring instead to join the rest of the family in the kitchen. Elodie tried to sit still but it was impossible – Molly's house was rarely as quiet as this, giving her clamorous thoughts only a little respite from the unremitting tick of the clock.

It was no good, she was going to have to go over to the shop alone. It was far better she do something to keep her mind occupied than sit here drinking tea and letting her thoughts run amok.

Then, to her relief, Elodie heard voices entering the hallway and she recognised Molly and Mary Jane's chatter as they entered the house, leaving the twin perambulator on the pathway outside.

'There's fresh tea in the pot.' She rose from the fireside chair as Molly popped her head around the parlour door.

'Good lass,' said Molly beaming, 'Mary Jane has just been to the clinic to have the babies weighed, and they've put on another half-pound each since the last visit, thanks to your excellent advice.'

'Glad to be of help.' Elodie beamed following the two women into the back-kitchen, knowing Mary Jane was having no trouble feeding her babies any more, thrilled that they were thriving.

'Look at this.' After regaling her with the health of her children and enjoying a cup of tea and a slice of fruit cake, Mary Jane proudly showed off her slim figure. 'I can get back into the baking overall I wore before I started having the twins.'

Elodie was glad of these two women and of the way they had befriended her and had taken her into their confidence since she arrived in Beamer Street. They offered her an invaluable abundance of friendship she never had back at Lavender Green, not since her mother...

She must not think of that now. She must concentrate on the good fortune she had in her new and abiding friendships and look to the future, instead of looking back at the tragedy of the past.

'There's something I must tell you,' Elodie said not knowing if what she was about to say would ruin the wonderful friendships she now enjoyed. Nevertheless, she decided, the time had come to tell Molly the truth of why she had come to start a new life in a place, she never imagined she would ever be able to settle.

'Lady Elodie Caraway!' Molly's jaw dropped and her eyes were wide. 'Well, lass, I knew you had something about you, but I never would have took you to be married to Lord Silas. I remember him, the man is a well-known bloody tyrant, excuse my language.'

'I am so relieved to get everything out in the open,' said Elodie, 'you don't know how many nights I've lain awake praying for the courage to tell you the truth.'

'Oh, poor girl,' said Molly, 'I wish I'd known... I should have known... I have daughters of my own.'

'No, Molly, you would never have known if I didn't say anything.' Elodie gave a wan smile. 'Circumstances, my marriage, my inability to care for myself the way I cared for others, made me adept at hiding my feelings.'

'Well, rest assured it makes no difference to our friendship,' said Molly, 'you'll always be Ellie Kirrin to this family.'

'Thank you so much,' Ellie began to feel the weight of her lie fall from her shoulders, 'but there is one other thing, which you might find a little hard to stomach.' What she was about to tell Molly, who had come to mean so much to her, might cut their friendship dead, but Elodie knew that now the door had been opened she could not close it again on another lie.

'It's about my Melissa...' Elodie began as Molly poured more tea into their cups. 'She is not his daughter.' There was a quiet hush as the women digested the words she had never spoken out loud, except to Aiden.

And, as she waited for the older woman to react to her confession, the ceiling did not fall down on her head, nor the floor open up and take her to the flames of hell. The woman sitting opposite her at the table, did not run screaming from the house at the horror of her audacity. Nor, if truth be told, did she look shocked at her admission.

'I don't think any less of you for telling the truth,' said Molly. 'But I knew it,' she exclaimed suddenly, scraping her chair back on the stone-flagged kitchen floor.

'Knew what?' Elodie asked, puzzled as she watched Molly cross the kitchen.

'When I first saw Melissa, I knew she reminded me of someone, but couldn't put my finger on who it was, all I knew was the resemblance was so striking, but let me show you something.' Molly reached up to the shelf and took down the family photograph she had taken before her Bert was killed in the war.

'Can you see it?' she asked Elodie, 'there's no mistaking the resemblance.'

'Good grief!' Elodie gasped, barely able to believe her own eyes.

'That's our Daisy. Can you see it, the resemblance?' Molly waited for Elodie to answer, and Mary Jane nodded in agreement.

'You're right.' Elodie tried to hold back the tears blurring her view. If ever proof were needed this would be it. 'Melissa is Aiden's daughter.'

'Listen, lass,' said Molly, 'nobody needs to know anything about what you have told me, it will never be spoken about outside this room.'

'Thank you!' Elodie, feeling light-headed, took a huge gulp of air.

When, sometime later, Elodie took Molly across the road to see the shop, they waved to Daisy, who was working in the bakery, and made their way to the apothecary. Elodie's hands were shaking with excitement when she pushed the key into the lock and opened the shop door.

'Look at this,' Elodie said, thrilled when she stepped inside and flicked the electric light switch with her finger, flooding the room with light. There were blinds at the front and side windows, which she liked, knowing some of the people who visited the apothecary would appreciate the discretion.

'I remember the day I took over my bakery,' said Mary Jane, who sauntered in, 'it was the best day. This shop is almost identical with its L-shaped counter.'

'I can't wait to scrub the dusty wooden shelves,' said Elodie, 'Ma kept our apothecary spotless.'

'Just goes to show the length of time the shop has been empty,' said Molly, 'but it won't take you long to get this shipshape, making it your own, and loved.'

But to Elodie this place could not be more perfect.

'The windows are in desperate need of a thorough cleaning,' said Mary Jane, as was the whole shop.

'That doesn't worry me,' said Elodie, 'I'll have it sparkling in no time.' Elodie knew she could not make her treatments anywhere that was less than spotless. She was here to cure, not to ruin the health of the dockside dwellers.

'I'd love to stay and help you,' said Mary Jane nodding in the direction of her new babies outside, 'but I've hungry mouths to feed first.'

'You have enough on your plate,' said Elodie, then turning to Molly, 'and you also have a family to feed, so off you both go,' She ushered the two women to the door, not wanting to make them feel unwelcome, but she needed to be alone when Aiden arrived. 'I'm looking forward to getting this place just the way I want it.'

There were three wooden steps behind the counter, which she climbed, and when she reached the slightly higher room, she noticed a door to her right. Opening it, Elodie saw the stairs leading to the rooms above and decided to go and investigate further, to see if one of the rooms would be suitable for storing her stock. She was amazed at the size of the large flat, with high ceilings and vast floorspace.

Along the landing, the front room, like the shop downstairs, had windows at the front and side and even one at the corner. *An all-round view of the neighbourhood*, she thought, her heart pounding against her ribs. *This would be ideal accommodation for a family.*

She stopped that train of thought in its tracks. Yes, it was true, she and Melissa could be comfortable here. She had been a bit hasty offering the flat to Aiden. But then again, Melissa had been uprooted enough and was so happy with Bridie and the Haywood family. She dare not imagine what it would be like to live here with Aiden and Melissa, a proper family, all she had ever wanted. But it was impossible. She was a married woman, and Silas Caraway would never give her a divorce. The idea of being Aiden's wife was more than she ever dared dream of.

She was upstairs when the front doorbell rang, which momentarily startled her but, quickly regaining her equilibrium, she brushed back a few stray, damp hairs with the palm of her hand and made her way down to the shop.

The top half of the door was frosted glass covered with the same blind as the other windows and when Elodie opened it, she was thrilled to see Aiden standing there, a battered cardboard suitcase at his feet, while holding wooden boxes of plants.

'Come in!' she gasped. 'You will never guess how big this place is – the upstairs is vast, big enough to house a whole family, so much too big for just a stockroom, and then there are the rooms at the back of the shop. Can you believe it!'

Elodie didn't even stop for breath, so Aiden had no choice but to silence her with a kiss.

Elodie melted into his arms, their lips eager, hungry. This was the first time they had been truly alone since Armistice Day – and look what had happened then, Elodie thought, deliriously happy when she remembered that day back at the summer house, when Melissa was conceived.

'I want to show you something,' she said, eagerly taking his huge, strong hand and pulling him behind the counter, up the steps, and into the back of the shop. 'Look out there.'

Aiden looked and let out a long slow whistle. 'That is a big garden – big enough for a couple of greenhouses and it's got soil, instead of being cobbled over like some backyards.'

'Isn't it wonderful,' said Elodie, 'my own piece of countryside. Well, it's only small compared to Lavender Green, but I will be able to inhale the fragrance of nature in all its colourful glory come spring.'

'Much earlier than that when I get those greenhouses up,' said Aiden, caught up in the excitement of a new beginning for Ellie and Melissa, 'and I've already measured up for a potting shed, too.'

'Well, we don't need the stable,' Elodie said.

'It's more than adequate,' Aiden said eyeing up the wood for the new shelving, 'it will also double as a handy workshop.'

'This is going to be the best apothecary in the land,' Elodie said. 'As well as the usual ointments and liniments, I will sell beauty balms, which the wives of affluent men favour.' Elodie saw no reason why the local women should not benefit from a bit of pampering too. Why should they miss out on nature's gifts just because they did not live in the countryside.

'The majority of working-class women never come within a mile of the healthy rural area,' she told Aiden, 'and their families are more prone to chest complaints due to the smoky outpourings. Another reason I feel my services are desperately needed.'

By keeping up with the news of the day, Elodie knew Prime Minister Ramsay MacDonald had encouraged improvements for a healthier way of living, especially after the influenza epidemic that had stolen so many lives. However, the vision proved more costly than the country could afford. Elodie wished there was some way she could bring more than just cures to the neighbour-hood, knowing these people deserved to feel green grass beneath their feet and fresh air in their lungs.

Keeping abreast of the country's financial status, she could see health insurance had increased for the working man. But there were still no noticeable changes in the benefits they received. 'The insured workers receive some income when they were laid off due to illness, and also given free medication and basic appliances from panel doctors, who take part in the scheme,' she explained.

'But their families, like the uninsured, have no such entitle-ment, is that what you mean?' Aiden asked and Elodie nodded.

'So, if they became unwell, they have to go without medical assistance. Unless, of course, they joined some kind of "friendly society" and paid their "clubman" every week. If the illness became serious enough, or someone in the family needed long-term medical treatment, some families could be in debt for years. It seems clear that this place is going to need my help.'

'That special light has returned to your eyes.' Aiden had not seen her look so happy since her sixteenth birthday, and he was glad. He always knew the girl he loved was in there somewhere, and to see her return was a joy. His heart swelled with love for her, and he knew that today was not the time to tell her what he knew about Silas Caraway coming to Liverpool, to judge a murder case at Saint George's Hall.

'Come and have a look upstairs.' Elodie was so excited, she was like a child at Christmas. 'You will never believe the size of it.'

'Sounds fascinating,' Aiden joked, following her up. When Elodie showed him the vast rooms, he knew as well as she did, the place was big enough to rear a family. 'This place has everything we could possibly need.' Except for the freedom to enjoy it together, she thought.

Taking her in his arms, he tried to resist her womanly charms but knew neither of them could resist the temptation to consummate their love, one more time...

22

'Did you hear what I said, Elodie?' Mary Jane asked. Sitting at her table in the warm, kitchen, as Elodie pushed around a slice of rich fruit cake on her plate, which she had made earlier and, smiling, went on to explain that she had wanted to call her son after his father, but Cal was adamant the boy should have his own name. 'I never even thought of two names,' Mary Jane said over a hot cup of tea, which was always on offer. 'I never contemplated having twins.'

'Two names?' Elodie said as if in some kind of stupor. In her head, she was still in that room over the apothecary, lost in Aiden's loving arms, the imprint of his kiss still on her lips. 'Two names, of course!'

'Is something bothering you, Ellie?' Mary Jane could hardly keep her face straight she had seen that far-away expression before and suspected it had something to do with Aiden.

'Mary Jane, can I tell you something?' Elodie suddenly felt nervous. 'It's about me and Aiden...' She hadn't told Mary Jane the whole story, as she had with Molly.

'I thought it might be.' Mary Jane smiled.

For the next half an hour, Elodie told Mary Jane about the love she still felt for her lifelong champion, about him going to France, her mother's death, about marrying Silas having Aiden's baby, then finding out Silas was impotent. 'That is the reason I had to leave Lavender Green. I am sure, if my husband finds me and Melissa, he will kill one of us – or both.'

Mary Jane said nothing for the time being, as if trying to sum up everything Elodie had just revealed about her past. Whilst Elodie hoped she had not just talked herself out of the premises, where she hoped her future lay. Lifting her chin, Mary Jane looked her in the eye and hesitated, her lips between her teeth as if trying to stop the words escaping.

'I'd appreciate a straight talk,' Elodie said, encouraging Mary Jane to speak her mind, which was something she respected most. The two women, Mary Jane and Molly with their practical advice and outlook, would let her know where she stood – and she could work with that, improve on it, and be guided by it.

'You're better off out of that marriage,' Mary Jane said bluntly, 'living a lie takes its toll on a body.' For, didn't she have to do that very thing when she first came to Beamer Street. 'None of us are saints. Well, I'm certainly not.' Mary Jane gave a wry laugh, she had given birth to little Hollie out of wedlock and waved aside the superstitious belief, some of the less educated had, that she would be damned for all eternity for giving birth without the blessing of the church.

'We are human, and we have failings, that's all there is to it.' Mary Jane was trying to lessen the shame Elodie must have been feeling all these years. Mary Jane had suspected Ellie had a story, as most of the women in Beamer Street did, but she had never imagined that story would be as big as this.

'A high-court judge – I've read about him in the newspaper,

they call him the hanging judge,' Mary Jane said, 'he is not a man you want to cross.'

'That is why Aiden is moving into the flat above the apothecary,' Elodie explained, 'he says it is to help me with the business, but I think he is making sure Melissa and I are well protected.'

'You don't think your husband will come looking for you here?' Mary Jane asked, and Elodie gave a hopeless shrug.

'He has the contacts.' Elodie said simply, 'but I doubt he would suspect I would move here, tucked away in a dockside backstreet, not a blade of grass to be seen, not a flower or a tree. No, Silas would never dream of looking for me in a place like this, and I am so thankful I have Aiden to look out for me.'

'Moving yourself and Melissa here sounds sensible, if not a bit dangerous.'

'In what way?' Elodie asked and Mary Jane raised an eyebrow.

'I know what you are going through, I felt exactly the same way about Cal, the first time I set eyes on him, even though I would not let myself believe it for a long time.'

'Do you think I'm being foolish?' asked Elodie.

'Only foolish because you married the wrong man, but that could happen to any woman.' Mary Jane paused for a moment as if choosing her words carefully. 'But I don't think you are foolish now, in fact, I wish you the best of luck, your secret's safe with me.'

'What secret's that, then?' asked Molly, who bundled into the kitchen with Bridie, Melissa, and Hollie who had joined the group.

'Names,' exclaimed Mary Jane knowing Molly was aware of Elodie's situation, but it wasn't her place to say anything, 'we were just discussing names and Ellie said she had a secret crush on a handsome film star.'

'Is it Rudolph?' Young Bridie's eyes lit up, she had been to the pictures with Molly to see *The Son of the Sheik*, and Rudolph

Valentino's dark good looks had set her twelve-year-old heart pitter-pattering. 'I've got a picture of him, which I cut from a magazine, it's at the side of my bed!'

'Looks like your secret's out, Ellie,' Mary Jane said innocently, and Elodie laughed. She loved living in Beamer Street.

'I said Rudolph too,' Hollie giggled, 'but I meant the reindeer,' and Melissa joined in too, although Elodie doubted that her daughter had any idea what she was laughing about. She loved being part of this big extended family, where she was never alone, and glad that her daughter too always had someone to talk to or play with.

'I don't think Rudolph would fit in with the people around here, lovey,' said Molly, urging Bridie and the little ones out of the room so the adults could talk in private. 'Our Bridie does come out with some daft things lately.'

'Well, Cal wants his only son to have his own name,' Mary Jane said when the children were out of the room, 'so I am going to call him Laurence.'

'Like Lawrence of Arabia?' Molly said.

'No after Cal, it is one of his names. Charles Adam Laurence Everdine.'

'I think that's lovely,' said Molly.

'Now, all we have to do is organise his christening.' Mary Jane did not want a lavish affair, but she did not want it to be as quiet as Hollie's had been, when she did a nice tea of ham salad for the family, in the parlour when they got back from church. Cal was Hollie's godfather, and Molly, with whom she lodged, was her godmother.

'Cal is Hollie's godfather?' Elodie looked perplexed and her brows creased.

'That was before Cal and I got married,' Mary Jane explained in hushed whispers. 'As far as Hollie is aware, Cal is her daddy.

The only one she has ever known, and that's the way we want it to stay.'

'Mam! Come quick!' The women turned towards the kitchen door when it burst open, and Daisy came flying into the room. 'You'll never guess what our Bridie's gone and done.'

'Not unless you tell me,' said Molly, who was used to family dramas and rarely rose to a panic. But neither did Daisy, usually. So, Molly knew that it must be something catastrophic to have her eldest daughter act in such a manner and she followed Daisy out of Mary Jane's parlour at a run.

Hurrying up the passageway of her own house, Molly froze when she reached the room, where a huge pair of scissors lay on the table, and a row of girls innocently stood, unaware their fringes ranged from, cut-to-the-root-tufts to a jagged line from roots to eyebrows.

'They wanted me to do it,' Bridie said, her own fringe in the same kind of mess.

'I don't know what their mams will say!' Daisy's face was ashen. 'They'll go mad.'

'Is there any way you can fix it?' said Molly, when she finally found her voice, sure she knew exactly what their mothers were going to say.

'I doubt it, Mam. She's cut it right up their forehead. Our Melissa has even got a bald patch!'

'That's because she would not keep still,' said Bridie by way of explanation. 'It kept going all wobbly, so I had to cut it shorter,' Bridie explained, seeing nothing wrong in her 'masterpiece'. 'I told them I'm going to be a hairdresser, after I saw our Daisy getting her hair cut. It looked dead easy.'

'Well, now you know it isn't, don't you,' said Daisy, dreading taking Ina King's daughter, Lottie, home to her mother in this state. But knowing she had to because her mam certainly wouldn't. So, she'd best get on with it.

Most of the mothers were understanding and philosophical, and like Molly said, it would grow again. But when Daisy took the last girl to her mother, Ina King roared fit to burst. 'What has she done to my child, I'll scull-drag her, the little demon, she's done this on purpose, she's done this out of spite.'

'For what?' Daisy asked, deciding that next time their Bridie got herself into a tricky situation, Mam could come and sort it out instead of leaving it to her. 'Why would she want to do this out of spite? She thought she could cut their hair, and then found she was out of her depth.'

'I'll give her out of her depth,' said Ina. 'I'll take her to the Cut and drown the little mare.'

'You won't do that, Ina, because I wouldn't let you.' Daisy knew it was best to stay calm where Ina was concerned. 'And your Lottie's fringe is not as bad as some of them.' The Herculean ability to keep a straight face deserted her, and Daisy began to laugh. 'It'll grow again, Ina, and if you want me to, I will straighten her fringe.' She could cut a pattern for a new dress with ease, so a fringe shouldn't be too much of a problem.

'You will do no such thing.' Ina was eager to get a free haircut out of the situation. 'I will take her to a professional hairdresser, one that's qualified, to see what can be done, and your mother will be paying for it.' When there was any sign of possible high ding-dong or dealing with authorities, Daisy was the one to handle it. Molly always said her eldest daughter was the diplomatic one, because of her dealings with the public in the shop.

'Well, take this for your trouble,' said Daisy, offering Ina a shilling, knowing her neighbour would put a pudding bowl on the child's head, cut the fringe herself and pocket the money. But handing over the shilling was the least she could do, thought

Daisy, glaring at her young sister. 'Come along, Bridie,' Daisy said in her best 'schoolmarm' voice, gripping her sister's arm and all but dragging her across the road.

'Daisy, do you think I'll make a good hairdresser?' Bridie asked, nonplussed at the chaos she had caused, not to mention the cost. 'I like cutting hair.'

'I noticed,' Daisy said straight-faced, 'and you will be, but only when you're trained, but not before. So, you'd better start saving for your indentures now.' Daisy sighed, making a mental note to keep the scissors under lock and key in future.

23

Daisy's practised eyes travelled the length of the long table, flanked on both sides by friends and family who had been invited to the christening of the twins Laurence and Neave. As the boy's godmother, Daisy was determined that everything should be exactly right, and had overseen the preparations, as well as making the most sumptuous christening cake for the occasion, which now took pride of place in the middle of the top table in Cal and Mary Jane's spacious, high-ceilinged front room, while Elodie, who had become good friends with Mary Jane, had been asked to be godmother to Neave.

The table was set out in a T shape, with Cal, Mary Jane, and godparents at the top, Mary Jane's brothers, all doctors, who had come over from Ireland, especially for the christening. Opposite Daisy was a business acquaintance of Cal's, Henry Beamer, son of the founder, Jeremiah, of Beamer's Electricals.

The tables, groaning under the weight of some of the most amazing food Mary Jane, Daisy and Molly had prepared, were a treat for the eyes, with no expense spared.

Daisy had searched the society pages for the best celebration food and was pleased when the ham, glazed and thinly sliced, was deemed a revelation, leaving the awestruck residents of Beamer Street open-mouthed. There was roast duck, with its sticky orange and honey glaze that made the skin so golden crisp, which Daisy assured Mary Jane had become widely popular at all the best parties she had read about in the women's magazines.

'Waldorf salad,' Daisy had suggested to Mary Jane, 'made famous by the American hotel.' It was something Daisy had longed to try, and she was thrilled to hear the appreciative comments made. 'Then there are the pastry pigs.'

Mary Jane and her mother had given Daisy a quizzical look.

'Little sausages wrapped in puff pastry blankets,' Daisy had explained. 'And the star of the table – the pineapple upside-down cake.'

Now, Molly's jaw dropped, and she patted her cheek. 'I've never seen the like in all my born days!'

'I had to send away for the fresh pineapple specially.'

Daisy threw her head back and laughed out loud, when she offered her mother a slice and Molly's face puckered, her left eye scrunched, involuntarily closing.

'It's lovely,' Molly said. 'I bet nobody in Beamer Street will have tasted a cake like this. Oh, you are so clever, our Daisy,' she said proudly.

'The article in *The Society Lady* magazine said pineapple, a rarely seen fruit, is the most exotic,' Daisy whispered proudly, interrupting her mother. 'Pineapple is unaffordable to all but the rich, you know, Mam. My baking tutor said so when I told her I was making the upside-down cake.'

'Well, it goes without saying, our Daisy.' Molly looked as pleased as if she had bought the pineapple and made the cake herself. 'Look at them all tucking in.' She nodded to the *oohs and aahs* rippling around, as the light fluffy cake with the sweet sticky topping was cut, served, and devoured by every guest.

'We'll still be talking about this cake next summer,' said one guest and Molly gave her daughter a little wink before informing the guest, 'My Daisy invented it, so tuck in.'

'No, Mam,' Daisy sighed, her mother always had to go one better, 'I only copied the recipe.'

'Don't be hiding your light under the bush, Daisy,' Molly misquoted, encouraging Melissa to tuck in.

'An adequate job you made of it too.' Henry Beamer raised his voice above everybody else's.

'Who does he think he is? Adequate indeed,' Molly leaned across the young man sitting next to Daisy and whispered.

'His father owns Beamer's, Mam,' Daisy whispered back, 'our Freddy's new boss.'

'I don't care if he owns the House of Lords, he's no right talking business at the table.'

'What do you mean, Mam? What business?'

'Apparently,' Molly whispered, 'and keep this under your hat, but Mary Jane told me Cal wants all the houses in Beamer Street electrocuted.'

'Electrified, Mam.' Daisy smiled, knowing her mother, a fount of all local information, was not always spot on with her words. 'Beamer won that contract during the war, making munitions and such.'

'They say if ever there is another war, God forbid,' Molly made the sign of the cross on her chest, 'his son will continue the tradition. But this is not the time to dwell on such unpleasantness.' Molly kept her voice low, but it took a great deal of effort to do so. 'This is a happy day, and as such, we owe it to those brave men, your sainted father among them, who gave their lives so we can enjoy ourselves.'

'Any sign of you walking down the aisle, Daisy?' said one of the guests and Daisy forced a smile.

'No fear,' she said. 'I intend to set up my own catering company, hosting parties and functions for the rich and famous.' She had no intentions whatsoever of popping out babies at a rate of knots like some girls did. 'Where would I find the time?' She rolled her eyes and gave a little shake of her glossy, shingle-bobbed hair.

'If ever I did marry, and the chances are slimmer than a flat-chested flapper,' she said recalling the disastrous date with that awful Max, who ran out on her and had not been seen since. 'Any would-be husband, would have to be a very understanding man,' she told her neighbour, 'one who didn't mind coming home to an empty house of an evening, and who would have to cook his own tea.' She would be far too busy doing her own work. 'And, as far as I can see,' she informed her neighbour, 'there aren't many of those type of understanding men about.'

'Who could blame them?' said Molly. 'Who's ever heard of a man coming home from a hard day's work and cooking his own tea! You live in cloud cuckoo land sometimes, our Dais.'

'There you go, Mam,' Daisy said, believing her mother had finally got her intention not to marry – at least, not until she found the man who thought the same way she did. 'With that thought in mind, you now understand why I am not on the lookout for a husband, and I'm not particularly fond of children either.' She looked across the table to where her sister Bridie was sitting between Ellie and Mary Jane tucking into their upside-down cake.

'Wouldn't you like a family of your own, Dais?' her mother asked, and Daisy's sympathetic gaze wandered towards the poor mites who had been the victim of Bridie's hairstyling enthusiasm, and whose huge, ribboned bows did not quite cover the bald patches at their foreheads, and she silently prayed to Saint Mary Magdalene who, Daisy believed, was the patron saint of hairdressers, hoping their hair would soon grow back again.

'I'm busy enough with the family I've got, Mam,' Daisy said. She had thought Max would be the type of bloke she would like to promenade the shoreline at Blundellsands or go for a picnic in Derby park, but that was never going to happen now. Not after his disappearing act left her in the lurch. When, and if, the right man did come along, she would know immediately. The realisation would be so sudden and so strong it would hit her between the eyes like a thundering boxing glove.

Now she was managing Mary Jane's Kitchen full-time, her time never seemed to be her own any more. But these were the things she had to endure if she were to have a successful catering business of her own. There had been so much organisation needed in making this event look effortless. Daisy made sure everything she did was perfect, knowing it would enhance her future reputation.

'Ladies and gentlemen.' Mary Jane's brother raised his voice over the general buzz of conversation and the room descended into silent expectation. 'First of all, may I thank you all for coming to celebrate this happy occasion. And may I say how beautiful Mary Jane looks today.'

'She looks beautiful every day,' Cal piped up, encouraging a ripple of laughter from the guests.

Not a strictly religious man, Henry Beamer knew these gatherings were good for commerce. He was sitting next to Cal and had no interest in the speech, wanting to talk business.

'As I was saying,' he said, as he polished off his Scotch whisky in one gulp and gestured to Ina King for a refill.

'Maybe talk of business can wait until after the speech,' Cal said with a smile.

Ina, brought in to help with the catering, had been listening to the speech and let out an audible tut at being summoned, showing her annoyance as she uncrossed her arms, swiping a bottle of King George IV 'Top Notch' Scotch whisky from the sideboard, to refill his glass.

'As if I've got nothing better to do,' Ina whispered as she passed Daisy's chair, 'and I've still got the champagne flutes to fill.' Another tut indicated her displeasure as she poured Henry's drink.

'So, as you all know,' Henry said to Cal, after imbibing another glass of the golden nectar, 'holding the views I do, it is against my principles to hobnob, to any great extent, with the bourgeoisie.'

'The bore-zhwa-what?' asked Ina and Daisy could not contain a low chuckle.

'It means the common people,' Daisy whispered, knowing the comment had incensed Ina when she plonked the flute on the table with a thud.

'I hope he's not talking about us,' Molly said to Daisy.

'He should be on the music hall, Mam.' Daisy decided she wasn't fond of the music hall, not after last time when she was unceremoniously stood-up.

'You never did tell us about your night out, our Daisy?' Molly looked puzzled. Daisy had been acting very strange lately.

'No, Mam.' Daisy raised her eyes to the high ceiling, and she wasn't going to either.

'Common people?' Ina's outrage was almost palpable. 'Bloody cheek, I'll give him common people when I spit in his drink.'

'Ina,' Daisy gasped, momentarily forgetting the disastrous date that still made her cringe to this day, 'you will do no such thing.' Henry knew all the right people and could be a valuable conduit for a girl who intended to have her own catering company one day.

'Of course not, madam, it was just a little joke,' Ina answered facetiously, which did nothing to put Daisy's mind at rest. She wanted this party to be perfect.

'I cannot help but feel that today, what with this being a christening and all,' Henry told Cal, 'that we should all be mindful and therefore—'

'Punch? Mister Beamer,' Mary Jane interrupted sweetly while he was in mid-flow.

'Don't tempt me,' said Ina under her breath. 'What an overblown gasbag,' she shook her head as she filled Daisy's glass, 'using a lot of words to say nothing at all.'

'Let's hear the speech.' One of the guests was not in the least bit interested in what Beamer had to say.

'Hear, hear,' said Molly, who had no time for pomposity at the best of times and did little to lower her voice when she said, 'We're in no mood to listen to some toffee-nosed pipsqueak spouting rubbish, when we should be listening to Mary Jane's brother – and then we can get on with our pudding.'

'Well said,' Elodie whispered, feeling sorry for Mary Jane and Cal who had put on a wonderful spread, which the guests were eager to continue.

'Thank you, Henry,' said Daisy in her sweetest voice, 'I think Cal, who actually paid for this wonderful spread, would now like to say a few words before we commence eating.' She motioned for her neighbour to stand up and get on with the speeches before a riot broke out.

'I bet you can't wait to host a bash like this,' said the young man sitting beside her, and Daisy's brow furrowed into a deep 'V'. She could not think of anything more disagreeable. All her life she had run around after her brothers and sister, helping Mam out when she needed a bit of time to herself.

'Only if I get paid a decent rate for it,' she said, her retort abrupt.

'I thought a pretty girl like you would jump at the chance of marriage and babies.'

'Well, you thought wrong. Mam needs me,' Daisy answered. 'I couldn't just up and leave her, not when she has three children to bring up alone, and certainly not after everything she had sacrificed for us.'

'You've done a very good job on this spread.' The young man knew he had said the wrong thing and decided to quickly change the subject. 'A very professional job if I may say so.'

'Oh, thank you,' Daisy answered, smiling, feeling her body relax. She had been quick to judge. 'I do want to start my own catering company, but I am biding my time. Mary Jane has been particularly good to me, and I do not want to leave her in the lurch.'

'I'm Jasper,' he said, his fair hair flopping onto his forehead as he held out his hand. Daisy shook his hand respectfully, 'I'm Henry Beamer's nephew.'

Ina reluctantly dragged herself away from eavesdropping the conversation when there was a knock at the front door, and she opened it to a young man with his camera and his tripod, followed by another young man, who sent a deep shade of pink shooting to the roots of Daisy's shingled bob.

'Hello, Dais, fancy seeing you here!' Max beamed as he took a notebook out of his top pocket. 'What a lovely spread, did you do this?'

Daisy gave him an incredulous look, surprise etched on her face, and she was momentarily robbed of words, knowing exactly what she would like to say to this gadabout, but she could hardly say it in polite company, nor did she want to let him know his vanishing act had caused her to lose her self-confidence for ages afterwards. 'I am also a godmother,' said Daisy, not sure what Max was writing on that pad.

'In my new position of reporter on the *Daily Herald*,' he looked proud of the fact, 'I don't always get assigned the best jobs, like murders and scandal.'

'I'm not sure I would want to read that kind of thing.' Daisy wrinkled her slim freckled nose.

'Most of the jobs I get are boring, weddings, christenings, birthday parties, that kind of thing, but I live in hope of a nice juicy murder.'

'Oh, really,' Daisy was not impressed. 'Well, don't let me keep you.'

'Look, Dais,' he said, making his way to her seat and crouching down beside her chair, sitting on the back of his two-toned leather brogues. 'I'm so sorry about that night at the music hall, and not coming into the shop to explain...'

'Really, I hadn't noticed.' Daisy gave an exaggerated sigh to show his explanation had not impressed her.

'I was sent on a hush-hush assignment and even though I asked...'

'You're asking for a fourpenny one, if you ask me.' Daisy could tell when she was being soft-soaped.

'Look, Daisy, can we talk a bit later when I've got everything I need.'

'I think you already have everything you need,' Daisy answered, 'so when you're ready to leave, I will personally show you the door.' What she wasn't prepared for was his usual easy laugh and twinkling eyes as he leaned forward, unable to contain his amusement.

'I can see I've put my size elevens in it,' he said apologetically, without actually apologising.

'That's the first thing we can agree on.' *Size elevens*, she thought holding back a smile, *get you and the price of fish.*

'We'll talk later,' Max said, 'much as I have to drag myself away from your sparkling conversation, I must do what I'm being paid for.' He moved from her chair and, nipping along the table, invited guests to share their good wishes, while putting everybody at their ease with a witty quip or two.

Daisy, feeling a rush of heat to her cheeks, flicked her hand as if swatting a fly.

'Max is one of the good guys,' said the photographer, 'he's going to make a first-class news reporter.'

'He's certainly out to impress,' Daisy answered, hardly able to keep her eyes from him. Then when she realised her mother was watching her, she stiffened, her words clipped, 'Not that I've noticed.'

'I think that reporter's taken with you, Dais.' Her brother, Davey, gave a gentle laugh when she shrugged off his comment, telling him not to be so daft, and felt an unusually warm glow that seemed to travel right through her veins. Davey gently shook his head, amused, he could always tell when his competent older sister was feeling a little flustered.

There was another knock at the front door and Ina gave a long, martyred sigh. 'It's like Lime Street Station in here today,' she said. She returned a moment later and whispered something to Ellie, who rose from her seat, excused herself and went out to the hall.

'Aiden!' Elodie felt her heartbeat quicken at the mere sight of him.

'I'm sorry to interrupt your party, Ellie, but there is something I must tell you.' Aiden removed his cap, and circled it through her hands, a sure sign he was nervous about what he was about to say.

'What is it, what's happened?' Elodie felt her heart sink. Aiden looked so serious, looking down at the floor, speaking into the air without making eye contact.

'Will has just been to see me,' said Aiden, his handsome face expressionless, his laughing eyes solemn. 'I'm sorry to interrupt the party but there's something I must tell you. It's about Lord Caraway.'

'What about him...?' Elodie could feel the rising panic that had once been part of her daily life engulf her once more.

'Will told me...' Aiden stalled for a moment. 'Look is there somewhere quiet where we can talk? There is something you need to hear.'

'We can go next door. Everybody is here so we won't be interrupted.'

When they were in the parlour of Molly's house, Aiden put his arms around Elodie.

'Will has just dropped Silas off at The Adelphi Hotel. He is hearing a murder case at Saint George's Hall,' Aiden said and felt every muscle in her body tighten, the colour draining from her face.

'No!' Elodie said a moment later, trying to stifle a terrified scream slicing through the fog in her brain. She would have to leave Liverpool. 'I can't stay here.' She shrank from him, her mind in turmoil knowing she did not have long to get herself and Melissa organised and out of Beamer Street.

'You can't leave now,' Aiden said, 'you've worked hard getting the shop ready to open, and what about Melissa, her friends, her schooling?'

'We can start again somewhere else,' Elodie cried. 'At least I will know we are safe.'

'And what will happen if he should go to that place? Will you keep on running?'

'I can't let him get to Melissa,' Elodie cried, 'he has never cared for her... She is my life.'

'There is something else.' Aiden drew her to the sofa, knowing she was going to have to sit down to hear what he had to say next. The time had come when Aiden knew Elodie needed to know the truth about her mother and how she died.

He had left Oakland Hall to make sure Silas Caraway never got within touching distance of Elodie or Melissa. For as God was his judge, Aiden vowed he would see the man dead before letting him touch one hair on either of their heads.

'That's not all,' said Aiden, and, as tactfully as he could, he told her everything that Will had told him, about the day he collected the medicines and watched Lord Caraway hang her mother's limp, dead body from the rafters. 'He made your mother's death look like suicide.'

'No!' Elodie gasped and felt her stomach lurch. She was going to be sick. This was too much. Aiden understood the dark pleading expression in Elodie's eyes, and he put his arms around her, holding her close, letting the raw, unresolved grief pour from her once more. 'I will ask Molly to keep a close eye on Melissa, my darling. I won't let anything happen to you or our daughter.'

'But why didn't Will say something?'

'He is terrified of Silas,' Aiden said, 'where else is he going to find a job and a house? He's half blind, with no prospects. His family depend on him for the roof over their head, and the food on their plate...'

'Everything is so much clearer now,' said Elodie, remembering how Silas lured her into marriage when she was still grieving, unable to think straight. Elodie believed she had lost her mother, as well as her lifelong best friend, Aiden, her only love. 'He made me believe I would have nothing if I didn't marry him.' Elodie's body rocked under the power of her sobs. 'I had no choice.'

'Shh, my darling.' Aiden was worried she was going to lose herself to hysteria. 'I am here, I will take care of you now.'

* * *

Ina King couldn't resist eavesdropping on their conversation when she went to find Elodie to tell her the photographer was looking for her. She noticed the pair slip out and go into the empty house next door. *So, Elodie Kirrin isn't as saintly as she makes out to be.* Ina strained to listen at the closed parlour door. *I knew there was something about her. I just couldn't put my finger on what it was. But now I know.*

'Is everything all right, Ina?' Mary Jane asked, she too had come to look for Elodie, as the photographer was ready to take pictures of the godparents, when she found Ina coming back through Molly's front door.

'I thought I heard someone crying.' Flustered, Ina scuttled past Mary Jane to the kitchen, and she wondered what the old crone had been up to.

Aiden, on Molly's step now, had his arms around Elodie, and Mary Jane knew there must be something wrong.

'He's here,' Elodie cried, when she saw Mary Jane. 'Silas is here in Liverpool, he is hearing a murder trial at Saint George's Hall.' Elodie's voice grew shrill with each word. 'He knows Melissa isn't his child, and worse still, he killed my mother!'

'Good Lord!' Mary Jane's hands flew to her face.

'Mary Jane knows everything,' Elodie told Aiden, and he nodded.

'Ina does too,' Mary Jane said solemnly, 'she was listening at the door.'

'No!' Elodie exclaimed and Mary Jane gently put her hand on her shoulder.

'Leave Ina to me, I'll sort her out, she won't be saying anything to anybody,' Mary Jane promised. 'Aiden is close by in the flat over the apothecary, we won't let that evil man anywhere near you or Melissa.

'You two go into Molly's house and talk, you can't talk here there are too many earwigs around,' Mary Jane said. 'I'll go and have a word with Ina.'

24

Max sat in the straight-backed chair next to Daisy after taking details of guests who wanted to impart their good wishes onto the children.

'That's a lovely dress,' Max said, admiring the way Daisy filled the long-sleeved pale blue silk dress, complemented by a square neckline, dropped waist and long glass beads that rested on her lap. 'That colour suits your complexion.'

'Pasty-faced, you mean,' said Daisy, not sure if he was making fun of her, again, 'and seeing as it's February, we haven't had much sunshine lately.' Daisy didn't want to talk to him, but she did want to know why he'd stood her up after buying her an ice cream six weeks ago! 'If you hadn't noticed, the snow is two feet deep in some parts.'

'I know, I was out reporting on it this morning and nearly lost a couple of fingers with frostbite.' He looked at her for a moment before saying in a lowered voice, so nobody else could hear, 'I was going to say you have wonderful skin.'

'It covers me all over.' Daisy felt the heat shoot to the roots of her hair before noticing his earlobes turn bright red. 'Now go away, I don't want to talk to you!'

The words fell over themselves in the rush to be out of her mouth. She didn't want him to think she was one of those fast girls who smoked and went to dance halls. Far from it.

'You really must stop rejecting compliments, Daisy,' said Max while, her head bowed, Daisy looked up through her glossy, perfectly straight fringe and silently dared him to ask her what was wrong.

'So, what else do you like doing, Dais?' Max asked unperturbed.

'I used to like going to the theatre, as it happens,' Daisy did not even try to keep the cynical tone from her voice, 'not that I go very often. There was one chap who took me last time, he even bought me an ice cream, then he legged it, leaving me alone, never to be seen again until today.'

'I need to explain about that, Dais.' Max did look sheepish, but Daisy was staring straight ahead at the cameraman setting up the shot. 'You know those tickets I got?' She waited. 'Well, I should have taken my editor's niece to the show, but she couldn't go...'

'Oh, so now you tell me I was second choice,' Daisy did not look at him, 'I have never felt so insulted.'

'But, Dais, her uncle was there and...'

'I don't know what people thought when they saw me sitting there.' Daisy was getting into her stride now. 'On my own, left there like a cold cup of tea, stood up, by meself!'

'Say cheese, everybody!' the photographer called, and everybody bunched up to have their picture taken before the flash of his camera exploded.

'I was going to come and see you, Dais, honestly, I was,' Max hastened to explain. His practised smile was replaced by a worried frown, but Daisy was not in the mood to listen any more.

'I have to go and make sure everything is going well in the kitchen,' she said, rising from the chair.

'But, Dais, you've got to hear me out. I really didn't want to leave you on your own like that. I got sidetracked by Cecily's uncle and then...'

'Cecily? Is that who I was stood up for?'

'Well, then the following day I got mumps, it was awful, I looked like a squirrel.'

'Mumps? Pull the other one, Max, it plays "The Black Bottom".' He was taking her for a fool, and she wouldn't stand for it.

'So, you like dancing!' Max knew he was losing her attention, but he must explain.

'Yes, I like dancing, but I am very particular about who I go to the dance hall with.'

Max looked crestfallen and she felt a glimmer of guilt, but she wasn't going to let him see she was relenting to his charm. 'I'd love to take you to a dance,' Max pushed on.

'Why? So, you can leave me on the dance floor like a...'

'Cold cup of tea,' they both said in unison and Daisy couldn't help but smile.

'Did you really have mumps?'

'Oh Dais, like you wouldn't believe, it's not something I can discuss in polite company, but they hurt something rotten.' He looked so crestfallen she couldn't help but believe him. 'I'm sorry,' Max said. 'Your mam tells me you made that dress yourself, the colour really suits your lovely skin,' he said, then quickly changed the subject, 'your eyes! I meant your eyes.'

Daisy's eyes widened.

'If I said I like your hair, would you bite my head off?' He was determined to make an impression, and Daisy laughed, suddenly relaxing. Her feelings towards him thawed.

'It's a good thing I don't hold a grudge,' Daisy said, 'I'm too busy concentrating on my career to think about scatterbrained boys who have a memory like a sieve and forget they have taken a girl to the music hall.'

'Your career?' Max raised his eyebrows. 'And what about husband and children...?'

Daisy shook her head and enlightened him to the fact she was not even thinking of marriage, nor was she looking for a husband. She was only eighteen years of age and had no time for that sort of thing.

Daisy looked towards her mother who was in deep conversation with Percy, who made the dough and pastry at the back of Mary Jane's bakery. It being Sunday, he too had the day off from working and seemed to be enjoying the party enormously.

'Do you like being a reporter?' Daisy asked, imagining what it must be like to tramp the streets in all weathers looking for something to write about.

'I live in hope of finding the next big story,' said Max, 'something with a bit of action and drama that I can get stuck into.'

'I'm going to have my own business one day,' Daisy said dreamily, 'and live in a big house by the sea.' It might take years to happen, but she could dream.

'I like the sound of that, Dais,' said Max, impressed with her vision, 'you can do anything you put your mind to, I'm sure.'

'Girls like me don't earn enough for seaside houses, but the thought keeps me going when I'm so tired I could sleep on a clothes line and motivates me to want to do better.' Although she could never leave Mam on her own.

'You have such a down-to-earth view on life.' Max smiled and as he did, his eyes danced. 'It is so refreshing, especially after some of the film stars I am used to dealing with.'

'I thought you got all the boring jobs?' Daisy shot him a cautious glance that did nothing to hide the twinkle in her eyes.

'Sometimes I get other jobs too.' Max smiled, sure he had met the girl with whom he wanted to spend the rest of his life, one day.

'In your capacity as a junior reporter, do you get to meet a lot of film stars?'

'I much prefer interviewing a local lass who can make a mouth-watering cloud of a Victoria sponge cake.'

'So that's the way to a man's heart, is it?' Daisy said and suddenly felt the heat of a blush on her cheeks as she drew in a sharp gasp. She could not believe she had just said such an audacious thing.

'I really did enjoy taking you to the theatre, Dais,' Max sounded very contrite, 'but when I saw my editor, I thought my number was up, that he would tell his niece I was out with another girl – so I left the theatre and ran head first into a charabanc full of factory workers who gave me what for when the driver pulled to a sudden halt, and they all fell off their wooden seats.'

Daisy's lips puckered as she tried so hard not to laugh. This bloke was as funny as Charlie Chaplin. Run over by a charabanc, indeed.

'Mam's having a fine old time.' Daisy wanted to change the subject before she doubled up with laughter.

'Do you like working around here for Mary Jane?' Max asked.

'I've never worked anywhere better,' she answered, 'but I would like to own my own catering company, one day. You?'

'I intend to travel the world, report on the big stories, enjoy different cultures before I settle down,' Max answered, and Daisy tried to ignore the sudden dip in her heartbeat.

'Mam often says she has her children for life, because none of us are in any hurry to leave home and find a place of our own. But she loves having her family about her.'

'Mister Casey is enjoying himself too, I noticed,' Max said, looking along the table.

'Have you finished with that?' Ina King interrupted, glaring at Daisy's empty plate like it had just insulted her. 'I'm ready to serve the sherry trifle.'

Daisy nodded and smiled, allowing Ina to take the plate.

'She's a bit fierce,' said Max, watching Ina, busily whipping plates from the table, even before a guest had finished eating. 'I wouldn't leave her five-bob short in her wages.'

'Without a second glance, she could make cheese out of fresh milk, if she had a mind,' Daisy said, and Max threw his head back and laughed again. He did that a lot, she noticed.

'That's not for me to say,' Max answered, loving Daisy's quick repartee. When his laughter subsided, he informed Daisy, 'I did hear her telling your mother her corns were giving her gyp, as she'd been on her feet all day.'

Daisy refrained from telling him Ina was being well paid for her aching feet. 'I'm sure, as gossip is to my mother,' Daisy explained, 'complaining is as normal as breathing to Ina. She also likes lots of praise for her efforts, and woe betide anybody who doesn't comply.'

'That was a lovely salad,' Max said quickly, heeding Daisy's words, when his half-filled plate was removed without formality, 'very tasty.'

'I dread to think how much you would have left, if you didn't like it,' said Ina in her broad Irish accent, sweeping the plate onto her tray with a disapproving clatter.

'You've done Mary Jane proud,' Daisy tried to appease Ina.

'Everybody looks happy,' Max agreed, enjoying the gathering enormously, it made a nice change from some of the engagements he was accustomed to reporting.

'Mam's like a cat who got the cream.' Daisy smiled, enjoying the day even more now. 'She's good at overseeing things. When Mary Jane said she was getting Laurence christened, Mam was thrilled, immediately volunteering me, "leave it to our Daisy," she said, "she'll sort it out."'

'Well, you've done a first-class job,' Max complimented her.

'Mary Jane deserves to be happy.' As did her mother, who was always available for a bit of advice.

Daisy looked to where her mam was still talking to Percy, and she felt a little glow of warmth. It was nice that her mam was enjoying a bit of male attention, she wasn't that old. Everybody was having a good time and that was good enough for her.

As the afternoon wore on, and the table was cleared away, one of the guests took his seat at the piano, and as the drink flowed, the singing began in earnest.

Bridie, being as helpful as possible since she had ruined the hair of a few small guests, was keeping herself busy, fixing Hollie's huge satin bow onto the side of her hair. Mary Jane, looked proudly on while Cal was still in conversation with Henry Beamer.

'I'm sure your son will follow in your footsteps, too?' said Henry Beamer, slugging back the last of his drink and holding up his glass for a refill.

Cal silently nodded when Ina raised a questioning eyebrow.

'That Beamer fella's got hollow legs, if you ask me,' Ina said to Daisy, 'he must have for the amount of booze he's putting away.'

Daisy looked over to Beamer whose voice was getting louder with every sup.

'Your daughter will marry and give you lots of grandchildren, I'm sure,' Henry said, and his face fell when Cal replied.

'Mrs Everdine and I hope she will go to university, but the choice is hers alone,' said Cal.

'Don't you think university is wasted on girls?' Henry asked, his look of disapproval clearly etched across his inebriated face.

'Obviously,' said Max, who was watching with interest, 'the

jumped-up windbag clearly hasn't understood the rules of good manners and should keep his private thoughts to himself.'

'She will only waste a good education when she marries, to take care of her husband?' Henry continued.

'What makes you think that?' Cal's eyebrows shot to the roots of his hair. 'Things have changed since the war ended. Women have proved they are just as capable as men, even more so.'

However, Henry was having none of Cal's silly modern ideals, and he made no effort to hide the fact. 'A woman's place is in the home, looking after her family, she has no business showing him up by going out to work.' Beamer shared the nugget of misinformation with a pompous swagger, obviously expecting Cal to agree with him.

'Some women can manage more than one thing at a time,' a flash of annoyance darted from Daisy's lips – how dare he? 'Especially when she has a supportive family around her.' Suddenly she put her fingertips to her lips. She had said too much. This man was a guest of Cal and Mary Jane's, she had no right to antagonise him with her own views.

'I hear you,' said Henry as if pacifying a petulant child, enraging Daisy even further. 'But I would never allow any wife of mine to go out working.'

'I'd keep my voice down if I were you,' Cal said, only half-joking, 'if my wife heard such a ridiculous suggestion, she would frogmarch you from the room and give you a good talking-to.'

'I am so sorry,' Daisy mouthed the words across the table and Cal batted the apology away.

'My neighbour, Daisy, is a very modern young woman who shares my wife's ambition. They are very forward-thinking,' Cal said, giving Daisy a reassuring smile. 'Times have changed so much since the war. Women have discovered they do not need a husband to rely on for their very existence, and it would serve men well to heed those changes, because I doubt they are going to go away.'

'I don't think those kind of views will ever catch on,' said Henry. 'Men won't stand for it.'

If Henry Beamer couldn't see that some women had been earning their own money since before the war, a time when they discovered they were just as good as men when it came to keeping the country going while the men were overseas, defending this country, then, Cal decided, it was not his place to enlighten him.

He loved the way women had a say in how this country was run, and by whom. Women now voted and owned their own property, all without a man's permission. Such a blessing, he thought, remembering how his poor mother had been under her husband's thumb for so long. He wished she had still been here to meet his wonderful wife and family and share her absolute wisdom, as she had quietly done when he was a boy.

25

'That was a smashing christening,' said Elodie as the last customer left the shop the following day. She had promised Aiden one of Daisy's delicious meat and potato pies for his dinner and had just called in to collect it, hot from the oven.

'Aye,' said Daisy wrapping the pie in paper, 'Mam had a fine old time. She likes nothing better than a good old knees-up.' She looked up, about to remove the empty wicker basket from its usual place near the doorway, knowing the rush of customers had made short work of the surplus bread, freshly baked yesterday, and sold at a knock-down price today.

'That young reporter, Max.' Elodie noted a glint in Daisy's eyes. Passing the time of day with Daisy took her mind off yesterday's bad news. 'He certainly has his eye on you.'

'He most certainly does not,' Daisy said, feeling the creeping heat rise to her cheeks, 'and if he has got his eye on me, he shouldn't. Max is married to his job. Journalists don't stay in one place, he told me he is chasing the next big story, and I want to run my own catering company.' Daisy was angry for allowing her imagination to run away with itself. Fancy having her head turned by Max. She ought to be ashamed of herself.

'Here's our favourite pie maker,' Elodie whispered, giving Percy an innocent, closed-lip smile when he brought a new batch of bread into the shop and when he went to the back, Daisy busied herself taking Elodie's money and putting it in the till.

'Just don't mention Mam in front of Percy. I can't see her taking up with him even though he's a nice bloke.' Daisy knew her mother loved her father too much to take up with Percy. 'He's just friendly that's all.'

'It won't be long before you're all off her hands and living your own life.'

'I'll stay home and be an old maid, and look after Mam,' Daisy laughed.

'I think your mam's well able to look after herself,' Mary Jane said coming into the shop. 'Next thing you know she'll want you all off her hands.'

'She was a young wife when Dad was killed, but she seems content enough looking after her family.' Daisy had no idea what her mother thought of romance, never having mentioned such fanciful thoughts, she never thought to ask her.

'I suppose she's got enough on her plate looking after you lot,' Elodie laughed, thinking it would be lovely to see Molly getting a bit of male attention too.

'I want to make a go of the black-tie events.'

'Well, you are certainly good at them, I could see that from the very first day,' Mary Jane said. 'You're a natural.'

When Mary Jane secured these premises in 1922, Daisy became her first employee and had helped her run the business ever since. Now they were branching out, catering for black-tie dinners hosted by local dignitaries, which were becoming extremely popular under Daisy's watchful eye. And she took to it like she was born to run a company. Reminding Mary Jane of the girl she once was before becoming a mother to three young children, whom she loved with all her heart.

'I don't know what I'd do without you,' Mary Jane quipped, and Daisy rolled her eyes.

'Hush your flannel, Mary Jane, you sound like me mam.'

'One of these fine days you will take praise with quiet grace,' said Mary Jane, 'instead of pushing it away with full force.'

'I don't see myself as anything special,' Daisy, pragmatic as usual, said quietly.

The christening had showed her there was an optimistic change in the air. Women were allowed to be independent. But would she have the courage to be totally independent? she wondered. Did she want to be?

26

'It was all my fault,' Elodie told Molly. 'The death certificate said: "Death by suicide while the balance of her mind was disturbed." It allowed Ma to be buried, but she could not be buried in consecrated ground.' Elodie tried to keep the tremble from her voice, but it was impossible. 'But, Molly, her mind was not disturbed when I left her at the cottage that morning. I know how she died now, but I still don't know why.'

Elodie told Molly the whole story. About Lady Felicia visiting her mam and dying. Then, a year later, finding her mother hanging from the rafters of their home. She told Molly about Aiden going off to war and Silas Caraway taking her in when the cottage burned down, then about Aiden, reported missing, believed dead. 'I was so stricken with grief; I think I might have lost my mind... I must have done. Because why else would I marry such a cruel and vicious man?'

'You poor lass,' said Molly, putting her motherly arms around Ellie.

'Aiden is Melissa's father,' Elodie said, not looking at Molly who was sure to be disgusted in her.

'I thought as much.' Molly handed Elodie the cup and saucer that had been sitting on the tray. 'Drink this before it goes cold.'

'You're not shocked?' Elodie said.

'What gave you that idea, lass?' Molly asked. 'We look after our own around here, we don't throw them onto the street when there's a sniff of trouble. A blind man could see how much you and Aiden love each other.' Molly rolled her eyes to the ceiling as she sat in the straight-backed chair at her kitchen table. 'Something'll work itself out, you mark my words.' Choosing her words carefully, she said, 'I can only imagine what you must have been feeling about your mam's death. I felt I had been slammed in the stomach with a tree trunk when my Bert were killed. I couldn't believe this huge, momentous thing had happened to me, and I had no idea how I was going to cope with four young children, our Bridie only a nipper.' Lightly touching Ellie's arm, she felt the younger woman flinch, and knew for certain she had not had it easy, no matter what her posh clothes said.

'I felt I was abandoned by the one person I trusted with all my heart and soul when Mam died.' Elodie was glad she had found the courage and the strength to finally talk about her mother's ordeal. The news had been a long time coming. 'Mam's death didn't make sense to me,' Elodie had tears in her eyes, 'and it still doesn't. But Aiden has been there for me through everything, keeping me strong, if it hadn't been for him...'

'He's a good man,' Molly's eyes softened, 'always has been, even from a young lad, thoughtful, caring, one of the best, he will protect you from the evil husband of yours.'

'You don't know what Silas is capable of,' Elodie told her. 'If he finds me, the first thing he will do is have Melissa taken away from me, he will say I am an unfit mother, he can do those kinds of things.'

'I don't care how powerful he is,' Molly answered, 'he won't get Melissa.'

'I'm glad I told you.' Elodie felt an enormous sense of relief.

'A trouble shared is worth two in the bush.' Molly gave Elodie a knowing smile. 'You just continue doing what you set out to do and you'll be fine here in Beamer Street. We'll look after you.'

27

'Do you know anything about...' Ina King said the day after the apothecary opened, she looked down to her abdomen and mouthed the words, 'down there?' This was the first time Ina had stepped inside the apothecary, after telling every woman she met that she would never set foot in the place. However, for a long time she had been feeling out of sorts.

'In what way?' Elodie asked, knowing most women did not discuss matters of a delicate nature at the front of the apothecary, and certainly not in front of their children. She raised an eyebrow and nodded to the two children who accompanied their mother. 'Maybe you would like to discuss your worries in private?' Elodie realised she must set aside a room at the back of the apothecary for private consultations.

'Outside and play,' Ina ordered her children, pushing them towards the apothecary door, 'this is not for your ears.' When she came back to the counter, she asked if Elodie had anything for *women's troubles.*

'What kind of troubles?' Elodie was not certain what Ina was referring to, but she had a good idea. Although she could not give out any cure until she knew what she was dealing with.

'It's been nearly two years since my last *visitor*.' The last word was mouthed, not spoken, and Elodie nodded, she had discreetly dealt with many woman's ailments, before, during and after the childbearing days.

'Don't worry, Ina, you can discuss anything at all with me, it will go no further. I do not discuss anything I hear in here; discretion is of the utmost importance.'

'If you please.' Ina looked anywhere except at Elodie, who could tell the other woman was embarrassed talking about such matters.

'I strongly suspect you are now past the age of childbearing if it has been so long since your last menstrual period.' Elodie noticed Ina's colour turn a deep shade of pink and realised, for as brash as Ina most certainly was, there was still an innocence about her that to some would be hard to believe.

Ina nodded but said nothing.

'You can tell me, and I can help,' Elodie said in that calm, gentle way she had about her.

'It's during the night, I get so hot, and the bedclothes are soaked.' Ina was twisting the thin gold band on her the third finger of her left hand. 'My Paddy said it's like sleeping next to the oven with the door open. I got so angry I threw the frying pan at him!'

Elodie pressed her lips between her teeth and nodded, she expected Ina would be the last person to come and ask her advice, and she must show as much tact as possible. No matter what Ina had come into the shop for, she was bound to give a blow-by-blow account of the service she received to everybody she met. Elodie had no doubt about that.

For a long time, she patiently listened to Ina's complaints, some physical, and some just a good moan about life in general, but it gave her a good idea of what Ina was going through and, if truth be told, Elodie felt privileged that Ina had come to ask for the help she needed.

'I will make you up a herbal tonic, which will help you,' Elodie said eventually, eyeing up her shelves for the right herbs, explaining that when a woman goes through the menopause her body loses some vital benefits that the tonic would help restore. 'You can either come back in half an hour for the tonic, or you can wait.'

'I'll send my girl back for it, later,' said Ina, not wanting to be seen inside the apothecary.

Outside, she immediately bumped into Molly of all people.

'You not well then, Ina?' Molly asked and Ina looked sheepish.

'I only went in for a tonic, and she had me there all day.' Ina looked most put out. 'She asks more questions than a doctor. I couldn't understand a word she said, but it sounds serious.' Ina liked to add a bit of drama. 'I told her I'd send my girl in for the jollop later.'

Later, when she got in after closing the apothecary, Molly hurried into the hallway before Elodie had even taken off her coat.

'Is it true?' Molly asked, her face grey with worry. 'Is Ina very sick?'

'Ina?' Elodie's eyebrows pleated in confusion. 'Not that I know of, why, have you heard something?' She watched as Molly let out an exaggerated sigh of relief.

'Trust Ina to make a mountain out of an ant hill,' said Molly, 'she had me worried she was on her last legs, the way she told it.'

'I can't tell you what Ina said to me in confidence, no matter what she told you,' Elodie said with the tact and diplomacy her mother had taught her, 'but I can tell you one of my tonics will soon sort her out.'

* * *

Elodie smiled the following day as she looked out of the apothecary window. She was pleased with the way the business was going. At first, people were curious and came in only to ask all sorts of questions, which she was more than glad to answer, it was as if they were testing her to make sure she knew her stuff.

They wanted to know what the best cure was for croup, for a bad chest, for lumbago, for any amount of everyday complaints that might keep them from doing a day's work. In this economic climate, nothing was left to chance and Elodie did a roaring trade in cough linctus, made from her own herbal recipe, and also rubbing liniment that cut through the thick mucus building up on the chest of the old and inform. Her nit lotion was a best-seller and so too her solution to get rid of bedbugs. Children came in with a copper to buy her barley sugar and liquorice root that looked like a dried-up twig that they called *stickylice* instead of liquorice and chewed on it all day long.

Aiden had built the greenhouses and tended her seedlings, he then re-potted them in the old stable potting shed, and as the days grew warmer, Elodie expected trade to diminish, but it never did. If anything, the apothecary grew even more busy as the confidence in her ability, from people round about, grew stronger.

Elodie even offered a very discreet advice service to harassed mothers who had too many mouths to feed and not enough money, on how they could prevent 'falling' pregnant. Something, which the church and the medical doctors were not prepared to discuss in any detail whatsoever – and certainly not to a woman.

'It's a disgrace that men with money can consult their physicians on the best way to prevent their wives conceiving,' said Elodie one evening when she, Molly, and Mary Jane, were sitting on their front step taking a breather from a scorching bout of summer heat, 'and yet, those who need the help most, women with no money and even less chance of bettering themselves, pop out babies until they are worn out by it all.'

'It's been the same since Eve was a girl,' said Molly, 'and I can't see a change coming in my lifetime.'

'I went to a lecture given by Marie Stopes,' Elodie admitted, 'her ideas are forward thinking and, most importantly I think, she believes that having children should be a choice and not a given.'

'That's a huge statement,' Mary Jane gasped, 'I can't see mother church agreeing with you there.'

'I didn't say it was my view,' said Elodie, 'but I agree with her on some things. Why should women not enjoy the same pleasure as her husband, without fear of conception.'

'There's no such thing,' Molly gasped, 'women were put on this earth to have children, and men were put on this earth to provide.'

'Except, that is rarely the case,' said Elodie, 'working class women do not have the time nor the inclination to query such ideals, it would not cross their mind.'

'I can understand your reasoning,' said Molly who was always open to a lively and well-thought-out debate, even if she didn't fully grasp the belief.

'I can't see the parish priest agreeing with you,' Mary Jane gave a small chuckle, 'nor the local doctor come to that, but I understand your reasoning. The amount of women who try to feed five, ten, fifteen children on a docker's wage, and run themselves ragged in the effort to do so is a disgrace.'

'So that is why I offer a little advice, and in some very special cases, protection from multiplication.' Elodie stopped abruptly and the other two women understood why.

'I'm good at sums,' said Bridie, 'I got top marks in school for multiplication.' All three women looked to each other and could not resist laughing.

28

JUNE 1925

Silas Caraway's hostility charged the air so powerfully he could almost touch it. He had ordered Soames to bring the picture. Or to be exact, the black and white cutting from a newspaper.

'Will that be all, Your Lordship?'

'No,' Silas answered, giving no indication of what more he wanted from his long-time servant as Soames stood, straight-backed and rigid-shouldered near the door.

Snatching up the newspaper cutting, Silas glared at it with cold intensity.

'She looks happy and carefree, wouldn't you say, Soames?' The idea caused his lips to droop like there was a bad smell under his nose, and not even in his thoughts, did he use Elodie's name. 'Proudly holding the child – my child!'

'I would say she does look proud and happy, Your Lordship,' Soames answered stiffly, knowing the picture was the only thing salvageable from a tattered newspaper, into which Cook had been wrapping potato peelings, when he saw the picture of Lady Elodie.

'Which newspaper did this come from?'

'The *Liverpool Herald*, sir.'

The date was February 1925. Four months ago.

'Can you make out the address?' Silas asked his manservant who took the scrap of newspaper and studied the faded words.

'A place called Beamer Street, sir,' Soames said eventually, 'apparently, it is in the dockside area of the port.'

Lord Silas glared, red-faced, eyes fiery, his fists clenched, knowing he would soon enter enemy territory.

* * *

'I am going into town to pick up supplies for the apothecary,' Elodie said to Melissa as they ate breakfast at Molly's table. 'It's a lovely day, would you like to come with me?'

'Oh yes, Mam,' Melissa said, thrilled at the rare outing with her mother. 'Can we take Laurence too?'

'I don't see why not,' replied Elodie clearing the table of breakfast dishes and washing up while Melissa ran into Mary Jane's house next door to ask if they could take Laurence to town. Since Aiden had moved into the flat above the apothecary, Elodie had felt more settled, even protected from the nightmares of her past. Molly and her lively brood kept her and Melissa entertained, taking them into their hearts as if they were part of the family, and as the days grew warmer and longer she began to relax. Life felt better than it had in a long time.

Aiden was within shouting distance. Much closer than he had been at Oakland Hall. They could talk freely without fear of being overheard and reported to Silas Caraway, even if they could not be together as they would have wished, because no matter how they felt and however much they longed to be a proper family, Elodie was still a married woman.

The apothecary was a great success, and her herbal remedies were in popular demand, cheaper than a doctor's visit, most remedies did exactly what they were supposed to do, which gave Elodie the confidence she had been sadly lacking in the past years.

'Mary Jane said we can take baby Laurence,' Melissa was so excited, 'but she will keep baby Neave at home because she is teething.'

'I have prepared a herbal powder for Neave,' Elodie said and they went to Mary Jane's house to administer the teething powder.

'She's been so crotchety,' said Mary Jane, 'and she's usually so pleasant, poor lamb.'

'She'll be right as ninepence in no time,' Mary Jane said. 'We'll take this little fellow off your hands for a couple of hours, give you a little time to yourself.'

'Putting two dozen nappies on the line has always been a dream,' Mary Jane laughed, 'but at least I can get them done while the little one sleeps.'

'Well, I'll leave you to it.' Elodie pushed the pram onto the step and Mary Jane helped her down. In no time, Melissa was skipping alongside the perambulator while singing a nursery rhyme.

In the shadow of the Portland stone, neoclassical façade of the new Empire Theatre, which had opened in March of that year, Silas watched, as if in some kind of stupor of disbelief, the woman pushing a perambulator. He had walked from Lime Street Station and was on his way to Saint George's Hall, where he was the trial judge in a controversial murder case. Although, he did not have to hear the case until Tuesday, but he had decided to spend a few days in Liverpool to enjoy the galleries and museums – some of the finest in the land.

Waiting for a break in the flow of trams, trolley buses, horse and carts, and motorcars, he was about to step into the road when he caught sight of Elodie pushing a perambulator, the girl, Melissa, was running wild, holding her arms open wide and scaring the pigeons. *Unruly child, she will never amount to much.*

But she was no concern of his. His interest lay only in the baby. This city was the last place he expected his wife to be, but it did answer a question that had been concerning him... Elodie had denied him the opportunity to be the father he longed to be. To shape his son into the man he would become. Proud. Fierce. Unchallenged. But her days of calling the shots were over. He was having none of her nonsense! The boy was his. She had played her part. Now her time was over. He would show Elodie who she was dealing with. She would not deny him his son.

He would follow her. No matter how long it took. The boy would be in his rightful place at Oakland Hall, and Elodie could go to hell.

29

'Bridie Haywood, don't you go wandering off with the baby, d'you hear me?' Molly called to her young, adventurous daughter when Elodie returned from her outing with young Laurence and Melissa.

'Given the chance,' Molly told Elodie, 'our Bridie will be off to the park or down to the shore with Mary Jane's baby and would not give a single thought that a six-month-old baby would need to be fed or have nappies changed.'

'I'm only going to walk up and down the street, with Melissa, Ma,' called Bridie through the open door of her own home, which, along with everybody else's were opened first thing in the morning and stayed open till last thing at night.

'Mary Jane asked me and Betty to mind them, seeing as it's Whit weekend and the shop is mad busy with women buying bread, because the shop is closed on Monday, what with it being a bank holiday an' all.' Bridie never used one or two words when she could string out fifty.

'Well, you just make sure you don't both go wandering off and forgetting where you left those twins.' Molly knew it was not beyond the realms of possibility her harum-scarum daughter would go off to play, forgetting she had the babies with her.

'I won't be long, Mam,' called Bridie, 'I'm just going to the shops with Betty and we're taking Melissa too.' She and Betty were pals who went everywhere together when they had finished their chores.

Making sure the children's covers were straight and that they were settled, Melissa put her hand on the handle of the pram as they waited for the return of Bridie's friend who had gone to borrow her mother's headscarf.

When she got back to where Bridie and Melissa were waiting, the two girls each put a headscarf on their head. Bridie pushed the brake off the pram with her toe, and Betty did the same, parading down Beamer Street like a pair of miniature housewives, chatting away like their mothers did.

* * *

From the shadow of the narrow, redbrick-walled alleyway, he watched Melissa and the two young girls clearly, without any danger of being observed. They were jabbering. Words he could not hear. Each imitating their elders as they pushed perambulators up and down the street. He took a long swig of the dark liquid from a bottle marked 'Laudanum'. Letting the elixir work its magic. He knew which perambulator held his son, such a fine coach-built vehicle he would have chosen himself, had he been made aware of dear Elodie's delicate condition.

Whether it was because of his addictions or because his anger and poisonous bile had addled his brain, Silas Caraway took a disjointed look at his life. In his mind, Elodie was his loving wife who had, for some strange reason, took it upon herself to come to this dirty place and give birth to his son.

A low chuckle forced itself from his throat. He knew all along the doctors were wrong. Elodie would obviously have been concerned he would be angry, lest she burden him with another female child. But he never would have been angry with her, knowing, as he did now, she had given birth to the son he so desperately wanted.

That he had been diagnosed barren by a Harley Street specialist was not a matter for speculation. No physician was infallible, his diagnosis had merely been a misunderstanding. In his mind, Elodie was not the godmother in the newspaper picture, she was his mother and he, the boy, was his rightful heir.

Only the Lord God above could decide if man was infertile. He, Judge Silas, was all-powerful, untouchable. How would it be possible for him to be barren? The proof was lying in the carriage being pushed with abandon by that young maiden.

He must remedy the situation and claim his son. He would take him back to Oakland Hall where he belonged, and Elodie could accompany him or do as she pleased. He had all he ever wanted before him. He would hire a nanny immediately.

Watching the three young girls go inside the bakery shop, he seized his chance.

* * *

When Bridie came out of the bakery, she noticed the pram she had been pushing had gone. Looking up and down the street, there was no sign of the pram or the baby. Her mother was going to have a fit. To teach her a lesson, Mam had taken the baby home. Then she saw him. An old man in a posh velvet-collared overcoat, smoking a huge cigar and pushing the pram! The sight was so unusually startling, Bridie dropped the loaf she had just purchased and ran down the street as fast as her legs would carry her, while Betty ran ahead, and Melissa did something she was not allowed to do alone – she crossed the road to the apothecary.

'Hey, Mister! Here, you can't take that baby!' Bridie yelled at the top of her lungs.

Mam is going to scull-drag me for this. She'd only been in the shop for two minutes to tell Mary Jane they were going to take the babies to the park.

Not knowing what to do, she ran to her own house.

'Mam, come quick!' Bridie's high-pitched voice carried up her mother's hallway. 'Some man has stolen Mary Jane's baby!'

In a flash, Molly was hurrying from her kitchen, her heart racing, as the pastry for the steak and kidney pie she had just finished making was left on the floury table waiting to go into the oven.

She knew it was possible their Bridie might be making mischief; she had been on her best behaviour for too long and these things happened when she wasn't getting the attention she felt she deserved.

'If you are playing tricks on me, girl, I will tan your hide, good and proper,' said Molly, who had rarely felt the need to raise a hand to her children, unlike some.

As she followed her rapidly worried words, Molly could see by her daughter's colour-drained face, that Bridie was not having her on.

'Jesus, Mary and Joseph!' Molly gasped, making the sign of the cross over her ample bosom, and she began to run faster than she had done in years. Stopping only long enough to yell into the bakery, 'Mary Jane, you've got to come quick, someone's pinched your baby!'

Molly only had enough time to issue the warning before she hurried down the street towards the train station. But Mary Jane was faster, and Aiden, who had just come out of the wide gates at the side of the apothecary where he had been working, turned into Beamer Street, was faster still. Cal was coming around the corner when he was met by a rapidly expanding line of racing neighbours.

'Cal!' Mary Jane gasped. 'A man... he's got the baby!' Terrified tears streamed down her cheeks and Cal did not need to hear any more as he sprinted down the alleyway, quickly followed by the full complement of Beamer Street children and adults. They took off in all directions, but Lord Caraway had a head start, managing to reach the London and North Western railway station at Oriel Road, opposite the town hall.

Mary Jane's piercing scream ripped the evening air, as Silas Caraway stopped dead and the pram teetered on the edge of the platform.

Elodie, reaching the platform, stopped only when she caught sight of him.

'Silas, what are you doing?' Elodie's words were calm, in complete contrast to every rattling nerve in her body. 'This baby belongs to Mrs Everdine, and she's terribly upset, as you can imagine.'

'You are a liar. This child is mine.' Silas glared at her with the finality of his chosen profession. 'I saw you in town. Why would you be in charge of another woman's baby?'

'The child is not yours, Silas, you must give him back to his mother.' Elodie knew Mary Jane was behind her, being held back by Cal.

'Tell her, Mother.' Silas looked to the back of the station and appeared to be talking to someone, but there was nobody there. 'You must tell her I will look after my son from now on.' Silas was worried the shadowy figure of his dreaded mother would rebuke him for doing something wrong. 'You know the child is mine.'

'I know full well the child is not yours.' The words that

sounded so much like his mother, came from Elodie's lips. 'You must give him up.'

'Why would I?' Silas said. 'You have never been a mother to me, my father was the only person who ever showed me affection.' He took a bottle of laudanum from the pocket of his overcoat and took a long draught.

Quickly realising Lord Caraway would take no notice of a woman, Aiden stepped forward.

'If you may permit me to take the baby carriage, my lord.' Aiden's words were soothing to Lord Caraway's ears. 'I can help you.'

'Don't let the child out of your sight, Newman.' His gaze took in every member of the gathered crowd of onlookers and Silas added, 'I am not a fool.'

'The train will be here any minute, sir,' Aiden stepped forward, his voice a little more commanding now, 'if you allow me, I will assist you.' Aiden knew the next train to come through here was the five forty-five mail train, which was not stopping at this station. However, Lord Caraway was too far gone to realise. 'You can be home before the light fades.'

Lord Caraway's face softened at the thought.

'The child must go on the train with Nanny,' he said, hardly recognising Aiden as his former chauffeur. Then, turning to Elodie, he said, 'I am so sorry you have been put through so much heartache, but you must realise you were never anything more to me than a vessel to carry my son.'

He watched Mary Jane take the child from the baby carriage into her arms while Cal, who had hurried across the road to the police station, directed the police onto the platform.

When Silas caught sight of the uniformed enforcers, his face hardened into an ugly grimace, and he looked to Elodie.

'You tricked me!' He pushed the words through his gritted

teeth. 'How dare you?' He turned his attention to Mary Jane and said, 'Nanny here will escort me on the train to take my son back to Oakland Hall.'

'He is not your son,' Elodie cried. Then she went over to him and said in words that did not carry to the rest of the gathered onlookers, 'You, Silas, cannot have children of your own. The venereal disease you caught from a lady of the night made you barren. You were never going to have a son. You brought all of this on yourself.'

'You dare to spout my private business,' Silas growled. 'You were nothing before I took you in.'

'You did not take me in, Silas,' Elodie answered, desperately trying to hold on to dignified self-control, even though she knew what he had done to her mother, 'you left me no choice but to marry you. I would have been destitute. You engineered the whole sequence of events, timing your own craving to when I was most vulnerable, too weak to see sense.'

'Your mother thought she could trick me, too.' He moved forward slowly, menacingly, and the police constable inched towards him, truncheon at the ready should the need arise to defend Elodie. 'She told me I would never have her precious daughter... She goaded me until I could take no more...'

'You killed her!' Elodie knew the truth of the situation because of what Will had seen. Silas Caraway's mind was putrid, through laudanum and strong alcohol, and she felt he still wanted to inflict as much pain on her as he could. She had to know what had caused his hatred of a good woman. 'Why did you kill my mother?'

'She killed my Felicia,' he answered without emotion. 'So, I had no choice but to sentence her to hang by the neck. As is fitting for such a heinous crime.' There was no energy behind his eyes, no life, or even emotion, Elodie noticed, they were as dead as a cold fish. 'I made it look like suicide. Justice must be seen to be served.'

'I always knew my mother would never kill herself. You are an evil, evil man.' Elodie moved forward and Aiden edged towards her, unsure about what she had in mind for her next move. Then, quietly, calmly, her voice just above a whisper Elodie said, 'I hope you burn in hell for all eternity.'

'I do not doubt it,' Silas gave a brittle laugh, 'but I will never be judged in a court of law, nor will I hang by the neck until I am dead.'

In the blink of an eye, before anybody could change the outcome, Silas Caraway nodded, leaned back, and swiftly threw himself backwards from the platform under the passing five forty-five mail locomotive that dispatched him to the darkness from whence he came.

The women turned away quickly, their hands covering their faces, while the men and the curious children stared in horror and disbelief at the sight they had just witnessed. Melissa screamed, running towards her mother.

'Come with me.' Aiden put his arm around Elodie's shoulders, holding her close, determined never to let either her or Melissa go. 'Melissa is safe. And so are you, my darling.' Aiden knew they would have peace from this day on.

* * *

'You can now rest in peace,' Elodie whispered to her beloved mother, now interred in her rightful place next to her long-departed father and the generations of wise women who populated their family plot, in the seraphic vault under the sweet-scented lilac tree on the edge of the village, against the backdrop of the Lancashire hills, a symbol of her gratitude to the countryside that had nurtured and sustained them both. From here Elodie would make her way to the ancient church.

Aiden's eyes were brimming with love for Elodie as she reached the altar. Joined by family and friends from the village and from Beamer Street he pledged his love for the only woman he had ever loved, and they would live together as the married couple they should have been, all along.

'Till death us do part...' Elodie said as she looked into the calm, loving eyes of her new husband, both standing at the ornate altar of the village church, filled with the people who were closest to her. People she could depend upon and trust.

'I now pronounce you man and wife,' said the minister as Aiden bent to kiss his new bride, the girl he was destined to be with and for whom he had waited for such a long time. The wait had been unbearable, but worth it, he knew. Walking down the aisle they passed the Caraway family pew without a glance, knowing there would be no more bitterness and anger.

Elodie also knew this was the final goodbye to the nightmares of the past, a purging of the horror of her first marriage, a sham of which she no longer wished to be reminded, knowing that this was the only place she could marry Aiden, for she must have good memories of this place too, where she and her mother had prayed together for better days to come. And over the choir's angelic voices, she heard her mother's voice telling her to keep up the good work she was already doing, and Elodie knew she would.

Elodie knew she and Aiden would not live in the village, nor in Oakland Hall, which was now called The Deborah Kirrin Retreat. The huge country estate, sitting in one hundred and fifty acres of spectacular land set deep in the valley, was surrounded by panoramic hills and woodland brimming with adventurous opportunities for children, which Aiden and Elodie knew it was better suited for. The house and land had been turned into a place where children who would not normally see the beauty of the countryside and all it had to offer would be able to come for some respite from the smoke and the narrow back-to-back streets of the dockland. The Deborah Kirrin Retreat would be a place for good.

She and Aiden had no desire to live there. The hall would be more useful in making new memories for youngsters from areas where trees did not grow in abundance, and who knew little of the wonders of mother nature and all she had to offer.

EPILOGUE
NEW YEAR'S EVE 1925

A lot has happened since this time last year, thought Elodie patting the sofa in their cosy flat above the apothecary, inviting Aiden to sit beside her. He had just come into the room after reading Melissa her bedtime story and she had been waiting all day for this time when they would be alone together. The best time to give him her good news.

'Did I tell you we are expecting a new arrival?'

'Oh, you clever girl,' he said, thrilled, and he kissed her, one of his most favourite pastimes.

'I think it was a joint endeavour, my darling,' Elodie laughed, and he kissed her once more.

'I could not be prouder,' he said, and Elodie knew he meant every word.

'And I have never been more content,' she told him, knowing Aiden loved this busy part of the world that never was still.

Aiden was growing herbs while Elodie used them to make her popular cures for the apothecary. Neither had any desire to live anywhere except Beamer Street.

Melissa had really come out of her shell and spent her time

between three houses – her own, Molly's and Mary Jane's. Elodie knew she would be thrilled when her new brother or sister came to join them. And even though their life was not the lavish one they once lived at Oakland Hall, with servants, they were far richer now with their extended Haywood and Everdine families and the many new school friends Melissa had made.

Elodie went over to the window and looked down into the street, intrigued to see a horse and cart piled high with furniture pulling up outside the empty house along the street. A new family were moving into Beamer Street. A fresh start, perhaps?

'I wonder what their story is?' she said to herself. Sure, that very soon she would find out, because nothing was kept secret for long in Beamer Street.

ACKNOWLEDGEMENTS

Writing a book is rarely a sole process, which is why I want to say thank you to some of the people who have taken the time and given their expertise, to bring *A Safe Haven on Beamer Street* to you, my lovely readers.

I would like to thank my agent, Caroline Sheldon, a wise, wonderful woman who is so supportive and knows publishing like the back of her hand.

My fabulous editor, Caroline Ridding, who has been wonderfully patient and supportive in what was a bit of a trying year, and also to Jade and Sandra, thank you.

I also want to acknowledge the whole amazing hard-working team at Boldwood, who put everything together, and make sure my books reach the most important people of all – my readers – thank you one and all.

Also, I want to thank the wonderful Julie Masie who narrates and brings my stories to life.

And to you dear reader, without whom, my stories would still be a distant dream, languishing on my hard drive. Thank you.

Sheila xx

ABOUT THE AUTHOR

Sheila Riley wrote four #1 bestselling novels under the pseudonym Annie Groves and is now writing the second of two saga trilogies under her own name. She has set her series around the River Mersey and its docklands near to where she spent her early years.

Sign up to Sheila Riley's mailing list for news, competitions and updates on future books.

Visit Sheila's website: http://my-writing-ladder.blogspot.com/

Follow Sheila on social media:

ALSO BY SHEILA RILEY

Reckoner's Row Series

The Mersey Orphan

The Mersey Girls

The Mersey Mothers

Beamer Street Series

Finding Friends on Beamer Street

A Safe Haven on Beamer Street

The Dockside Sagas

The Mersey Mistress

The Mersey Angels

Sixpence Stories

Introducing Sixpence Stories!

Discover page-turning historical novels from your favourite authors, meet new friends and be transported back in time.

Join our book club Facebook group

https://bit.ly/SixpenceGroup

Sign up to our newsletter

https://bit.ly/SixpenceNews

Boldwood

Boldwood Books is an award-winning fiction publishing company seeking out the best stories from around the world.

Find out more at www.boldwoodbooks.com

Join our reader community for brilliant books, competitions and offers!

Follow us
@BoldwoodBooks
@TheBoldBookClub

Sign up to our weekly deals newsletter

https://bit.ly/BoldwoodBNewsletter

Printed in Great Britain
by Amazon

54895506R00148